PRAISE FOR
DEATH OF A CRABBY COOK
BY PENNY PIKE

"With her aunt's business—and freedom—on the line, it's up to Darcy and Dream Puff Jake Miller to put the brakes on a crabby—and out-of-control—killer."
—Examiner.com

"A fun food-related series . . . [with] recipes to die for."
—Kings River Life Magazine

"Fun, fresh, and different."   —Open Book Society

"A page-turner that I needed to finish."
—MyShelf.com

"A thoroughly enjoyable read."
—Here's How It Happened

PRAISE FOR THE
PARTY-PLANNING MYSTERY SERIES
BY PENNY PIKE
WRITING AS PENNY WARNER

"An appealing heroine whose event skills include utilizing party favors in self-defense in a fun, fast-paced new series guaranteed to please."
—Carolyn Hart, *New York Times* bestselling author of the Death on Demand Mysteries

continued . . .

"The book dishes up a banquet of mayhem."
— *Oakland Tribune* (CA)

"With a promising progression of peculiar plots and a plethora of party-planning pointers, *How to Host a Killer Party* looks to be a pleasant prospect for cozy mystery lovers." — Fresh Fiction

"Warner keeps the reader guessing." — Gumshoe

"Grab this book. . . . It will leave you in stitches."
— The Romance Readers Connection

"Frantic pace, interesting characters."
— *Publishers Weekly*

"I highly recommend this book to all mystery readers, cozy or not. This is a party that you don't want to miss."
— Once Upon a Romance

"Presley is a creative, energetic young woman with a wry sense of humor." — The Mystery Reader

OTHER BOOKS BY PENNY PIKE

The Food Festival Mysteries
Death of a Crabby Cook
Death of a Chocolate Cheater

BOOKS BY PENNY PIKE
Writing as Penny Warner

The Party-Planning Mystery Series
How to Host a Killer Party
How to Crash a Killer Bash
How to Survive a Killer Séance
How to Party with a Killer Vampire
How to Dine on Killer Wine

Death of a Chocolate Cheater

A FOOD FESTIVAL MYSTERY

Penny Pike

AN OBSIDIAN MYSTERY

OBSIDIAN
Published by the Penguin Group
Penguin Group (USA) LLC, 375 Hudson Street,
New York, New York 10014

USA | Canada | UK | Ireland | Australia | New Zealand | India | South Africa | China
penguin.com
A Penguin Random House Company

First published by Obsidian, an imprint of New American Library,
a division of Penguin Group (USA) LLC

First Printing, June 2015

Copyright © Penny Warner, 2015
Penguin supports copyright. Copyright fuels creativity, encourages diverse
voices, promotes free speech, and creates a vibrant culture. Thank you for buying an authorized edition of this book and for complying with copyright laws
by not reproducing, scanning, or distributing any part of it in any form without
permission. You are supporting writers and allowing Penguin to continue to
publish books for every reader.

OBSIDIAN and logo are trademarks of Penguin Group (USA) LLC.

ISBN 978-0-451-46782-9

Printed in the United States of America
10 9 8 7 6 5 4 3 2 1

To my mother

Acknowledgments

Thanks to everyone who helped make my chocolate dreams come true: Colleen Casey, Janet Finsilver, Staci McLaughlin, Ann Parker, Carole Price, the guys at Pacific Puffs, the people at San Francisco Chocolate Tours, my wonderful agent, Andrea Hurst, and my incredible editor, Sandra Harding. I owe you all a big box of chocolates.

"What kind of monster could possibly hate chocolate?"

—Cassandra Clare, *Clockwork Angel*

"When I die, I'm not going to be embalmed. I'm going to be dipped."

—Adrianne Marcus

Chapter 1

"Darcy, did you know chocolate is a valuable energy source?" my sixtysomething aunt, Abby, asked as she handed me one of her homemade lattes. By homemade, I mean she used her instant one-cup machine, pressed a button, and voila. "I just read that one chocolate chip can give you enough energy to walk a hundred and fifty feet."

"Great." I took a sip of the steaming mix of milk and coffee and washed down a bite of a brownie I'd found on the counter. "I'm going to need about seven billion of them to get going this morning." It was a good thing I'd found the leftover brownie or I would have run right out and bought a bag of chocolate chips. Just the word "chocolate" made my mouth water.

Aunt Abby settled onto the empty barstool at her kitchen counter with her special "Lunch Lady" mug, her faithful long-haired Doxie, Basil, at her feet, wagging his tail. She was already dressed for the day in a pink blouse and black slacks, covered with her "Big Yellow School Bus" apron. She wore her Clairol-colored fire-engine-red hair in the same bubble cut she'd had in high school, and her overly mascaraed eyes and blushed dimples made her look like a Kewpie doll.

She picked up the San Francisco Chocolate Festival brochure she'd been reading from. "And it says here chocolate has great health benefits," Aunt Abby continued after adjusting her paw-print-decorated Peepers. "Chocolate helps alleviate depression; it can lower blood pressure, reduce tumors, and relieve PMS. . . ." She paused and shot a glance at me.

I frowned. "Are you hinting that I've been crabby the past few days?"

She raised a perfectly drawn brow. "I'm just saying, chocolate supposedly increases serotonin and endorphin levels, in case yours happen to be low."

I knew she was referring to my recent dark mood. Ever since I was let go from the *San Francisco Chronicle* a couple of months ago, I'd been helping my aunt serve comfort food from her Big Yellow School Bus food truck. Her "busterant," as she called it, was semi-permanently parked at Fort Mason, not far from her Russian Hill home. In order to make ends meet after losing my reporter's income, I'd regularly been making Bus Driver BLTs and dishing out Teacher Tuna Casseroles. And it looked like that would continue, at least until I sold my as-yet-to-be-completed-and-future-best-selling cookbook. I planned to feature recipes from food trucks, the culinary phenomenon that had swept the country. Maybe then I could move out of my aunt's Airstream, which was parked in her side yard, and get on with my life after Trevor the Tool, my cheating ex-boyfriend.

Unfortunately, life wasn't progressing the way I'd

planned. I was beginning to think I'd be serving Principal's Pot Pies and Custodian's Crab Mac 'n' Cheese for the rest of my days. The only respite from the daily food truck workout had been my budding relationship with Jake Miller, the dreamboat from the Dream Puff truck. I'd had a crush on Jake since the first time I tasted one of his cream puffs, and we'd recently worked together to save my dear aunt from a life serving jailhouse food. We made a great team. The only trouble was, I'd been sampling so many of his creamy concoctions, the results were beginning to show around my waist.

Until recently, that was. I hadn't had a cream puff in days; nor had I seen much of Jake. I looked away from my aunt's probing gaze and into my coffee mug. The color of my cooling latte was no longer a creamy rich caramel but had darkened to a morose drab brown, matching my mood.

I yawned, trying to wake up, and took another sip of the latte. "Are you sure this isn't decaf?"

Aunt Abby shook her head, absorbed in the Chocolate Festival brochure again. Her red curls bounced, then settled back into place. "Chocolate contains caffeine, you know. Maybe you should pour some chocolate syrup in that cup and throw it in the microwave."

"I'd have to add the whole jar to get the same amount of caffeine that's in a cup of coffee. Maybe I'll just have another brownie." I felt my jeans tighten at the thought.

Aunt Abby turned a page, then sat up straighter. "Did you know chocolate also contains iron, helps prevent tooth decay, and has antioxidants, which help minimize aging?" She patted her porcelain skin. The only giveaway to my aunt's years were the tiny laugh lines around her mascaraed eyes. I wondered how much chocolate she'd consumed in her lifetime.

"Stop!" I held up a hand. "I've gained five pounds from eating so many of Jake's chocolate cream puff samples, especially those Mocha Madness ones. They're killer. No more talk about chocolate! Pretty soon I won't be able to fit in my Big Yellow School Bus T-shirts. You'll have to get me Extra-Big." I put down the half-eaten brownie and sipped my coffee.

"Well, you'd better get used to being around a lot of chocolate," Aunt Abby said, "because I have a surprise."

"Oh?" I asked warily, peering over my coffee mug. It was too early in the morning for one of Aunt Abby's surprises.

"I just signed us up for the Chocolate Festival competition next month!"

I set my mug down with a *thunk*. Coffee sloshed inside like a mini tsunami. "But your specialty is comfort foods, not chocolate."

Aunt Abby frowned at me. "*Hmph*. Chocolate is the *ultimate* comfort food. And are you forgetting my chocolate-covered potato chips? My chocolate-peanut-butter sandwiches? My chocolate pasta? My chocolate pizza? I've seen you sneak plenty of those chocolate leftovers at the end of the day." She eyed the half-eaten brownie.

She was right. In addition to her usual fare of American comfort foods, with school-themed names like "Cheerleader's Chili," "Coach's Cole Slaw," and "Science-Experiment Spaghetti," my aunt Abby had dishes where she put her own chocolate twist on classic cuisine. Her chocolate-dipped, raspberry-iced Twinkie bites were worth the extra calories.

I loved just about everything on my aunt's Big Yellow School Bus menu, but I wondered if her chocolate offerings were good enough for the prestigious San Francisco Chocolate Festival competition. The annual event featured locally renowned chefs competing for some hefty cash prizes and appearances on Food Network shows. It seemed out of her league.

"Don't you think my chocolate goodies are award-winning?" Aunt Abby asked, as if reading my mind.

I cleared my throat and backtracked, worried I'd hurt her feelings. "Oh, of course they are . . . but it's a tough competition. Remember George Brown, the guy who owned Chocolate Bliss? He took home the grand prize with his Peanut-Butter–Chocolate-Chip-Cookie-Dough Cheesecake. Which, by the way, was to die for."

"Yes, I remember. George is an old friend. And this year he's one of the judges. But nothing beats the creation I've come up with for the contest." She smiled mysteriously. "Not even his grand-prize recipe."

"Really? You've got something new planned? What is it?"

"Top secret. If I tell you, I'll have to—"

"—I know. I know. Just give me a hint, then. Chocolate-covered snickerdoodles? Chocolate-dipped Danish? Chocolate-frosted cinnamon buns?" I teased.

She harrumphed. "Very funny. Now you'll just have to wait and see."

I shrugged in response to her secretiveness. "It's going to be a lot of extra work, you know, plus the cost of ingredients and the entry fee. Are you up to it, in addition to running your busterant?"

Not to mention the fact that I didn't have time for a lot of extra work. I had a book to write, a career to develop, a life to start over. And Jake . . .

"What extra work?" came a low voice behind me.

Basil barked in response.

"Quiet, Basil!" Dillon, Aunt Abby's twenty-five-year-old son, shuffled into the kitchen barefoot. Tall and slim like his deceased father had been, he wore a thin, shaggy robe over his bare chest and Superman boxer shorts. His curly dark-red hair looked as if it hadn't seen scissors, gel, or even shampoo in days, nor his face a razor.

I started when I saw his pet rat, Ratty, on his shoulder and backed away.

"Do you have to bring that thing in here?" I asked. "It's unsanitary!"

Ignoring me, he went directly to the pantry, opened the door, and stared at the loaded shelves. "Mom, you're out of cereal."

"Yes, dear," Aunt Abby said to her boomerang son. "And Darcy's right. Ratty doesn't belong in the kitchen. He's upsetting Basil."

After glaring at me, Dillon lumbered back down the hall, his rat clinging to the shoulder of his robe. Aunt Abby's son had been "asked" to leave the university due to some suspected hacking activity and had moved home to "reconfigure" his life goals. In other words, sponge off his mom, sit on his butt, and play computer games.

At least I paid rent.

He returned moments later, rat-free. "Got any more of those chocolate whoopie pies you made last night?"

"Dillon! Those were supposed to be top secret!" Aunt Abby looked at me. "Well, Darcy, now you know my secret weapon for the chocolate competition—my newest creation: Chocolate Raspberry Whoopie Pies. But both of you need to keep quiet about this. I don't want anyone to find out and steal my idea before the contest begins."

"Chocolate Raspberry Whoopie Pies?" I said, stunned at her entry choice. I wasn't even sure what a whoopie pie was.

"It's my own recipe," Aunt Abby said. "Instead of using regular chocolate cakey cookies, I use brownie cookies, and instead of vanilla filling, I use chocolate buttercream frosting with fresh raspberries. And then I dip the whole thing in melted chocolate and add sprinkles."

It sounded like overkill, but when it came to chocolate, maybe there was no such thing.

"So where are they?" Dillon said, looking around helplessly.

"In the fridge," Aunt Abby said.

Dillon opened the refrigerator door, brought out a plastic container, and set it on the counter. After withdrawing a double-decker-Oreo-sized "pie," he stuffed the whole thing in his mouth. It wasn't a pleasant sight.

Aunt Abby sighed. "Oh well. The secret's out now. You're sworn to silence, Darcy. Want to try one?" She picked up the container and brought it over to the kitchen island where I sat. Dillon followed her like a hungry puppy and plopped down on the barstool next to me, still chewing. Chocolate frosting had oozed out from the corners of his mouth.

I reached into the container and helped myself. Taking a tentative bite, I let the sweet morsel dissolve on my tongue. The flavor flooded my mouth.

Wow. Chocolate crack.

"This is incredible!" I said when I could talk again.

"Awesome, right?" Dillon agreed, then popped another one into his mouth. "You may actually have a shot at winning this thing," I said to Aunt Abby. "What's the prize?"

"Den fouszen dollars," Dillon answered with his mouth full.

"Ten thousand dollars?" I repeated. I was used to translating Dillon's food-obstructed speech. "That's a lot of money."

"And a chance to be on that Food Network show *Chocolate Wars*," Aunt Abby added, batting her feathered eyelashes in excitement.

I knew Aunt Abby's dream was to appear on one of the many TV cooking shows, especially *The Great Food Truck Race*, but it was the money that had caught my attention. I knew she could use it to make improvements in her bus. "When's the festival?" I asked.

"In two weeks," Aunt Abby said.

I gulped. "We'd better get to work!"

*   *   *

Half an hour later I was on my way to Fort Mason to help Aunt Abby prepare today's specialties in her Big Yellow School Bus. We would soon be serving comfort food to the usual hungry patrons. I hoped to see Jake, since he'd seemed too busy the past few days to stop by or meet after work. I wanted to tell him about Aunt Abby entering the Chocolate Festival competition. At least, that was my excuse for talking to him.

As I drove down Bay Street to the Marina, I thought about the annual festival and the competition. Although I'd covered the event as a restaurant critic for the newspaper, this would be the first time I'd get to see it from the contestants' point of view. The festival was held near Ghirardelli Square, home to one of the original chocolatiers of San Francisco. Last year twenty thousand people had paid the twenty-dollar entry fee to taste the mouthwatering wares of two dozen chocolate vendors and half a dozen contest entrants.

I'd learned from Aunt Abby that any legitimate vendor could participate in the festival and contest as long as he or she offered something chocolaty—and could make enough for hundreds of attendees. Each entry in the competition would be judged by a select panel of local experts in the chocolate industry. And while the thought of personally tasting all that chocolate had my heart singing, it was the winner's ten-thousand-dollar check that really had me excited. Aunt Abby had promised Dillon and me each a third if her whoopie pies won.

I pulled up to the permit-only parking lot at Fort

Mason in my coffee-colored VW Bug and headed for the circle of food trucks parked in an adjacent lot. The area was home to a dozen permanent vendors, including my aunt, but other trucks came and went, depending on how popular they were. There was always a long list of new trucks vying for the few nonpermanent spots. My aunt had been fortunate—her comfort-food menu was a hit with people who longed for "Mom's home cooking."

As I headed over, I spotted Jake outside his festive Dream Puff truck, decorated in giant-sized cream puffs. It had been too long since I'd caught more than a glimpse of him. He looked especially sexy this morning, even though he wore his usual Dream Puff T-shirt and denim jeans. A lock of his sun-streaked brown hair had fallen over his forehead, and he brushed it back with a tanned hand, causing me to quiver a little. Suddenly feeling shy, I took a deep breath for courage and walked over under the guise of telling him about Aunt Abby entering the contest. I was eager to see him, and snagging one of his Dream Puffs of the Day samples would just be the frosting on the cake. Or cream puff.

The hand-printed blackboard sign read TODAY'S SPECIAL: CHOCOLATE MOCHA MOUSSE.

OMG. Chocolate Mocha Mousse. It was all I could do to keep from drooling down the front of my Big Yellow School Bus T-shirt. Was it the thought of the cream puff, or Jake?

"Do you have anything with no calories?" I asked, coming up behind him as he filled bowls with toppings for his dreamy delights.

He whirled around and gave me that adorable, toothy grin. "Darcy!"

"Morning, Jake," I said, unable to stifle my own smile. It was good seeing him up close again.

"It's been a while," he said, looking me over. "You look . . . really nice."

"Thanks," I said, running my fingers self-consciously through my dark brown, bobbed hair. "I haven't seen you much lately," I said.

I'd told myself Jake had been too busy with his food truck to do much socializing, but in truth, I was beginning to wonder if his interest in me was starting to wane. Aunt Abby's situation had given us a reason to spend time together. But once that was over, it seemed like things had changed.

"Yeah, sorry about that, Darcy," he said as he arranged the condiments on the outside shelf. He looked incredible in his white Dream Puff T-shirt and faded jeans. "It's been crazy around here the past few days."

"Oh, I know how it is. Me too. You know . . . lots of stuff going on . . ."

Yeah, right.

"Actually, I've been dealing with something the past couple of weeks," he said, brushing his sun-lightened brown hair off his forehead again, "but, hey, if you're free later tonight, how about we get a drink and catch up?"

"Sounds great," I said, grinning at the thought of spending some alone time with him. "I've got some news to share."

"Really? What's up?"

"I'll tell you tonight," I said mysteriously. I just hoped Aunt Abby hadn't blabbed her news about entering the Chocolate Festival competition already. She had a habit of oversharing everything with anyone who would listen, including details of my personal life.

"Looking forward to it," Jake said. He reached in through the open truck window and pulled out a two-bite cream puff nestled on a paper doily. The delicate puff was filled with a mocha-colored cream, drizzled with dark chocolate, and topped with a perfect chocolate curl. "Want to try my latest?"

"Love to! Is it today's special?"

He nodded. "Let me know what you think."

I took a bite. The creamy mixture spread over my tongue and melted away in seconds, leaving the crunchy shell to savor. I felt a bit of the cool cream on my upper lip.

Jake leaned in, and with his fingertip, wiped away the mocha mustache I apparently wore. Then he licked the tip of his finger.

Whoa. I suddenly felt dizzy. I didn't know which had my heart racing so fast—Jake's dreamy cream puff or the mustache removal I'd just experienced.

I held up the remainder of the cream puff. "This is incredible," I managed to say.

"You like it?"

"You've outdone yourself."

"Great, because I just signed up for the Chocolate Festival competition, and that's what I'm entering."

I felt my smile waver. Oh no! Jake was entering the competition? With that killer cream puff? Suddenly my news about Aunt Abby's whoopie-pie entry didn't sound so exciting.

"Are you sure you like it?" Jake said, obviously noticing my reaction.

"Oh, yes . . . of course!" I said, mustering up some enthusiasm. "It's . . . great! I'm sure you'll do well in the competition."

"Hope so. I don't care about being on the TV show, but I can always use the money. The cream puff business isn't quite as lucrative as the litigation business," he said, referring to his former job.

"Well, it's definitely a winner." I pointed to Aunt Abby's bus. "Uh, I . . . gotta go. I'm going to be late. You know what a tyrant my aunt can be. See you tonight?"

He smiled and nodded.

I turned and hustled over to my aunt's school bus before I accidentally blurted out her news.

It wasn't that I didn't want Jake to win.

I just wanted us to win more.

How was I going to tell him we'd be competing against him?

As I reached the bus, something else Jake had said bothered me. It wasn't the contest, or the fact that we hadn't seen each other much lately. It was his comment about *dealing with something* lately.

Something important enough to keep him from spending time with me?

Or some*one*?

Before I started plotting his imaginary girlfriend's demise, I stepped into the school bus, wondering how I would break the news to Aunt Abby about Jake's entry into the competition. Not only would she be competing against some of the best chocolate chefs in the area, but now she'd be going up against her friend Jake Miller.

But instead of busily preparing today's menu selection, my aunt was sitting on a stool, holding her cell phone. The color had left her face and she looked dazed. She had her hand on her chest, as if she might be having a heart attack.

"Aunt Abby!" I rushed over to give her some support. "Are you all right? You look like you're about to collapse."

Aunt Abby sighed and lowered the cell phone to the counter. She stared blankly at it.

"What is it, Aunt Abby? Are you ill? Do you want me to call a doctor?"

She shook her head. "It's not that. I'm okay, I guess."

"Then what is it?"

Still staring at the phone, she answered, "That was Reina Patel. . . ."

I shrugged, not recognizing the name.

"She's the Chocolate Festival coordinator. The one who decides who's eligible for the competition, the one who handpicks the judges, the one who's in charge of the whole event."

"Did something happen? Are you disqualified from competing for some reason? Because if she says you can't participate, well, I'll just go down there and—"

"No, no," Aunt Abby said, cutting me off. "I'm still in the competition—"

"Good," I said, cutting her off this time. "Because I've got some news—"

She held up her hand to stop me. "Reina called to tell me they've had a little glitch in the competition. That's what she called it—a little *glitch*."

"What kind of glitch?"

Aunt Abby sighed again. Tears welled up in her eyes. Her shoulders sank. "Apparently, they're looking for a new judge to replace George Brown."

"Why? Did he quit?"

"No," she said. "George Brown is dead."

Chapter 2

One of the judges is dead? I blinked at the surprising news. "What happened?"

"Reina wasn't sure," Aunt Abby said, absently patting the phone. "Some kind of accident. She's looking for a replacement judge so the competition can continue. . . ." She drifted off.

She was taking this news pretty hard.

"You said you knew George Brown? Were you close?"

My aunt sighed. "You could say that. I met George years ago, when we were at culinary school together in Napa. After graduation, he went on to become editor of *Chocolatta*, a print magazine that featured anything and everything to do with chocolate. But the rag folded, like so many do these days. And now he's dead." Tears welled again.

"I'm so sorry, Aunt Abby." I rested a hand on her shoulder. I wondered if he had been more than a friend.

Aunt Abby seemed to read my mind. "George was a nice guy. Good-looking too. We dated a little while we were at the academy, but then Edward came along. We got married, and I forgot about George. I always figured George would become a pastry chef, since he loved desserts so much, but I guess he preferred tasting and writing to cooking and baking. I hadn't thought about him for years, until I heard he'd entered the competition last year—and won." A tear ran down her cheek. She turned away and wiped it off with the back of her hand.

So there *was* some history there. "Maybe we can check the Internet and see if there's a report on the accident," I offered, giving her a hug. Perhaps that would help with closure.

Aunt Abby said nothing, seemingly lost in her memories.

"Why did Reina call *you*?" I asked, thinking it odd that the woman running the festival would take the time to tell the contestants this news.

Aunt Abby shrugged and looked at the clock.

"Goodness!" she said, rising from the stool. "It's almost showtime!" She patted her face, brushed the wrinkles out of her apron, then took down a loaf of whole wheat bread from a shelf.

"Are you okay?" I asked, surprised at this turnabout.

"I'm fine," she said, handing me the bread. "Here, you slice this for sandwiches. I'll shred the cheese for the chili. Where's Dillon? That boy will be the death of me." In an instant, she was back to her old self.

Speaking of the devil, "the boy" bounded aboard the school bus, ducking his six-foot-plus frame to clear the doorway. The bus rocked on its wheels.

"Sorry I'm late," he said, grabbing an apron from the

nearby hook. At least he had changed out of his robe and underwear and now wore nearly suitable clothing. If you can call torn, saggy jeans and a threadbare Radiohead T-shirt clothes. Dillon refused to be caught dead in the Big Yellow School Bus T-shirt his mother had made for all of us.

"You're late again," I snapped, shooting him a daggered look. I attacked the bread with a serrated knife.

"Yeah, well, I'm here now," he snapped back. "And besides, I have a good reason."

I rolled my eyes. "What? Was the FBI chasing you? The CIA? The NSA?"

Ever since Dillon had left the university under the computer-hacking cloud, he was convinced the government was watching his every move. When he felt especially paranoid, he dressed up in disguises and slept in the school bus instead of at home.

"Or was it the PTA this time?"

"Ha. Ha," Dillon said, not laughing.

"Now, you two"—Aunt Abby handed Dillon a chunk of cheese and a grater—"cut it out or I'll make both of you wash the bus tonight. Speaking of which, wash your hands, Dillon."

"Well, if you don't want to hear the news . . ." Dillon pouted as he went to the sink and turned on the water.

"What news, dear?" Aunt Abby asked as she began stirring a pot of her popular chili. The woman had the patience of a school cafeteria lady.

Dillon turned off the water and wiped his hands on a paper towel. "One of the Chocolate Festival judges died last night," he announced.

We looked at Dillon. "We know," we said in unison.

Dillon frowned. "How did you know? I just found out."

"Reina Patel called this morning and told me," Aunt Abby explained. "It was George Brown, an old friend of mine. She said he had some kind of accident."

Dillon's eyes narrowed. "You knew him?"

"A long time ago. Before I met your father."

"Hmm," Dillon said. Then something clicked in his warp-speed brain. "Then you don't know what *really* happened to him?"

Aunt Abby stopped stirring. I stopped slicing.

"You know?" Abby asked. "Tell me!"

Dillon pulled a small notepad from the back pocket of his saggy jeans. I had a feeling this was going to be a long story. If that was the case, we were never going to be ready to open for business on time.

"Okay, so, I did some digging to find out more about the judges—you know, their likes and dislikes, stuff like that—to help us win the competition. Anyway, I went to hiddenhacker.com and a bunch of other sites and looked up each of their names, then dug a little deeper—"

"You mean you hacked into their personal information," I said, shaking my head.

"Hey. People are careless with their passwords," Dillon said. "It's not my fault they're stupid."

"Sooo?" I said, circling my knife, meaning, "Get on with it."

He rolled his eyes at me this time, then checked his notes. "So there are three judges, right? Simon Van

Houten works for his family-owned corporation called Cote d'Ivoire Industries. At least, that's what it says in his bio. But what it doesn't say is that the company, owned by Van Houten Senior—Simon's dad—owns a whole bunch of international import businesses under a bunch of fake names. Dad and son have practically cornered the market in—get this—chocolate. They have factories all over Africa, producing two-thirds of the world's cocoa."

"Huh," I said. "I thought most chocolate came from Central and South America."

"Me too," Aunt Abby said.

Dillon shrugged. "Whatever. It sounds like they have a worldwide monopoly on wholesale chocolate production. But that's not all. Junior and senior don't get along all that well. Apparently, Dad is old-school conservative when it comes to business, while son is more eco-geek."

"Interesting, but what does this have to do with the contest?"

"And what does it have to do with George?" Aunt Abby said before Dillon could answer me.

"I'm getting to him," Dillon told his mother. "So, the second judge is Isabel Lau, right?"

Aunt Abby nodded.

"It wasn't easy finding stuff on her," Dillon said. He glanced at his notepad. "Seems she's a regular judge on the dessert circuit, but I couldn't find out much more about her. It's like she came out of nowhere and suddenly became an expert on chocolate. No family history. No school credentials. Nothing. I did find an interview she gave in *Chocolatta* magazine. She claims chocolate is an aphrodisiac, and she puts chocolate on everything she eats, even salad."

"So, she likes chocolate," I said. "What woman doesn't? Did you find out anything about George Brown?" I checked my watch again. If Dillon didn't wrap up his report soon, we weren't going to hear the punch line until after we finished serving the last customer at the end of the day.

"Dude, get this," Dillon said. "George Brown used to be the *editor* of that *Chocolatta* magazine."

"We know that," I said, glancing at Aunt Abby for confirmation. "It went under."

"Not exactly," Dillon said. "Turns out Van Houten's company, Cote d'Ivoire, bought the magazine, changed the name to *The Magic of Chocolate*, fired everybody on staff, including George, and hired all new people."

Harsh, I thought. But it happened a lot in the magazine business, especially today, as print mags competed with e-zines. The competition was one of the reasons I'd been downsized at the newspaper.

Abby frowned. "Do you know what happened to George after he left the magazine?"

Dillon glanced at his notes. "Uh, let's see. He opened up his own chocolate shop in Fisherman's Wharf called The Chock'lit Shop, but it crashed and burned six months later. After that he started a gig writing an online blog he called Wicked Chocolate. Covered all the local chocolate news—reviewed chocolate shops, offered chocolate recipes, mentioned events, stuff like that."

"This is all very interesting," I said, "but do you have any idea what *happened* to him? Reina said it was some kind of accident."

"Dude, chill. I'm getting to that. So anyway, George wrote a blog about being a judge for the chocolate competition and said he was looking forward to tasting all the chocolates, blah, blah, blah. But get this. He published that blog yesterday. And last night he was killed."

"I thought it was an accident," Aunt Abby said.

"It was," Dillon said. "He was killed by a hit-and-run driver."

"Oh my God." Aunt Abby's face went as white as her still-clean apron. She held the counter to steady herself. "I thought it was just an accident, like a fall or something. That poor man! What a horrible way to die. Did they find the person who did it?"

Dillon shook his head. "I checked the police records. It happened at night, and the only witness said the car was a late-model SUV, probably black."

Aunt Abby sighed and shook her head. "I'm beginning to feel like Jessica Fletcher," she mumbled. "Lately it seems like everywhere I go, someone gets killed."

I knew exactly what she was referring to—the murders that had recently plagued the food truck businesses. She'd even been a suspect for one of the deaths.

"Who's Jessica Fletcher?" Dillon asked.

"You've never heard of Jessica Fletcher?" I asked. "*Murder, She Wrote*? I think the show is still on a cable channel."

"Before my time," Dillon answered. "Was she a cop or something?"

I laughed. "No. She was a meddling mystery writer who kept stumbling over bodies in Cabot Cove, Maine—a quaint New England town that happens to have the highest murder rate in America. It almost became a joke that if Jessica Fletcher was in the area, there would be bodies—and most of the suspects were her relatives."

"Sounds lame," Dillon said.

"I loved that show!" Aunt Abby said. "She was one smart lady, and smarter than the police. I always guessed the killer right along with her, just by studying the physical evidence instead of being distracted by what the suspects said. You can't argue with the evidence."

"We're getting off the subject, guys," I said. The clock was ticking. I could hear murmurs of a line outside the shuttered bus. "If George Brown was killed by a hit-and-run driver, it was probably an unfortunate accident. I don't think Jessica Fletcher is needed for this. It's sad, but right now we need to hustle."

Aunt Abby frowned and gazed into the distance. "On the other hand . . . it *could* have been deliberate."

"Seriously?" I stared at her.

She shrugged, smoothed her apron, and returned to stirring the pot of chili. "It's possible, although I don't know why anyone would want to kill sweet old George."

Was it possible? Nah. With all this *Murder, She Wrote* talk, we were being overly suspicious. George Brown's death was a tragedy, but there was no reason to suspect it was anything other than a terrible accident. Still, I wondered what he'd written in that last blog.

Aunt Abby glanced up at the clock. "Oh, goodness. It's time to open up."

I moved to the window, rolled up the shutter, and saw the long line of customers.

"Wait a minute!" Dillon said. "I haven't told you the best part. Don't you want to know who's replacing George Brown in the competition?"

"They already have a replacement?" I asked, glancing at Aunt Abby. "That was quick."

"Tell me about it," Dillon said, tapping his notepad with his fingertip.

"How did you find out?"

"I have my ways," he said, raising a thick, squirrely eyebrow.

"Oh my God, you hacked into the festival's computer too, didn't you!" I said, raising *both* my eyebrows.

Dillon glanced around. "Shh! You never know who might be listening."

Aunt Abby held up a just-a-minute finger to the first customer in her line. "So tell us. Who's the new judge taking George's place?"

He looked at his notepad. "This chick named Polly Montgomery. Ever heard of her?"

Aunt Abby shook her head.

"Uh-oh," I said under my breath.

Aunt Abby and Dillon looked at me.

"I know her," I said. "I mean, I know *of* her. She's the food editor at the *Times*. But we've never actually met. In person."

The truth was, Polly and I had had a couple of snippy exchanges via e-mail, when she disagreed with one of my restaurant reviews. She'd had the nerve to accuse me of making stuff up, which of course wasn't true. I had given the restaurant an honest review. The food was tasteless, the service was lax, and the prices were high. I later learned one of Polly's several ex-husbands owned the place.

I had a sudden thought. "Aunt Abby, did you put my name on any of the entry forms?"

"No. Just mine. Why?" Aunt Abby asked.

"No reason," I said. No sense in worrying my aunt that Polly Montgomery might be prejudicial if she knew I was part of Aunt Abby's team. Nor did I want to get myself kicked off the team and lose a chance at that prize money. I didn't know if Polly had that kind of power, but it wasn't worth taking the risk.

"What's this Polly person like?" Aunt Abby asked me.

I glanced out the window at the restless customers and said, "I'll tell you later—"

Dillon interrupted me and held up his notes. "She's quite the party girl. Her name came up in all kinds of social-type articles. It's rumored she's hooked up with the ex-mayor, the owner of Chez Paris, and one of the news anchors on Channel 4, at least. And get this. They say she also hooked up with the former editor of *Chocolatta* magazine—your George Brown."

Aunt Abby's face lost its pink color, but instead of tearing up again, she lifted her head, put on a smile, and she shoved open the school-bus service window. "What'll you have?"

Talk about bouncing back. What was going on behind those Kewpie-doll eyes of hers? Had her relationship with George years ago really been more than just friendship? Did she still have feelings for him? If her reaction to the news that the new judge, Polly Montgomery, had hooked up with her old flame, George Brown, was a barometer of her feelings, she was making a serious effort not to let them show.

And if the restaurant world was as interconnected as it appeared to be, the chocolate community was even more so. Just like Cabot Cove.

Chapter 3

The theme song from *Murder, She Wrote* played in my head the rest of the day. I wondered if George's death had anything to do with my earworm. Had he really died accidentally, as reported? Or was it something else, as Aunt Abby seemed to suspect?

My thoughts jumped around like popping popcorn. George's tragic death. His sudden replacement. The uncompromised competition. And now that my nemesis, Polly Montgomery, was to be the new festival judge, was I jeopardizing my aunt's chances of winning if Polly found out I was part of Aunt Abby's team? The woman clearly didn't like me or the pen I wrote with.

Maybe I should take a clue from one of Dillon's amateur spy tricks and wear a disguise to the Chocolate Festival. Dillon had a penchant for dressing up like Inspector Clouseau, if not Inspector Gadget, anytime he felt especially paranoid. But I had a feeling I'd just look silly wearing a deerstalker cap and a London Fog trench coat to the event. What would Jessica Fletcher do?

Exhausted by the time we had served our last customer and closed the counter window around four, I was really looking forward to relaxing with Jake. I'd missed him the past few weeks and hoped we could pick up where we left off. Besides, I craved another one of those new cream puffs he was entering in the contest. Hmm. Maybe if I ate up all of his supply he wouldn't have any left to submit for competition.

Bad Darcy.

"Quitting time!" Aunt Abby sang out, removing her chili-encrusted apron and dropping it into the portable mesh laundry basket. "I'm making a caprese pizza tonight. Hope you didn't nibble all day."

I took off my apron and tossed it on top of Aunt Abby's. "Actually, I have plans after work."

"With Jake?" she asked with a bright grin.

Nothing gets past my aunt.

"We're just having a drink. Maybe go to dinner afterward. I'm not sure yet." I felt my face flush. "No big deal."

"Well, it sounds lovely. I was beginning to wonder if you two were still an item."

"An item?" I repeated with a laugh. "You sound like a gossip columnist from the fifties. I told you, we're just friends."

"With benefits?" she asked, her grin widening.

"Aunt Abby! First you talk like a retro news gal; then you switch to teenage slang."

"You didn't answer my question," she said, eyeing me.

I shook my head.

"Just so you know, I have a sense about these things," she said.

"Yeah, as I recall, you had the same sense about Dillon and that hippy girl he was seeing in college. What did she call herself? Stormy Mountain? Steamy Magpie?"

"Starry Meadow."

"Yeah, how did that work out?" Before she could answer, I added, "And by the way, where *is* your wayward son? He left right after the lunch rush to get a coffee and never came back."

"I told him he could take the rest of the afternoon off. Mondays are slow here, and I figured we could handle it. Besides, he's doing some more digging for me."

Hacking was more likely, I thought, but bit my tongue. "What's he looking for now?"

She shrugged. "Just stuff—"

Something caught Aunt Abby's eye, and she leaned over to have a better look through the school-bus window. After a moment she pulled back, then glanced at me, her mascaraed lashes fluttering madly. Something was up.

I leaned over to see what had shut her up and caused her eyelashes to flap like startled butterflies.

It wasn't hard to miss.

Jake stood outside his truck talking to a woman. She was drop-dead gorgeous, with long blond hair, expert makeup, and a stylish suit made to fit her perfect curves. It took me a moment before I realized she looked familiar. I recognized Lyla Vassar, one of the feature reporters on Channel 2. She was talking animatedly to Jake.

Uh-oh.

Was she planning to do a special feature on Jake's Dream Puff truck for the upcoming Chocolate Festival?

Not fair.

Aunt Abby and I continued to spy on the two of them. I wondered what Lyla was saying to Jake but couldn't hear anything, thanks to the rumble of the food truck motors. Before I could sneak out and listen in, Lyla took a step closer to Jake. I froze as she laid a perfectly manicured hand on his chest. Then she leaned in and kissed him on the cheek!

I felt my stomach drop, along with my jaw.

Since when did TV interviewers kiss their prospective interviewees?

I glanced over at Aunt Abby, who was standing behind me, watching the scene unfold.

She gave me a pitying look and placed her hand on my back. "Darcy, I'm sure it's not what it looks like."

I stepped away from the window, unable to watch any more.

Aunt Abby continued to peer out. "She's leaving," she whispered, as if the couple might overhear her. Before I could see for myself, my cell phone rang.

The caller ID read JAKE MILLER.

I hesitated before answering, not sure I wanted to talk to him at the moment. I glanced out to see if Lyla was still there, but she was gone. Finally I took the call.

"Hello?" I said, unable to muster up any cheerfulness in my voice.

"Darcy?" came Jake's low, sexy voice.

"Oh, hi, Jake," I said, trying to sound casual, if not

completely disinterested. He'd just have to work harder if he still wanted that after-work drink and possible dinner we had planned. It was his punishment for flirting with Drop-Dead Gorgeous.

"Hi, listen, uh, something's come up. Sorry, but I have to cancel tonight. Rain check?"

My hands turned cold. My stomach dropped. I pressed my lips together. He was actually canceling our plans.

"Oh, sure. I understand," I lied. "Another time."

"Soon, I promise," he said. That was probably a lie too.

"No problem. See you later." I ended the call and stared at the phone as if it were a Ouija board about to give me an answer to my question.

What was up with Dream Puff Jake Miller and Drop-Dead-Gorgeous Lyla Vassar?

"You okay?" Aunt Abby asked.

"Of course," I said, trying to hide my feelings after seeing Jake's flirtation with Lyla and his cancellation of our date. He and I didn't have any kind of understanding, much less a commitment. We'd been on a few dates, kissed a few times. I'd wanted to take it slowly after my breakup with Trevor the Tool. Had I blown it?

"I guess I'll take you up on that dinner offer, after all," I said glumly to my aunt. "I'll see you at home."

She patted my back but said nothing. I glanced out the window to make sure the coast was clear—I wasn't in the mood to run into Jake after his phone call. And I sure didn't want to see his hot blonde. Awk-ward.

I made a dash for my car in the adjacent parking lot,

feeling wiped out physically, mentally, and emotionally. It had been a long day in the close confines of the school bus, feeding hungry patrons. I felt let down by Jake's cancellation. And I was worried that my old feud with Polly Montgomery might affect Aunt Abby's chances in the competition. I hoped a big glass of red wine, half a gourmet pizza, and a few whoopie pies would soothe my aching body and soul. Make that a half bottle of wine.

When I reached my VW Bug, I found a small white box on my windshield. I checked the area for lurkers, but no one was around. Hesitantly, I opened the box and found a lemon meringue cream puff and a folded note inside. I took out the note and read it:

> *Darcy, sorry again about having to cancel. I was looking forward to seeing you. I've missed you. I can't explain now, but I've been dealing with something that's taking up a lot of my free time. Hope to see you soon.*
>
> *—Jake.*

I smiled at the bittersweet note. Jake sounded sincere, and I wanted to believe him. But I couldn't shake the image of that woman touching him, kissing him, and even a dozen cream puffs wouldn't stop me from wondering what was going on. I assumed it had something to do with Lyla Vassar. Maybe she *was* doing a feature on him, but that kiss didn't look like a thank-you peck.

Out of the corner of my eye, I caught a glimpse of

the woman who had been flirting with Jake. She was texting on her phone, just outside her late-model BMW, so I got in my car and watched her from a distance. She frowned as she typed in her message, her demeanor completely different from the one she presented to Jake. I wondered what she was typing—and to whom—and imagined it had something to do with her encounter with Jake.

Finally, she put the phone in her purse and got into her car. With a quick look around, she backed out of the parking spot, then started driving forward.

She was headed right for me.

I ducked down like an idiot as she approached, but it was too late. She'd caught me staring at her. I was certain she would stop her car and confront me, but instead I heard her rev her motor and drive off.

Well played, Darcy, I scolded myself. She'll probably text Jake and ask him why that woman from the school-bus truck was spying on her in the parking lot just before she tried to duck down out of sight. I felt a wave of embarrassment pass through me.

Enough! I told myself. I started the car, backed out of the spot, and headed for the safety of my Airstream home so I could take a long, hot shower and get started on that bottle of wine. Maybe that would help me wash down the bittersweet cream puff from Jake.

Dillon was sitting at the table with his laptop when I entered Abby's home through the back sliding-glass door. I rarely saw him without an electronic device, except when he was helping Aunt Abby in the school bus.

Even then he brought his laptop and cell phone with him and checked them every chance he got.

"Darcy!" Aunt Abby exclaimed from the kitchen, as if she hadn't seen me in years.

She came over and gave me a big hug, followed at her feet by Basil, her Doxie, who barked a greeting. She cleared her throat to get Dillon's attention. He grunted "Hey," while keeping his eyes on the laptop screen. I sat down across from him, setting the small box with the untouched cream puff on the table. Aunt Abby immediately brought me a glass of Tournesol merlot—her favorite Napa Valley wine. I was tempted to chug it but didn't want my aunt and cousin to think I had a drinking problem.

"Thanks, Aunt Abby. Smells good in here."

"The pizza is just about ready. Enjoy your wine. Dillon has something to share with you—don't you, Dillon?" She rested a hand on his shoulder. Basil barked again.

Dillon blinked as if he were coming out of a trance and looked up at me. "Oh, uh, well. I've been doing some more research about the contest."

"You're calling it research now?"

"Dude," Dillon said, "if you knew how easy it is to breach someone's password, you'd be surprised."

"Okay, okay, you're a genius. So did you find out anything else on the judges that can help us with the competition?" I took a sip of wine and felt my legs and arms begin to melt.

"Not about the judges," he said. "But I did find out a few things about the other contestants."

I sat up straighter. "Really? You know who they are? I didn't think they were going to announce them until the night before the competition, at the preview party."

Dillon smiled. He could be so smug.

"All right, so what did you find out?" I asked, intrigued.

"It'll cost you that cream puff over there." He pointed to the box on the table that Jake had left for me at my car.

"How do you know it's a cream puff?" I asked.

He pointed to the printing on the box that read Dream Puffs. "Duh."

"Fine," I said. I hadn't had the stomach to eat it, nor the heart to throw it away. Now I wouldn't have to think about it anymore. I pushed it over to him.

"Okay," Dillon said, happy with his payment. "Like, there are five other contestants besides Mom and Jake. Ever heard of Frankie Nudo from Choco-Cheese Delights?"

I shook my head at both the name and the thought of chocolate and cheese combined. Maybe I didn't know what I was missing.

"Frankie's quite a character," Aunt Abby said. "He's divorced—something about his wife caught him cheating."

"You know him?" I asked, surprised at the number of people Aunt Abby had met after starting her food truck business.

"Like I said, it's a small community. Especially among the chocolate people. Frankie was one of the first to combine chocolate with cheese, and it's become quite popular. Isn't it amazing how many foods taste better with a chocolate coating?"

I nodded. "Do you think he has a chance of winning?" I asked.

Aunt Abby shrugged. "Probably not. While some people like the combination of chocolate and cheese, most are like you and won't even try it. I think you have to have a sophisticated palate to enjoy chocolate-covered Brie, you know?"

"Yuck," Dillon said simply. "Sounds disgusting. I wouldn't eat American cheese dipped in chocolate, let alone something like moldy old Brie."

"That's good mold, Dillon," Aunt Abby said. "It's called *Penicillium candidum*. The bacteria seep into the cheese and turn it into a wonderful, soft, tasty delicacy."

"A good mold?" he protested. "Right."

"It's true," Aunt Abby confirmed. "There are good molds, like the ones covering soft cheese, and bad molds, like on bread, which create toxins that will make you sick. When in doubt, throw it out, I always say. But not Brie."

"I'm still not going to eat it," Dillon said. "Let's move on. Next, there's Harrison Tofflemire from Chocolate Falls. His company makes those chocolate waterfall thingies."

"Chocolate Falls? I love those gizmos!" Aunt Abby interrupted. "That's the fastest and easiest way to cover foods with chocolate—strawberries, caramels, marshmallows, bacon."

Dillon winced at the bacon reference. "Anyway, he's gotten rich off them. Claims he invented them and he sues anyone who's tried to copy him. From his Chocolate Falls website, he sounds like a jerk. Whenever he gets a complaint in the comments section, he makes the person sound like an idiot, like whatever is wrong with the thing is the user's fault."

"Really?" Aunt Abby said.

"Yeah, like, one lady wrote in and said the chocolate doesn't flow evenly down the tiers. Harrison told the lady she didn't set up her machine right and should get someone who knows how to put things together to do it."

"Wow," I said. "Sounds like he's a little short on customer-service skills."

"Another lady said the chocolate is either too thick like pudding or too watery, never just right."

"What did he say to that?" Aunt Abby asked.

"He wrote back, 'Follow the directions better and use better chocolate, not the cheap stuff.'"

"Jeez. It's a wonder he's still in business with that attitude," I said.

"My favorite one was from someone who complained that the fountain was lopsided. He told her to put it on a level surface, as if she wouldn't already have done that."

Aunt Abby frowned. "Well, I'm not looking forward to meeting Harrison Tofflemire—that's for sure. You're right; he is a jerk."

"There's a bunch more like those," Dillon said. "Complaints about the temperature, the design, the weight of the thing, how flimsy it is. Plus how hard it is to get it fixed or get a refund."

"We'll have to see what his chocolate tastes like," Aunt Abby said. "If his Chocolate Falls machine is so shoddy, I'd imagine his chocolate will be too. It may be game over for Mr. Tofflemire."

"Maybe not," Dillon said, raising an eyebrow. "He may have an advantage at the festival—at least with the guys. Get a load of this." Dillon turned his iPhone toward them, revealing two beautiful, buxom girls dressed in skimpy cheerleading outfits.

"Who are they?" I asked.

"'Jezebel' and 'Delilah,' his college-age twin daughters. At least, that's what I call them. Apparently, they help out at his shop—and they wear those cheerleading outfits. According to Harrison, business is booming, with guys coming in off the streets to buy chocolate-covered whatevers."

Aunt Abby shook her head. "Well, he may pull in the most money, using those kinds of visual lures, but when it comes to the contest, taste will tell."

Dillon shrugged. "Next there's some chick named Mon-it Richards."

"Mon*et*," Aunt Abby corrected, pronouncing the name with a French accent: Mon-*nay*. "Like the painter, dear."

"You know her too?" I asked.

"I've heard of her. She owns a truck that makes ice-cream-cake cones in all kinds of flavors and colors. As a matter of fact, she's been trying to snag a spot for her I Scream Cupcakes truck at Fort Mason for months."

"Okay, so Moh-NAY," Dillon said, mocking the French pronunciation. "I suppose it's Ree-SHARDS, not Richards?"

Aunt Abby shrugged him off. "What did you find out about her?"

"She's hot," Dillon said, staring at his iPhone screen. After a few seconds, he turned the screen around so we could see.

She was hot.

She had shoulder-length dark hair that tumbled over one eye and a beauty mark under the other, heavily made-up eye. Her pouty lips were painted bright red, matching her red fingernails. She appeared to be posing in front of her truck in a tight black leotard-looking outfit, as if presenting her business—or herself—like Vanna White might do showcasing a winning prize. With that too-tiny waist, those larger-than-life breasts, and that self-confident smirk on her face, I hated her immediately. This competition was *on*.

"Better keep her away from Jake," Dillon added.

I glared at him.

"Who else?" Aunt Abby said, distracting us from a possible food fight.

Dillon checked his notes on his iPhone. "Some dude named Griffin Makeba. Calls himself the 'Pie Man' and owns the 'Piehole' truck." Dillon used air quotes at each pie reference.

"I've seen it around," Aunt Abby said. "He parks illegally at a bunch of different places until they run him off. Pies? How much competition can he be? Besides, he's just a kid." Anyone under forty was "just a kid" to my sixtysomething aunt.

"His pies are getting good write-ups on Yelp, Off the Grid, and Food Mafia. He says he uses his grandmother's secret pie recipe, the one she used to make as a cook for a plantation owner. He says the secret has African roots, but he won't give out the recipe or talk about the ingredients."

"Hmm. Secretive, eh?" I said, as if I were about to take on the role of Sherlock Holmes. "Interesting."

"I've never been a fan of chocolate pie," Aunt Abby said. "Too sweet, too gushy, too intense. My mother used to make chocolate silk pies for my dad for his birthday, but I only ate the ice cream that came with it."

"So that's why you've never made a chocolate pie?" Dillon asked. "Because you don't like them? Did you ever think I might want to try one?"

"Guilt trip," I whispered to Aunt Abby. "Just ignore him."

"Is that it?" Aunt Abby asked.

Dillon looked at his phone. "There's one more. Some old lady named Wendy Spellman. She supposedly has a little shop at Pier 39 called Candyland."

"Wendy Spellman?" Aunt Abby exclaimed. "Oh my goodness! Wendy's an old friend! I didn't know she was competing."

"Was she from culinary school too?" I asked, remembering her friendship with George Brown, now deceased.

"No. We met in high school. We used to be in the Cooking Club together at Balboa High. I lost track of her when I went to culinary school and she went to community college. After all these years, we reconnected again on Facebook."

Dillon rolled his eyes. Facebook was so yesterday for the younger generation, but the older folks had embraced it. I had closed all of my social networking accounts after I found out about Trevor cheating on me because I'd found out about it on *his* Facebook page.

"Have you talked to her in person? Do you know anything more about her?" I asked.

Aunt Abby shook her head. "All I know is from her Facebook postings. She posts about her candy shop a lot—the pictures of her candy creations are incredible— but she never mentioned she was entering the contest. I keep meaning to get over there and say hi, but I've been so busy."

"Didn't she stop by when Dad died last year?" Dillon asked.

"As a matter of fact, you're right," Aunt Abby said, looking off into the distance. "I forgot about that. She brought that lovely wreath made out of candy. How could I have forgotten?" She looked at Dillon. "And how did you happen to remember her with all those people who came to the memorial?"

Dillon made a face. "She seemed kinda crazy."

Aunt Abby huffed. "No crazier than I am. Besides, sane people are boring."

"What did she do that makes you say that, Dillon?" I asked, curious about Aunt Abby's old friend and now competitor.

"Well, first, she wore that bright-colored dress and big hat full of flowers, as if she were going to the Easter parade or something."

Aunt Abby nodded. "She always did have a flair for fashion."

I kept my snort to myself.

"Then she went around tasting all the food without taking any on a plate, like she couldn't commit to any one thing and had to have it all. It was weird."

"She's a culinary artist, like me," Aunt Abby said. "We taste things. It's the way we roll."

I had to stuff another snort at her choice of hipster lingo. My aunt, the gangsta/thug wannabe.

"That's not all," Dillon said, raising an eyebrow. "She was, like, flirting with everyone there." He suddenly turned bright red.

"Oh my God!" I said, grinning. "You think Wendy Spellman came on to you!"

Aunt Abby blinked. "Are you sure, Dillon? I mean, she's my age. I hardly think she'd be interested in a college boy."

"Oh yeah? Well, when she hugged me, she put her hand on my butt."

I didn't think Aunt Abby would have a comeback for that bombshell, but she surprised me and said, "Well, you're a very handsome young man, Dillon."

I could no longer hold back my laughter.

Dillon glared at me and slammed the laptop closed. "That's it. You want my help? Forget it."

"Oh, don't be that way, dear," Aunt Abby said. "We're very grateful for all that you do. I don't suppose you found out what the other contestants are making for the competition."

Dillon's frown softened. "Not yet. It's apparently top secret. But I will." The gleam was back in his eye.

At least I knew what Jake was making—those killer mocha cream puffs. But I hadn't had the chance to tell him that Aunt Abby was in the competition too. I wondered what he'd think of that.

Not that I cared.

Aunt Abby brought the caprese pizza to the table, along with a fresh green salad filled with cherry tomatoes, Kalamata olives, and mozzarella cheese. Everything looked and smelled delicious. No one could beat Aunt Abby's cooking, even if she'd honed her skills at the local school cafeteria. I took another long sip of wine in preparation for my first bite.

"Well, the competition doesn't sound too stiff," I said to Aunt Abby. "I'm sure you'll cook them under the table, so to speak." I helped myself to salad and a slice of pizza, putting everything on my plate. "Although Jake may have a slight edge," I added quietly.

"What?" Aunt Abby said, frowning.

I looked up at her. Uh-oh. Did I just say that out loud?

"What do you mean?" she asked.

"Nothing," I said, trying to spear some lettuce leaves with my fork.

"Darcy . . . ," Aunt Abby said.

"Really, it's nothing. That woman we saw him talking to? I didn't tell you, but that was Lyla Vassar. She's a feature reporter for Channel 2."

Aunt Abby's eyes widened. "Uh-oh. Don't tell me she's going to do a story on him for TV."

I shrugged and looked down at my food, not wanting to see the disappointment in Aunt Abby's face. "Even if she is, I wouldn't worry. It won't help him," I finally said, trying to reassure her. "Granted his cream puffs are great, but your whoopie pies are out of this world."

I glanced at Dillon for reinforcement, but he was busy on his laptop again. It must have been important enough to keep him from eating. Ordinarily, nothing came between food and Dillon's mouth.

"Dillon?" I asked. "Did you find something else?"

Dillon frowned, keyed in a few more strokes at rapid-fire speed, then eventually looked up at me. "Uh . . . I don't think Jake's getting a special feature on TV from that news chick."

"Why not?" I asked. "You didn't see them this afternoon. They were having quite the conversation. She was flirting her ass off with him."

Dillon closed his laptop. "I think they call it nepotism or something."

I frowned at him. "What are you talking about?"

Dillon sighed. "That reporter—Lyla Vassar?"

"Yeah. What about her? Did you find something?"

Dillon hesitated.

"What? Tell me!"

Still frowning, he looked up at me with his big brown eyes. "Lyla Vassar is Jake's ex-fiancée."

Oh my God. Jake had never told me her name, and I had never asked.

What the hell was his drop-dead-gorgeous ex doing sniffing around Jake again?

And touching him.
And kissing him.
There could be only one reason.
She wanted to be friends . . . with benefits.
Or more. She wanted to get back together.

Chapter 4

The San Francisco Chocolate Festival couldn't come fast enough. I needed something to distract me from thinking about Jake. I hadn't seen him much in the last two weeks, mainly because I'd been avoiding him after spotting him with his ex. Plus, Lyla had been by several more times to see him, disappearing into his cream puff truck for who knows what.

I made the mistake of checking her out on the Internet. As a feature reporter for Channel 2, she was all over the place. Black-tie charity event for Children's Hospital? She was there, dressed in a black-and-white suit and interviewing the mayor. Bay to Breakers run? She was there, making her souvenir T-shirt look like an exclusive designer top as she chatted with the station's sports reporter. Gay Pride Parade? She was there, draped in a rainbow of colors and talking with Gavin Newsom, a leader in San Francisco's gay rights causes. Polar Bear Plunge? She was there, wearing barely anything more than a bikini and goose bumps as she plunged into the freezing water at Aquatic Park.

And hardly a long blond-highlighted hair out of place.

So this was Jake's ex? Beauty-queen looks, workout body, and popular TV personality? With her back in his life, no wonder he hadn't been available lately.

I did a little more research, suddenly obsessed with Lyla Vassar, and found so many links, it would have taken days to read every detail. I decided to focus on her Facebook page and had easy access to her "Lyla Vassar, Channel 2" page. Her personal page offered little information to people who weren't friends, so I put in a request, hoping she'd think I was a fan and maybe give me clearance. In the meantime, I scoured her professional page and learned five useful tidbits:

1. She'd been at Channel 2 since leaving college six years ago, after winning the titles of "Miss California Animal Rights," "Miss Keep California Green," and "Miss Gilroy Garlic Festival."

Great. She really was a beauty queen.

2. Her relationship status was "single."

Uh-oh. I thought Jake had said she'd taken up with the DA who prosecuted him.

3. She was "super grateful" for the award she received for her exposé on the city's homeless pigeon population.

Seriously?

4. She thought San Francisco was the "Best City in California!"

and

5. She was "totally psyched" about her upcoming feature on the San Francisco Chocolate Festival.

I was doomed. Now that I knew she was "single" and "psyched" about the Chocolate Festival, I was certain something was going on between her and Jake. When Jake did call, I let it go to voice mail, and when he stopped by, I told him I was too busy to take a break. There was no way I could compete with Drop Dead, and after my breakup with Trevor the Tool, I wasn't about to get my heart broken again so soon. By the end of the week, he seemed to have gotten the message. The calls and drop-by visits had stopped and I hardly missed him.

Crap. Who was I kidding?

Luckily, I had lots to keep me busy. With the Chocolate Festival a day away, Aunt Abby had Dillon and me making whoopie pies until I was sick of the sight of them. She hoped to collect a bunch of tickets from attendees for her contest entry, win that ample prize money, and hopefully gain fame from being featured on the Food Network show. Success came down to a bite-sized melt-in-your-mouth dark-chocolate-and-raspberry-mocha-cream sandwich.

At seven p.m. the night before the festival was to

begin, I stood in Aunt Abby's kitchen, dressed in black slacks and a black silk blouse, waiting for my aunt and Dillon to finish dressing so we could head for the preview party. Reina Patel had invited the judges and contestants to a private soiree at the Maritime Museum, so we could all get acquainted, taste the chocolate contest entries, and celebrate the hard work it took to participate in the Chocolate Festival.

I hadn't wanted to go, knowing Jake would be there, but Aunt Abby insisted, and I couldn't let her down. However, I planned to keep a low profile, hence the black outfit, and hopefully go unnoticed not only by Jake, but also by Polly Montgomery. I was worried if she found out I was part of Aunt Abby's team, she'd vote for anyone but my aunt.

"I'm so nervous!" Aunt Abby announced as she entered the kitchen, little Basil scuffling at her feet. She was fiddling with an earring, trying to insert it into her pierced left ear. It was a tiny silver spoon that went perfectly with the tiny silver fork that dangled from her right ear. She wore a pink floral blouse over slinky pink pants, with matching pink heels and a pink shrug over her shoulders. I'd never seen her so dressed up. She looked like a strawberry ice cream confection.

Dillon sauntered in behind her, this time rat-free. To my surprise, he'd changed out of his usual slacker garb and was wearing what looked like brand-new black jeans and a collared button-down black shirt I didn't know he owned. He'd even added some product to his normally porcupine hair in an attempt to tame it, and he held a white tie in his hand as if it were a snake. His only concession to his normal style were his red Converse athletic shoes.

"Mom, why are you nervous?" he asked his mother.

Aunt Abby and I stared at him, openmouthed.

"What?" he asked.

"You look . . . nice!" I blurted.

"My handsome son!" Aunt Abby added, grinning. "With a tie!"

Dillon actually blushed. "Chill out. It's just a costume. I'm going as a waiter to blend in and do a little eavesdropping at the party."

"Clever," I said. "All you need is one of those half-aprons those avant-garde servers wear."

"You mean, like this?" he said, pulling one of Aunt Abby's aprons from a drawer and folding it over before tying it around his waist.

"Perfect!"

"So, Mom. What are you nervous about? The competition?"

"No, no. I plan to ace that." Aunt Abby checked her reflection in her shiny kitchen toaster. "It's this damn party! I hate these fancy froufrou things."

"Well, you look adorable," I said. "Cute earrings. And with that outfit you're going to *kill* at this party as well as at the competition."

She shrugged. "I'm only going so I can chat up the judges like all the other contestants are probably going to do. Thanks to Dillon, I know something about each of them, so I can carry on a decent conversation."

Dillon had been researching the judges and contestants on the Internet and filling his mother in on what he'd found. I doubted any of his information would help her win the contest—the proof would be in the pudding, or in Aunt Abby's case, the whoopie pies—but I supposed a former cafeteria lady could use all the help she could get.

Dillon turned to me and frowned. "Why are you dressed like me?"

"I'm not going as a waiter, if that's what you mean," I said. "I'm just keeping it simple. We're only backup players in Aunt Abby's gastronomic theater, remember?"

Dillon shook his head. "Copycat."

"Dork," I said under my breath.

"Time to go!" Aunt Abby announced before we started a food fight.

I put on my black linen jacket and led the way. We would have taken my VW, but the backseat was a little snug. Dillon's dirt bike was out of the question, so we opted for Aunt Abby's Prius. I drove us to the Maritime Museum on Beach Street, located between Aquatic Park and Ghirardelli Square in the Russian Hill area of San Francisco.

It would be hard to miss the museum, even on a foggy night. The Works Progress Administration had funded the construction of the Art Deco Moderne building back in 1939 as a public bathhouse, but today it was part of the San Francisco Maritime National Historic Park Service. From the outside, the museum looked like a ship, painted white with round portholes, two decks, and a naval flag at the top of the third story. The inside had been renovated several times and currently featured colorful murals from the WPA era by artist Hilaire Hiler. The building included a steamship room, showing the evolution of sailing power, photo murals of the city's early waterfront era, scrimshaw art and whaling weapons, and an intact shipboard radio and teletype.

I found parking on the street and squeezed the Toyota into a space between a Smart car and a Fiat to avoid valet parking. Tonight's party was being held on the veranda overlooking the bay, so we entered through the gray double doors, held open by a man wearing a crisp naval uniform, and headed across the room and out the door. Outside, the area was filled with round tables covered in white tablecloths, each featuring centerpieces made of long-stemmed chocolate roses. I glanced at the spectacular view of sparkling yachts moored at Aquatic Park, and Alcatraz, Angel Island, and Tiburon beyond. Although the spring night was clear—unusual for San Francisco in any season—most of the guests still had on their suit jackets or elegant wraps against any sudden chill, as they drank from fancy wineglasses and champagne flutes to warm their insides. The conversations seemed animated—no doubt focused on the topic of chocolate. A three-piece jazz band played softly in one corner, mostly ignored by the attendees.

We checked in at the welcome table and found our name tags. I looked around for the bar and spotted it on the far side of the veranda. Before I could sprint over, Abby managed to swipe a drink from a passing waiter, then took a deep breath and headed into the crowd. Dillon, apparently forgetting he was dressed as

a waiter, snagged a fancy-looking appetizer from another waiter, who frowned at him, and popped it in his
mouth. I helped myself to what turned out to be a
chocolate-dipped asparagus tip, which was oddly tasty.
All I needed was something to wash it down with, like
a giant glass of wine.

I made a beeline for the bar and surveyed the offerings. Besides the usual chardonnays and merlots, the
choices included a chocolate red wine, a chocolate stout
beer, a white chocolate champagne, and chocolate cor-
dials in edible chocolate shot glasses. I opted for a chocolate chardonnay, took a sip, then felt hot breath on the
back of my neck.

I whirled around to find Dillon standing right behind me.

"What are you doing?" I asked.

"Nothing," he said. "Just getting a drink like you."

"Well, don't sneak up on me like that," I said.

"Why so jumpy?" he asked.

"I'm not jumpy," I argued. But I was, and I knew why.
Jake. Where was he?

I took the glass of wine from the bartender and
stuffed a dollar into the tip jar. Dillon asked for the
chocolate stout, garnering another eyeballing—from
the bartender this time—which he ignored. After I took
a long sip of my drink, I stepped back into the shadows
to observe the crowd. Dillon joined me and began
pointing out the various judges and contestants.

"How do you know who's who without reading
their name tags?" I asked, squinting to see if I could
make out any names.

"Their pictures are in the program," he said, holding up a folded piece of paper I had somehow missed. He handed it to me.

I took another mouthful of wine. The drink had a weird aftertaste of chocolate, but the alcohol was beginning to do its trick. I felt more relaxed with every gulp.

Dillon nodded to a man with dark curly hair and a Mediterranean complexion who was talking to a blond woman with her hair up in a twist, wearing an eye-catching red velvet gown.

"That's Frankie Nudo," Dillon whispered, as if worried someone might hear us over the animated conversations coming from the crowd. "He owns the Choco-Cheese truck."

I glanced at the paper Dillon had given me and read Frankie Nudo's short bio. Most of it I already knew, thanks to Dillon's Internet sleuthing. But the program included something even Dillon hadn't been able to discover—Frankie Nudo's entry in the chocolate competition.

"Chocolate Goat Cheese Truffles?" I made a face. "That doesn't sound good at all." I studied the man a moment. While he seemed to be talking animatedly with the blond woman, his eyes darted around the room, as if he were looking for someone.

Dillon's eyes narrowed. "Who's the woman he's talking to? Her back is to us."

"Looks more like flirting to me," I said. "She keeps leaning in and putting a hand on his arm. Get a load of that ring on her finger. Is that a diamond?" The sparkler on the woman's finger must have been the size of a chocolate M&M—and about the same color. A chocolate diamond?

Frankie seemed to spot someone he recognized and frowned. Then he quickly downed his beer, gave the woman in red a superficial hug, and made his excuses. I watched as he headed into the crowd and disappeared.

As soon as he turned to go, the blonde looked around, no doubt for someone else to flirt with.

I recognized her immediately from her picture in the newspaper.

"Oh my God, that's Polly!" I whispered to Dillon. "I hope she doesn't spot me."

Dillon frowned. "Why not?"

I filled him in on the negative review I'd given to one of her ex-husband's restaurants.

"I doubt she cares or even remembers," he said.

"I'm not so sure, and I don't want to ruin Aunt Abby's chances for winning if Polly is still holding a grudge against me." I turned away to make sure she didn't see me. "What's she doing now?"

"She just chugged the rest of her drink," Dillon said. "Now she's setting the glass down on a table . . . and she just snatched another drink off a waiter's tray. Looks like she's not one to let her mouth go dry for very long."

"You said she's supposed to be quite the party girl," I said, not surprised at Dillon's observation. "Is she talking to anyone else yet?"

Dillon shook his head, then said, "Wait. . . . She's heading for another guy. . . . I think it's Harrison Tofflemire, the Chocolate Falls guru. What did he enter in the contest?"

I was about to scan the brochure when a woman came up to me holding two empty wineglasses. She wore a long chocolate-brown sheath, slit up the side and embellished with sequins and rhinestones. Her black shoulder-length hair framed her face, and she'd emphasized her dark eyes with a heavy layer of eyeliner, making her look even more exotic. Her long nails were painted chocolate brown, and one sported a diamond stud that matched the tiny diamond in her pierced nose. A long silk scarf, light beige and dotted with silk-screened chocolate chips, was draped over her neck.

I was about to admire her themed scarf when she said, "Why are you two just standing there? You're supposed to be circulating the drinks and hors d'oeuvres. I didn't hire you to help yourselves and stare at the guests."

My mouth dropped open. Apparently she believed Dillon was one of the waiters, but did she actually think I was part of the serving staff too?

"I'm sorry, but I'm—," I started to explain, but Dillon cut me off.

"Yes, we're sorry. We'll get right to it." He bowed his head subserviently.

I blinked at Dillon's response but kept my mouth shut and watched as he took the two glasses from the woman's hands. She gave us the once-over, then said, "See that you do, or you won't be working for me again." With that she turned on her dark brown high heels and returned to the crowd.

"What a beeotch!" I said. "Who does she think she is?"

Dillon hushed me. "That's Reina Patel, the event co-ordinator. She's the one who's running this show, and she can get us kicked out of here if she feels like it. Mom says she's a bit of a diva. She's even having the event videotaped to submit to one of those Food Network shows—a kind of behind-the-scenes thing. Starring her, of course. Mom said this is her first year hosting the Chocolate Festival, so she's probably worried about every little thing."

So that was the woman who had called Aunt Abby and told her about George Brown's death. "Why didn't you tell her I'm part of the competition? Why did you let her think I was staff?"

Dillon grinned. "It's more fun this way. When she realizes we're both on Mom's team, she'll be all flustered and embarrassed. And besides, it might work to our advantage if we act like waiters. No one will notice us, so maybe we'll hear things. . . ."

Dillon was always scheming.

Moments later the videographer appeared from out of nowhere. His digital video camera was focused on Reina, obscuring his face, but from his clothes he looked like a typical college student in jeans and a T-shirt. He followed Reina from a distance of a few feet as she began greeting the various guests.

I returned to the program to see what Harrison Tofflemire was entering in the contest. "It says here he's created something called Chocolate Kahlua Falls. Sounds interesting."

I studied the man who was currently talking to Polly. He was hefty—dare I say fat—as if he'd been enjoying many of his own Chocolate Falls over the years. Balding, with glasses, a rosy gin-blossom nose, and pudgy fingers wrapped around the wineglass stem, he looked like a man who'd had success early and then gone to pot. But his less than appealing appearance didn't seem to stop Polly from fawning all over him. She alternately straightened his bow tie, patted his Buddha tummy, and giggled at his jokes. Jeez. Next to him stood two bored-looking young women in identical skimpy tight dresses more appropriate for clubbing than a reception.

Dillon nudged me, causing me to nearly spill my drink. "Careful!" I said.

"Check it out," he said, ignoring my complaint. "It's that French chick."

"Monet?" I scanned the area, trying to pick out someone who looked French, then realized that was impossible. "Where is she?"

"Over there." He pointed her out. "She's headed straight for Polly and Harrison, and she doesn't look happy."

I watched as the frowning, thin woman joined the twosome. Harrison's attention suddenly shifted to the attractive newcomer, who had obviously pleased Harrison, while Polly seemed taken aback by the intrusion. While Polly was still trim and in good shape for a woman her age—I guessed fortysomething—she had nothing on the younger, prettier French pastry chef. Monet sported white blond hair cut in a smooth bob, her makeup expertly done. She wore a skintight silver sheath, the top cut low enough to reveal ample pale breasts and bottom cut high enough to show off long, slim legs. She towered over Polly and Harrison in her silver stiletto Manolos. Harrison looked downright hypnotized by her.

"Wow."

I glanced at Dillon. Like Harrison, he was staring trancelike at Monet. "Close your mouth, Hacker-Boy," I said.

Men.

I wished I could hear what Monet was saying to the other two guests, but the noise of the crowd prevented any eavesdropping. She kept glancing around the room while she talked, and I wondered who she might be looking for. I checked the program to see what the Frenchwoman was offering for the contest. "Hmm. It looks like the girl from I Scream Cupcakes is entering something called Chocolate Scream Cakes, whatever that is. She probably doesn't want to give away too much before tonight's preview tasting."

Dillon still hadn't broken his gaze. I waved a hand in front of his frozen face. "Earth to Dillon."

"Uh, what?"

I sighed and checked the brochure. "Never mind. Any sign of Griffin Makeba, the Pie Guy, or Aunt Abby's friend Wendy Spellman?"

Dillon tore his eyes from the dessert called Monet, searched the room, then pointed to a young African American guy sitting alone at a table, seemingly reading the brochure. "That's him."

Griffin appeared to be in his late twenties or early thirties. He was sipping what looked like a glass of water while glancing up occasionally to observe the other mingling guests. Much like the videographer, he had not dressed up. Instead he wore faded black jeans and a T-shirt with a graphic of a pie in the middle. Underneath were the words "Fill Your Piehole." He, too, was frowning.

I checked the program. "Griffin's entry is called Chocolate Cherry Tarts."

I glanced back up to see an older woman with short gray hair, wearing a long Victorian-style dress, join him. They shook hands, said a few words, then sat sipping their drinks in silence and watching the crowd.

"Oh boy. That's Wendy Spellman, my mom's friend," Dillon said, indicating the older woman sitting with Griffin. "I hope she doesn't see me. I don't need another butt massage."

At that moment, Wendy spotted Dillon, gave him a big smile, and waved him over. Dillon smiled meekly and waved back, muttering to me through clenched teeth, "Great. If I'm not back in five minutes, come and rescue me."

I giggled and watched Dillon pick up a tray from the bar, set two waiting drinks on it, and head over to join his mom's friend at the table, still posing as a waiter.

I was about to take a sip of my wine when I heard a familiar voice behind me. "Can I buy you a drink?"

Recognizing the voice, I turned around.

Jake Miller.

Apparently my waiter disguise hadn't fooled him.

I sucked in my breath when I saw what he was wearing—a smart black suit fitted perfectly to his muscular body, paired with a bright Grateful Dead tie. I'd never seen him so dressed up before. Had he looked like that when he'd worked as an attorney? I had a feeling all he had to do was smile at the women in the jury box and they would have voted his way.

"Jake!" I said, feeling a sudden heat wave envelop me. "Uh . . . you made it."

Lame, I thought. But what was I supposed to say at an awkward moment like this? How's your ex?

"You look really great," Jake said, eyeing me up and down.

I felt my face burn and let out a half smile. "Oh, this? I'm just trying to keep a low profile. It's Aunt Abby's night tonight."

"Well, you'd look terrific in anything. Here." He handed me a brown-colored drink in a champagne flute.

I set down my empty wineglass and took the one he offered. I held it up to the light to examine the unusual color. "What is it?"

"Mocha champagne. It's not bad."

I took a sip. Like the other chocolate drinks, it tasted weird, but at the moment, I figured I could use another boost of courage from the alcohol.

"Sorry we've kept missing each other these past couple of weeks," Jake said.

"Yeah, you know . . . I've been helping my aunt get ready for this event, and you've been—" I stopped myself.

He nodded. "I was surprised when I heard your aunt had entered the competition. You never mentioned it."

I wanted to say, "I never got the chance with your ex around," but I didn't. I kept it light instead of snarky. "Yeah. How about that?" I sipped the champagne. "So how've you been?"

"I've missed you," Jake said quietly. I turned aside so he wouldn't see the hurt on my face, but I could feel his eyes on me as I watched the party guests.

"I missed you, too," I said as casually as I could. "I know you've been busy too." I wondered if he'd get my drift and confess he'd been seeing his ex.

Instead, Jake took the drink out of my hand and set it down, along with his. He took my hands and turned me toward him. "Listen, I really am sorry about being out of touch lately. Like I said, I've been dealing with something and it's taken up a lot of time. But I don't want to jeopardize our friendship. . . ."

"Friendship?" I repeated. Was that what he thought this was? I pulled my hands away.

"Darcy, I've wanted to tell you what's been going on, but . . ."

I took a deep breath. "But what, Jake?"

"But it involved another person."

"I figured as much." I looked out at the crowd. I knew who he meant—Lyla Vassar.

He took my chin and turned my face toward him. "You know I was engaged before, right?"

"I vaguely remember," I said. *Oh boy. Here it comes.*

"Well, Lyla—that's her name—she came by a couple of weeks ago—"

"I know."

Jake blinked in surprise. "You know?"

I nodded. "She seems to make regular visits to your Dream Puff truck. I assumed—"

He cut me off. "Oh . . . you assumed . . . No, no, Darcy. She needs my help."

I'll bet, I thought.

"She wants me to help with her divorce."

So she can marry you.

"Brad—the guy she married, the guy she left me for—he was the DA who prosecuted me when I got disbarred. When I lost everything, she dumped me and ran off with him."

I suddenly felt sorry for him, but it still didn't change anything.

"Now," Jake continued, "she wants out. She found out he's been having an affair with the court stenographer, and now Lyla wants a divorce."

I frowned, trying not to show my skepticism. Had this Brad guy really cheated on Jake's ex-fiancée? Or had Lyla come to her senses and realized what a great guy Jake was? Possibilities poured through my mind like a chocolate fountain.

"Sorry to hear that," I said evenly, "but I thought you weren't practicing law anymore. How are you going to help her? And why? You don't owe her anything."

But I knew why. In spite of everything his ex had done to him, Jake was a genuinely nice guy, and not the type to hold a grudge. Besides, she was drop-dead gorgeous. And maybe he was still in love with her.

"I'm helping her because her parents asked me to."

I remembered that Lyla's parents would have lost

their life savings if Jake hadn't helped them out back when he was a corporate securities attorney. When he discovered one of his clients was bilking investors out of their money—including his ex-fiancée and her parents—he told them to pull their money out in order to protect them. But he was indicted for securities fraud and disbarred for breaching the attorney/client privilege. That's when he turned to creating cream puffs.

Still, why would Jake help his ex-fiancée and her parents now?

"Jake, you're not a private detective. You're not even a divorce lawyer. Why doesn't Lyla just hire a professional to do all of this? Why get you involved?"

He shrugged and looked away. "Honestly, I'm not sure I understand it either." He shook his head. "Guilt, maybe."

"What do you have to feel guilty about?"

"I was a workaholic when I was at the law firm. I know I neglected her. That's probably why she left me. Brad gave her the attention she wasn't getting from me. That's part of the reason I didn't try to get reinstated to the bar. I realized after all was said and done that I didn't have much of a life outside of work, and I wanted to change that."

"Jake, are you sure she's not just trying to get you—" I stopped myself.

"Back?" Jake broke into a grin. "Darcy . . . are you . . . jealous?"

"What?" I felt my face turn the color of Aunt Abby's dyed hair. "No! I'm just trying to look out for you. . . ."

"You actually think Lyla wants to get back together

with me?" He laughed. "I'm flattered, but there's not a chance in hell of that happening."

I started to ask if he was really that naive, but my response was interrupted by a scream. The room went deadly silent.

I immediately looked for Aunt Abby to see if she was all right. I spotted her sitting at the table with her friend Wendy. Both were staring openmouthed at the table next to them, as were the rest of the guests who had heard the scream. I leaned in to see what had happened.

The limp figure of a woman lay facedown on top of the table, not moving.

I recognized her from the blond twist of hair and red gown.

Polly Montgomery.

Chapter 5

"Oh my God!" a woman shrieked. "Is she dead?"

The festival judge lay sprawled across the round table. She wasn't moving.

Jake pushed through the encircling crowd, shouldering his way to the table. I was right behind him. "Someone call nine-one-one!" he said as he reached in to feel Polly's neck.

I heard a muffled giggle and looked around to see who was rude enough to laugh when there was a dead woman lying in the middle of a table.

It was the dead woman. She raised her head and blinked her glassy red eyes.

The crowd gasped.

She rolled over onto her back and giggled again.

So, Polly Montgomery wasn't dead after all. She was simply dead drunk.

"Whoopsh!" she said, grinning as she looked up at Jake. "How about a li'l help, handshome?"

"She's all right," Jake announced to the onlooking crowd. "Everyone, give her some space."

Polly waved her arm around. The chocolate diamond on her finger sparkled in the light. "Hello? Need a hand here, big boy."

The crowd began murmuring at the spectacle Polly was presenting. Like a gentleman, Jake took Polly's arm and hoisted her up to a tenuous sitting position on the table. She shook her head as if trying to clear her vision. "Whoa!" she said. "Why is the room spinning?"

"Are you okay, Ms. Montgomery?" Jake asked.

"'Coursh I am," Polly replied, as the crowd whispered around her. She glanced at the table. "Must a' shlipped on a wet spot."

"What were you trying to do? Stand on the table?" Jake asked.

She shrugged. "I just wanted to make an announshment."

"Well, next time don't try to stand on a table in heels," Jake admonished.

"How else was I 'posed to get everyone's attenshun?" She swung her feet onto a chair, using it as a step down from the tabletop. She swayed precariously on her perch.

"Well, you've got their attention now," Jake said. "Why don't you come down and make your announcement? It's a lot safer."

As Jake reached to help Polly down, Reina Patel came rushing up, her dark eyebrows pinched in a frown. "What happened? What's going on? Get her off the table this instant!"

"Calm down, Reina." Polly leaned into Jake's strong arms. "I just got a little dizshy. I'm fine, but I could use a drink." She winked at Jake.

He took Polly by the waist and guided her feet to the floor. Polly's hands lingered on Jake's arms a few seconds too long for my liking before she brushed off her gown and touched the back of her French twist. She snatched up a half-empty glass of wine from a nearby table and downed it. "Great party, Reina."

Reina reached for Polly's free hand. "I think you need to come with me—"

Polly cut her off and yanked her hand away. "Wait a sec. I wanna tell everyone who I'm gonna vote for tomorrow so they can all relaxsh."

The crowd hushed, waiting to hear what Polly was about to say. Before she could speak again, Reina took her by the arm, more forcefully this time.

"Come on, Polly. You need to get your beauty rest before the big day tomorrow. Besides, we don't want to spoil the fun for everyone tonight."

Polly blinked slowly, then stared at Reina as if just recognizing her. "Ooookay," Polly said, nodding like a bobblehead doll.

Reina relaxed her grip and led the intoxicated woman toward the doors. Polly stumbled a couple of times along the way, tripping over her long gown. I noticed the videographer a few feet away, taping the scene, and wondered if this was something Reina wanted to capture on tape.

"J.C.!" Reina snapped. She swiped her fingertips across her throat, signaling "cut" so he'd stop taping. "Help me, would you?" The twentysomething man named J.C. lowered the recorder and took Polly's other arm.

"I'm fine! I jus' need another drink," Polly mumbled before she and her two escorts disappeared behind the exit doors.

"Where are they taking her?" Aunt Abby whispered to me.

I shrugged. "They're probably sending her home in a cab."

"Wow," Dillon said, as the party guests slowly resumed their conversations. "She's totally wasted! But I guess that's normal for her. I saw a bunch of selfies on her Facebook page, and she looked shit-faced in about half of them. Plus, I overheard some people talking about her drinking problem."

"What did they say?" I asked Dillon.

He shrugged. "Something about how much she was drinking tonight and how her glass was never empty."

"I wonder how she expects to judge the contest with the hangover she's sure to have tomorrow," Aunt Abby said.

"It sounded like she's already made up her mind," I answered. "And we haven't even tasted the entries yet."

Aunt Abby glanced at Jake. "She'll probably choose your cream puffs, Jake."

Jake shook his head. "I'm sure it'll be your whoopie pies, Abby."

"They're both fantastic," I said, rolling my eyes.

"Actually, I don't think it's going to be either one of you," Dillon interrupted.

"What?" I asked.

"I've been doing a little recon," Dillon said.

"Recon?" I raised an eyebrow.

"Yeah, you know, surveillance. I wanted to see if I could get a line on the other judges—Simon Van Houten and Isabel Lau. Figure out their tastes."

I perked up. "You mean, you've been spying on them."

Aunt Abby's eyes widened. "What did you find out?"

"Not much. As soon as Polly joined them, they got real quiet and looked kind of nervous."

I frowned. "Did Polly say something to them?"

Dillon shrugged. "Yeah, but I couldn't hear what it was. All I know is, Van Houten's face turned red and Lau looked like she'd seen a ghost."

What had Polly Montgomery said to the two judges to make them react that way? Did it have anything to do with the death of Judge George Brown?

Too bad I didn't have time to do some eavesdropping of my own. Sirens interrupted my plans. Someone must have called 911, because moments later EMTs and police officers burst in and all conversations came to an immediate halt.

Jake handled the cops—he happened to know a couple of them from his years working as an attorney. One in particular was an attractive Asian woman who wore the equipment-laden uniform as if it were a fashion statement. He explained the situation, told them Polly had left, and suggested they talk to Reina when she returned if they wanted to know anything else. With no real harm done, the cops and paramedics took off. I was ready to head home too, done in by all the party drama at the end of a long day of helping Aunt Abby prepare her chocolate entry.

"Attention, everyone," came a voice over the sound system. Reina Patel was back, as was the camera guy, J.C. If he was trying to be unobtrusive, it wasn't working, not in those baggy jeans, Avengers T-shirt, and wild hair Reina didn't seem to notice or care, as long as he was filming. She stood in front of the band, holding a microphone, looking tired, with dark circles under her eyes. She smoothed a few strands of mussed hair as she waited for the murmuring crowd to quiet down.

"Attention, please!" Reina repeated. She nodded to J.C., and he began recording the audience, finally focusing on Reina. With her hair limp, her lipstick faded, and her designer scarf missing, it appeared this event was taking a toll on Reina. I felt for her. The scene with the drunken judge must have been her worst nightmare.

"Thank you, everyone," Reina said. She glanced at J.C. as if to make sure he was recording before continuing. "I appreciate all you're doing to make this year's Chocolate Festival the best ever!"

The enthusiasm in her voice rang false, but I admired her for trying. She nodded and smiled as the group halfheartedly applauded themselves.

"I'd like to share a little background on the Chocolate Festival with you," Reina continued.

Seriously? I thought. Now? Wasn't it a little late for a history lesson? Poor Reina didn't seem to understand that the party was essentially over. But the crowd politely stood listening and sipping their drinks.

"As many of you know, the first Chocolate Festival was held back in 1849, the year after gold was discovered in California. What you might not know is, Frankie Nudo's great-great-grandfather, Dominic Nudo, came over from Italy to strike gold, but instead found another type of gold—liquid gold in the form of chocolate—which he sold to the miners at profitable prices. He was so successful, he opened up the Nudo Confectionary Company a few years later, and that's when he really struck it rich. If it weren't for him, we wouldn't be hosting our annual Chocolate Festival this weekend, right here where it all started. Keep in mind, the event also raises money for the city's homeless population, a very worthy cause."

Dillon mumbled under his breath, "Maybe it should go to the Diabetes Association."

I elbowed him, hoping no one else had overheard his snarky remark.

"Today," Reina continued, "the annual Chocolate Festival has evolved into a two-day celebration encompassing nearly a full city block. It features more than fifty booths of chocolate vendors as well as various food trucks, plus live music, chef demonstrations, chocolate-eating contests, and of course, the chocolate-tasting competition. And you get ten tastings for twenty dollars!"

A cheer and more applause broke out. Glasses clinked. I searched for the other contestants and caught a glare between Frankie and Monet. Interesting. Harrison said something to the twins that made them roll their eyes. Griffin stiffened and blinked nervously several times. Wendy stood by my aunt, the two arm in arm like the old friends they were.

"This year, our twentieth year, I'm proud to be your event coordinator. I've added a few new features, including a Wine-and-Chocolate Pairing, where you can taste wine and chocolate together, a Chocolate-to-the-Death Ice-Cream-Eating Contest, where contestants down bowls of ice cream without using their hands, and a Chocolate College, where folks can learn all about making and cooking with chocolate."

Murmurs of pleasure and interest filled the room.

"But tonight, as special guests of the festival, I have a treat for all of you, to show my appreciation for your participation in the competition." Reina smiled broadly. She seemed to have gotten a second wind. "Please follow me upstairs to the second-floor ballroom."

She signaled to J.C. to turn off the camera and led the way out of the room.

The crowd mumbled as they headed for the stairs or elevator, most still holding their champagne flutes and wineglasses. I looked for Jake and spotted him in the corner talking on his cell phone. I wondered who was on the other end. Drop Dead?

Aunt Abby, Dillon, and I took the stairs to the second floor. I was initially curious about the "big surprise," but with Polly's recent intoxicated performance, I felt I'd had enough surprises for one night.

We entered the lavish ballroom, where I imagined many a fancy event had taken place over the years. Giant colorful murals covered the walls, depicting scenes from under the sea, along with old sailing ships. The tiled floors meant there had been dancing, and the mini stage was obviously set up for a live band.

Currently the stage area was occupied by a giant plastic vat the size of my VW. It was filled three-quarters full with a dark, thick liquid. One sniff and I knew immediately it was melted chocolate. Two large rollers, half-submerged in the liquid, churned the contents inside the vat, creating a roiling mini ocean of fragrant dark brown waves. I had to admit, it was impressive.

Reina stood next to the vat, holding her microphone. As soon as everyone was assembled in the room, she began addressing the crowd again.

"Welcome to one of the largest vats of chocolate in the nation!" she said proudly, as if she'd constructed it herself. The audience applauded, probably because it seemed the right thing to do.

"The chocolate will be on view to Chocolate Festival participants during the two-day celebration, but you're getting a preview of this magnificent beauty." She smiled at the camera.

The crowd didn't seem as excited as Reina. Her smile fell, and she segued into the next part of her speech, reading from index cards she held in her hand.

"As most of you chocolate connoisseurs probably know, chocolate was made from the Theobroma cacao trees in Mexico and South America for more than three millennia. We can thank the Maya and Aztecs, who created the very first chocolate drink. Unfortunately, it was a very bitter drink, and it wasn't until the Europeans added sugar and fat that it became the delicious and popular chocolate we know today."

Several people in the audience yawned. I wondered where all this Wikipedia stuff was going. I glanced over to see if J.C. was still recording. Indeed, he was capturing every moment.

Aunt Abby nudged me. "You know, those same chemicals can kill dogs and cats. I never give Basil any chocolate, no matter how much he begs."

I smiled at Aunt Abby's comment, then turned my attention back to Reina.

"Now, most of our cocoa comes from the Ivory Coast, thanks to Frankie Nudo and his successful family business."

Reina gestured toward Frankie, dressed tonight in an ill-fitting suit, his dark hair slicked back. The crowd turned to him. He humbly bowed his head, and they dutifully applauded.

When the applause died down, a voice called from the back of the room, "I wonder if his business would be so successful if he didn't use child labor!"

The crowd gasped and looked for the heckler. J.C. turned the lens of his camera on the young black man wearing jeans and a T-shirt that read "Fill Your Pie-hole." Griffin Makeba, the Pie Guy. I glanced over at Frankie, who stood a few feet away. He'd turned beet red.

Reina snapped back, "I'm sure I don't know about that, but I doubt it's true. Child labor is illegal."

"Not in Africa!" Griffin called out.

"Hey, buddy!" Frankie Nudo stepped up through the crowd. "You don't know what you're talking about! My people aren't involved in that kind of thing, so shut your piehole!"

Griffin mumbled something under his breath, then downed the rest of his wine, turned on his heel, and left the room.

"All right, everyone," Reina said, forcing a smile, "as I was about to say, we're here to celebrate chocolate, not complain about it." She laughed self-consciously into the camera. "Did you know that cocoa beans were so valuable in the past, they were used as currency?"

Aunt Abby nudged me and whispered, "Will work for chocolate."

I nudged her back.

"These days there are two types of chocolate entrepreneurs," Reina continued. "Chocolate makers, like Frankie, who harvest the beans and process the chocolate." She waved her arm in his direction. "And chocolatiers, like many of the rest of you, who use the finished product to make your treats." Reina pointed them out as she mentioned their names.

As she continued, the crowd began side conversations, and I had the sense she was losing their attention. She seemed to realize this, and after a brief pause, she gestured for J.C. to shine his camera light on the vat next to her.

"Ladies and gentlemen," she said into the microphone. "Next to me is a vat of liquid chocolate that's being mixed by a process called conching. Inside the container are metal beads and giant roller blades that grind, refine, and blend the chocolate, keeping it in a liquid state of one hundred thirteen degrees. The more conching, the better the chocolate. This batch will be conched for about seventy-two hours, to produce the highest quality."

Unfortunately for Reina, the natives were growing restless. Even the vat of chocolate wasn't enough to hold the crowd's attention during her lecture.

"And finally," Reina said, winding up her speech.

Thank God, I thought.

"The health benefits of chocolate are impressive." Reina continued to list all of them. That got some appreciative *ooh*s and *aah*s from the audience.

"Now," Reina said, "to thank you all for your hard work to help make this a successful Chocolate Festival, the servers will be bringing out samples of tomorrow's contest entries for a sneak preview. Enjoy!"

The partygoers gave it up for the hostess, then sipped their drinks and waited for the tasty finale. Servers in black uniforms appeared carrying silver trays, each one laden with chocolate treats. I saw Aunt Abby's whoopie pies and Jake's cream puffs go whooshing by faster than I could grab them. I was able to snatch only a knife-shaped chocolate from a platter filled with edible silverware—one of many novelty chocolates Aunt Abby's friend Wendy Spellman had made—before the rest were devoured by other guests. Unfortunately, I missed out on the remaining entries, which were gone seconds after they arrived.

"Well, that was disappointing," I said to Jake and Aunt Abby. My aunt looked a little bewildered at the speed in which the treats had disappeared. Moments later Dillon appeared holding a napkin filled with an array of chocolate goodies.

"How did you get all those?" I demanded, noticing a smear of chocolate on his right cheek. "I barely managed to nab a chocolate knife, and your mother didn't get a bite of anything."

"Stealth," he said with a mouthful of something brown and gooey. "And it helps to look like a waiter. You get your own tray."

Yeah, Dillon was about as stealthy as a sugar-crazed kid in a candy shop. I tried to snag one of the delicacies off his napkin, but he pulled it away just in time.

"Greedy," I said.

"Jealous," he returned.

"You just said chocolate causes health problems," I reminded him.

"Better than all that coffee you drink," he countered.

"Children! Hush!" Aunt Abby said sternly, then checked her Mickey Mouse watch. "It's late, and I need to get home and make sure I'm ready for the festival tomorrow."

"Good luck, Abby," Jake said. "I'm sure those whoopie pies are to die for."

"You too, Jake." Aunt Abby gave him a hug. "May the best chocolatier win."

Jake reached out and touched my arm. "See you tomorrow?"

I nodded and bit the tip off the chocolate knife I was still wielding.

Suddenly, someone screamed.

The crowd froze and hushed.

Not again, I thought. Was Polly back for an encore?

I turned to Reina, still standing on the stage. She was staring at the vat of chocolate next to her, her hands over her mouth, her eyes wide with horror.

Through the crowd, I strained to see what had happened.

I wished I hadn't.

I could just make out a human hand, pressed against the inside of the clear plastic vat.

Chapter 6

While most of the crowd turned away from the horrifying sight, I couldn't take my eyes off the vat of chocolate. Maybe because I couldn't really believe my eyes. Was there really a body in there? The hand, bobbing slowly with each turn of the mixer, convinced me it was. In spite of the fact that I'd helped to solve a double murder recently, I'd never actually seen a dead person. I always wondered how I'd react. Now I knew. It was surreal.

"Turn it off!" Reina screamed, shaking me out of my hypnotic stupor. "Turn it off!" she screamed again over the incessant humming of the vat's churning rollers.

At first I thought she meant the digital camera, which was still capturing every moment of the unfolding drama. But Reina was pointing to a power cord that led from the vat, off the stage, and across the floor to an outlet. Jake rushed over and yanked the cord from the socket.

The motor went deadly quiet.

"Everyone out! Now!" Reina shouted.

The hushed crowd stared at her.

"I said get out!" She waved her hands wildly as if that would shoo everyone away.

After another shocked moment of silence, the crowd began whispering and mumbling and pulling out cell phones. Two staff members started guiding the guests out of the ballroom and herding them downstairs. As soon as one of the staff announced the bar was still open, the displaced crowd made a mass exodus to collect their medicinal antidotes to the disturbing incident.

Only Jake, Aunt Abby, Dillon, J.C., and I remained with a visibly distraught Reina. I spotted Jake on his cell phone, no doubt calling the police again. Thank goodness there was at least one level head in the chaotic scene. Aunt Abby rushed to Reina's side to help console the trembling hostess, while Dillon craned his neck to stare at the vat, as if trying to see the rest of the victim through the chocolate sludge.

"Oh my God!" Reina kept repeating as Aunt Abby helped her down from the stage. "This can't be happening! The Chocolate Festival will be ruined! Oh dear God!"

The festival? Was that uppermost in her mind? What about the poor chocolate-covered victim who had seemingly fallen into the vat and drowned in hot liquid? I had to cut Reina some slack. She was probably in shock.

Abby eased Reina into a nearby chair, then looked at me for help and shrugged. I shrugged back, also feeling helpless. Jake hung up the phone, said something to a staff member who was milling around, then headed over to me.

"You called the police?" I asked.

He nodded. "They'll be here any minute. I told the waiter to make sure no one leaves the building. The police will want statements."

"I think most of them are in the bar downstairs."

Jake touched my arm as if to reassure me before heading out of the ballroom to double-check on the crowd. I looked for Aunt Abby, avoiding eye contact with the vat, and saw her sitting with Reina at a small table, her face buried in her hands. Dillon was talking to J.C., the camera guy, no doubt asking him inappropriate questions about his camera. I wondered how much J.C. had captured on his camera. I headed over to tell them the police were on their way, still averting my eyes from the body in the chocolate, and caught Dillon in midsentence.

". . . must be a woman," he said, nodding toward the vat.

Before I could stop myself, I turned to look at the Plexiglas tub, wondering what had made him say it was a woman. How could he possibly tell? The only thing I could see was that hand, pressed against the side of the plastic container.

And then I saw what he'd seen—what I had missed the first time I'd looked at the vat. There was a ring on the hand. Even though it was covered in chocolate, it was unmistakable—a diamond the size of an M&M.

Oh my God.

Polly Montgomery?

*　　*　　*

Before I could say anything, a deep voice bellowed from the doorway of the ballroom.

"Where's the victim?"

I turned to see three uniformed officers—two men and a woman—accompanied by a large black man in a black suit. It was none other than Detective Wellesley Shelton, my nemesis and my aunt's crush.

Detective Shelton had handled the homicide investigation I'd been involved in a while back and had even brought my aunt in for questioning, since she'd had a public altercation with one of the victims only hours before the murder. I think my aunt mistook the detective's initial attention for personal interest and she'd flirted with him shamelessly. But ever since he'd visited her in the hospital, he'd warmed to her. Now I suspected he had a genuine affection for her. They'd been dating for several weeks, and Aunt Abby seemed happier than ever.

Aunt Abby lit up at the sight of the detective and waved. I saw a crinkle at the side of his mouth when their gazes crossed. The beginning of a smile? Before I could be sure, the expression disappeared.

"What are you doing here?" he asked her bluntly. He spotted me, then Dillon, and shook his head. "Not again."

Before Aunt Abby could reply, Dillon waved from across the room. "Over here, Detective," he said, pointing toward the plastic tub.

Detective Shelton frowned. "Stay here," he ordered before heading over.

"What's his problem?" Aunt Abby whispered to me.

I shrugged. "He's working, Aunt Abby. I'm sure it's nothing personal."

Dillon took a few steps closer to the vat and pointed at the hand.

The detective stepped up on the small stage, leaned over the edge of the vat, and rubbed his curly, graying black hair. "How in the hell . . . ?"

Good question, I thought. How could anyone end up like that without help? The top of the vat was as tall as the detective's waist. You have to lean over pretty far to fall in.

The detective turned back to the six of us and verbalized my thoughts. "Do any of you know how this happened?"

We all shook our heads.

"Any idea who it is?"

When no one said anything, I ventured, "I think I know."

Detective Shelton focused his dark gaze on me. "That figures . . . ," I thought I heard him mumble. "Well?" he said louder, prompting me to continue.

"I think it's one of the judges for the Chocolate Festival competition. If I'm right, her name is Polly Montgomery."

The others looked at me, mouths agape at my announcement.

"And how would you happen to know that, Ms. Burnett?" the detective said, eyeing me.

"The ring," I replied simply, as if that would be enough for a smart detective to figure out.

Detective Shelton turned back to the vat and studied the chocolate-covered hand pressed against the clear wall of the container.

"That's quite a ring," he said, looking back at me for confirmation.

"She was wearing it this evening," I offered.

"Yes!" Reina suddenly spoke up. "That's Polly's ring! It's called a chocolate diamond. She was showing it off to everyone."

"A chocolate diamond?" the detective said. "Never heard of it."

"It's basically a brown diamond, but retailers don't think that sounds very attractive so they call them chocolate diamonds," Reina said. "I'd love one, but I can't afford it. The hundred-carat ones are pretty rare and very expensive. I think hers was cinnamon. You can get them in cinnamon, champagne, honey, cognac, or clove."

Wow, this lady knew a lot about diamonds.

"I'm sure that's Polly's diamond," Reina said, tearing up. "Oh my God . . . poor Polly. . . ."

I was afraid Reina was about to turn into a blubbering mess, but she controlled herself and accepted the tissue Aunt Abby offered from her purse.

"Did you know her well?" the detective asked Reina. He pulled out his notebook, ready to write down any details he deemed important.

"Not really," Reina said. "But everyone knows *something* about everyone in the food business—at least a little bit. It's a small community."

The detective nodded and wrote something in his

notebook. "Any idea how she might have ended up . . . in there?" He gestured toward the vat with his pen.

"I have no idea," Reina said, tearing up again. "She was a little intoxicated—"

"She was a lot intoxicated," Dillon tossed out.

Reina shot him a sharp look before continuing. "She may have had a little too much to drink, but—"

"I'm telling you, she was crunk," Dillon said, unable to keep from interrupting.

"Crunk?" I repeated.

"Crazy drunk. Wasted. Hammered. Smashed. Trashed. Faded . . ."

The detective held up a hand to Dillon. "I got it." He turned his attention back to Reina. "All right, so she was intoxicated. How does that explain how she ended up in there?"

"Fell in, maybe," Dillon offered.

I shook my head at him. The guy didn't know when to keep quiet.

"Fell in?" The detective repeated the words, his eyebrows raised skeptically.

Dillon shrugged. "It wouldn't have been her first fall."

"What do you mean?" Detective Shelton asked, frowning.

Jake stepped up to explain. "I think what Dillon means is, at the party this evening, Ms. Montgomery tried to climb up on one of the tables to make some kind of announcement. She slipped and fell facedown on top of the table."

"A bunch of us thought she'd dropped dead," Aunt Abby said, her eyes wide. "Then she rolled over, laughed, and asked Jake to help her off the table."

"After that, Reina sent her back to her hotel," J.C. said. He held the camera up as he spoke, obviously recording the detective's visit. Anything for ratings, I thought, even on a food show.

"Turn off the camera," Detective Shelton ordered. "What's on the tape?"

J.C. shrugged. "It's digital, not tape. Nothing about Polly falling into the vat of chocolate, if that's what you're asking. Just some party footage for the Food Network."

"I'm going to need that tape or whatever it is," the detective said. He nodded to one of his officers to retrieve it.

J.C. lowered the camera. "I told you, it's digital. I'll have to send it to your computer. But there's no way you're getting my camera. There's never been a death on a cooking show before. The audience will eat it up."

I stared at J.C. as if he'd just admitted to pushing Polly Montgomery into the chocolate himself for ratings. Was reality TV coming to this—adding murder to the mix?

"The camera," Detective Shelton said. His eyes narrowed at the young man. "Now, or I'll arrest you for interfering with a homicide investigation."

"Not without a court order," J.C. said. "I know my rights."

Detective Shelton turned to Jake. "Miller. Got any

judges who owe you a favor?" Jake knew Detective Shelton from when he was an attorney and from the recent homicide investigation.

Jake nodded and opened his cell phone to make the call.

"I said I'd download it to your computer," J.C. argued. "I just need a computer."

"Dude," Dillon said to him, "I've got my laptop in my mom's car. You can download it now."

"Awesome!" J.C. said.

"Is that okay, Detective?" Dillon asked Detective Shelton. He nodded. While Dillon and the detective weren't exactly friends, Dillon had learned to trust the cop, which was something new for him, being a part-time hacker.

Detective Shelton nodded. "Hurry back," he added. He checked his notes and then looked at Reina. "You said Ms. Montgomery was intoxicated."

"Yes. I thought it best if she got some sleep before the event tomorrow. So I put her in a cab, gave the address to the cabdriver, and sent her home."

"So how did she end up in there?"

"I have no idea," Reina said. "Maybe she got out of the cab. Maybe she came back. Maybe someone brought her here. I don't know."

Detective Shelton thought for a few minutes, then said, "All right. So somehow Ms. Montgomery made it back here, went upstairs while you people were partying downstairs, climbed up onto the stage, leaned over the top of the vat, got knocked over by one of those mixer thingies, fell in, and drowned. Have I got that right?"

No one said anything. The whole idea sounded ludicrous. Yet what other explanation was there? Polly had been drunk. And falling into the vat was certainly possible.

The only other option was unthinkable. Someone had intentionally pushed her into that vat of hot chocolate.

Chapter 7

My imagination was running away with me, as usual. Of course, the last time that had happened when there was a dead body, my suspicions proved to be true. Statistically, the chances of Polly Montgomery's death being deliberate were pretty slim. Still, I'd be curious to hear what Detective Shelton determined after his investigation.

After telling one of the officers to go downstairs and begin questioning the guests, the detective moved us to a small room adjacent to the ballroom, leaving the crime techs to do their work until the ME arrived. Dillon returned with his laptop and set it up for J.C. to use.

"I'll be interviewing each of you," he said, once we were assembled. "Ms. Patel, I'd like to talk to you first. The rest of you, please just sit quietly."

Reina followed him to a table across the room, just out of listening range, leaving the rest of us sitting together at another table. Although I couldn't hear what she said, I could see her twisting the tissue Aunt Abby had given her as she answered Detective Shelton's questions. We sat in silence as J.C. downloaded his footage, Dillon texted on his cell phone, Aunt Abby tapped her finger on the table, and Jake frowned.

Ten minutes later, Reina returned to our table.

"Your turn," she said to J.C.

The camera guy stood up, yanked down his ragged T-shirt, and smoothed back his wayward hair, as if preparing for a job interview. Grimacing, he picked up his camera and the laptop and headed over to where the detective sat waiting for him. Reina slipped into his seat.

As soon as J.C. was out of earshot, Aunt Abby turned to Reina and whispered, "Can't you go?"

Reina shook her head. "Not until everyone is done. He said he may have more questions."

"What did he ask? What did you tell him?" Aunt Abby asked her quietly.

"Nothing." Reina shook her head, still twisting the tissue that was nearly shredded. "I can't tell him anything because I don't *know* anything about Polly's death. Like I said earlier, I left her in a cab—she was nearly passed out—and the next thing I knew, she was floating in that vat of chocolate." Polly shivered.

"What else?" Aunt Abby asked, eyes wide with interest.

"Quite, please!" Detective Shelton called from across the room.

Aunt Abby slunk down. She waited a few minutes, then whispered, "What else did you tell him?"

Reina stole a glance at the detective, who was concentrating on J.C.'s statement. She whispered, "I told him Polly had been drinking most of the night. Everyone knows she has a taste for wine . . . and beer . . . and scotch and whiskey and vodka."

What, no cough syrup? I thought. Was Reina throwing poor Polly under the bus?

Reina seemed to read my mind—or was it my frown—and quickly added, "Not that her penchant for anything alcoholic is relevant, but the fact that she was intoxicated has to be the reason why she fell in."

True, Polly had been bombed. But if she'd woken up from her drunken stupor and left the cab, why would she go into the upstairs ballroom and not return to the party? And what would possess her to lean into that vat of chocolate?

We sat quietly, contemplating our thoughts. After a few minutes, J.C. returned, his face flushed. He set his camera and the laptop on the table, then nodded to Dillon. "Thanks. I sent the footage over to his e-mail, so I can keep my camera. You saved me. I owe you." He turned to Jake. "You're up."

Jake stood, glanced at me, and headed for the detective.

Once again, Aunt Abby began her own whispered third degree, leaning in to J.C. conspiratorially. "What did you say to Wes . . . I mean, Detective Shelton? Was there anything on your camera that showed what happened?"

J.C. shook his head. "Nope. Nothing. I saw what the rest of you saw, only through my camera lens, and now he's got everything I have. But this stuff is going to be golden for the TV show." He patted his camera.

"How so?" I asked. "All you've got is some party

footage. You just said you don't have anything showing Polly's death—or do you?"

"No," J.C. said. "But there's still plenty of drama.
And when it gets out that one of the judges died—
especially the *way* she died—the ratings will be huge."

I shook my head, disgusted at the videographer's
callousness about the tragedy. It was all about exploiting a woman's death just to garner ratings.

"Quiet!" Detective Shelton commanded. "Don't make
me put each of you in isolation."

Jake ambled over and tapped me on my shoulder.

I knew what that tap meant.

I stood up. "I don't know why he wants to talk to
me," I said, "but here goes nothing."

I joined the detective at the small table and sat across
from him.

"Ms. Burnett," he said in his low voice. "Nice to see
you again."

I doubted that. "I think you can call me Darcy, seeing
as how you're dating my aunt—don't you think, Detective?"

He winced. "Darcy, then." His facial expression softened, and he looked at me as if I'd lost a close relative,
when I hardly knew the woman. I figured it was a trick
he used to get people to relax and unburden themselves. I, however, had nothing to unburden. This was
a colossal waste of time.

"Darcy," he repeated, "did you see anything that might
help clarify what happened to Polly Montgomery?"

"Sorry to disappoint you, Detective, but I didn't see
anything unusual. Yes, I was at the party and she was

there, but it was a party like any other party. Lots of drinking, lots of flirting, a little drama when Polly Montgomery collapsed on the table and we all thought she was—" I stopped.

"Dead?" the detective finished the sentence for me.

I shrugged. "But that time, it turned out she was just tipsy. Then Reina and J.C. took her away, and that's the last I saw of her until . . ."

He nodded again. "Did you happen to notice what Ms. Montgomery did during the party—besides fall on the table? Who did she talk to? Did she have an argument with anyone? Did she slip off somewhere with another guest?"

I thought back, trying to remember what I could. "She was hard to miss in that red velvet dress and the rock the size of a chocolate truffle," I said. "Plus, she was very flirtatious and outgoing."

"Uh-huh." The detective made a note in his notebook, then looked up at me, waiting for more.

"Umm, she seemed to talk to just about everyone at the party, flitting from person to person—mostly the men. Dillon noticed that she had an odd conversation with the other two judges, but I wasn't there so—"

He cut me off. "I'll talk to Dillon about that. Just tell me what *you* saw or heard."

"Okay, well, like I said, she seemed to chat up everyone," I said. "Made the rounds. Besides the judges, I think she spoke to the contestants, the camera guy, Reina, even Jake. I think I was the only one who didn't catch her eye." And that had been deliberate.

The detective sat up straight. His body language

was clear. He was done with me. "Well, Ms. Burnett—Darcy—if you think of anything else, you'll let me know?"

"Of course," I said as I got up to leave.

"Oh, Darcy?" he added. "Would you ask Dillon to join me?"

I nodded. I was suddenly feeling exhausted by the events of the evening. Tomorrow was going to be the first day of the festival, and I desperately needed some sleep. I wished I could leave, but I had to wait for Dillon and Aunt Abby, so there was no point in asking.

"Sure," I said. I headed back to the table. "Dillon, he wants you now," I said, trying to keep a light tone. But inside I felt uneasy. Something wasn't right about Polly's death. And I was curious to learn what the crime techs and ME would eventually discover.

"Where's Jake?" I asked the others after I sat down.

"He got a text and said he had to go," Aunt Abby said.

"But the detective said we had to wait. . . ." I tried not to show my disappointment. "Did he say anything before he left?"

Aunt Abby looked at me with a sympathetic face. "No, dear."

I hate sympathetic faces.

J.C. was still reviewing the footage he'd shot, while Reina was busy texting on her smartphone. I wondered how the death would affect the festival or the contest. When prospective attendees heard the news, would it keep them away? Or would it bring in ambulance chasers and the morbidly curious?

I waited with Aunt Abby until Dillon had his turn, wondering where Jake had run off to, then waited some more for Aunt Abby to have her turn. Still no sign of Jake.

As soon as Abby returned, I stood to leave, hoping the detective didn't have any more questions for us.

"Thank you all for your patience," Detective Shelton said, ambling over. "I'll get in touch if I have more questions."

Reina stood up, grinning at her cell phone. "Good news!" She glanced up at us. "I don't have to cancel the contest! I've found another judge to take Polly's place at the last minute! A man named Delbert Morris. He's the chocolatier at Toujour Truffles. We're saved!"

With that, she picked up her small beaded purse and practically ran out of the room.

So much for mourning the loss of Polly Montgomery.

As Dillon, Aunt Abby, and I left the Maritime Museum, I spotted Wendy Spellman on the sidewalk, looking a little befuddled.

"There's your friend," I said to Aunt Abby. My aunt turned around, waved, and headed over, saying, "I'll be right back."

No, she wouldn't, I thought. She'd be yakking with her friend for the next hour if I didn't do something. "Come on," I said to Dillon, and we met up with Aunt Abby and Wendy a few yards away.

"Aunt Abby—," I started to say.

She cut me off. "Darcy! I want you to meet my oldest and dearest friend, Wendy Spellman."

I smiled and offered my hand. Wendy's delicate, pale hand shook mine softly.

"I think we met," she said, frowning, as if trying to recall the meeting.

"Not formally," I said, "but I was at the party. It's nice to finally meet you."

I glanced at Dillon, who was spinning on his heels, glancing around the area and trying to avoid eye contact with Wendy. The woman really seemed to make him uncomfortable.

"And Dillon!" Wendy said, spotting him standing behind me. She gave him a big, motherly hug. I checked to make sure.

"Wendy," Dillon said, after clearing his throat. "I hope the cops weren't too hard on you."

"Not at all, you sweet boy," Wendy said. "They just asked us a few questions, like where we were when the body was discovered and did we know the victim well. That's about it. This has been quite a night, hasn't it? Just like on one of those TV cop shows like *Law and Order*. I love that show."

Wendy seemed more excited about the events of the evening than disturbed.

"Did you know Polly?" I asked, curious by her lack of empathy for the deceased.

"No. Never met her—until tonight. She was one of the judges, wasn't she? I wonder if the competition will be canceled. I hope not. I spent hours working on my entry."

Aunt Abby explained what she'd learned from Reina— that a replacement had been found. Wendy gave a big sigh of relief.

It was getting late and cold. "We'd better get going, Aunt Abby," I said to her. "Big day tomorrow."

My aunt turned to her friend. "Wendy, can we give you a lift? I've got my car."

"That would be lovely, Abigail. Thank you so much."

The two women began walking arm in arm down the street, while Dillon and I followed.

"I'm not getting into that backseat with her," he mumbled.

I grinned. Wendy Spellman hardly looked like the man-eater type Dillon had described. As soon as we arrived at the car, Dillon opened the front passenger door and pulled the seat forward. "After you," he said to Wendy. Aunt Abby went around to the other side and climbed in to join her friend in the backseat.

I drove the four of us to Wendy's apartment on Gough, following her directions, while listening to the two old friends talk about the old days. When the name George Brown came up, I paid closer attention.

"I remember him!" Wendy said. "Didn't you date him before you met Ed?"

"I might have gone out with him once or twice," Aunt Abby conceded humbly. "It was no big deal."

"I thought he was cute," Wendy said. "You could have passed him on to me."

Maybe Dillon was right. Maybe this sweet old lady was really a she-wolf after all.

Aunt Abby giggled. "I seem to recall you were perfectly capable of getting your own guys."

"Married three times," Wendy said proudly. "And three times a widow."

A black widow, I thought fleetingly, then mentally reprimanded myself.

"This is it," Wendy said as I pulled up to the curb in front of her apartment building. "Thank you so much for the ride. See you all tomorrow. And best of luck to you, Abigail." She gave a quick peck to Aunt Abby's cheek and stepped out of the car.

Aunt Abby reached out of the window to give her friend's hand a squeeze. "You too, Gwendolyn."

"We won't need luck now that we've got a new judge!" Wendy let go of Aunt Abby's hand and stepped back, then waved us off.

On the ride back to Aunt Abby's house, I found myself exhausted from the party, the drama, and the interrogation by Detective Shelton. And what about Jake? He seemed to have completely disappeared, and I couldn't help wondering if he was meeting his ex somewhere.

Not that I cared. Not at all. Nuh-uh.

I was glad for Aunt Abby that Reina had found a replacement judge so the contest could continue. Like Wendy Spellman, my aunt had worked so hard preparing hundreds of her chocolate whoopie pies. Frankly, if the whole thing had been canceled, I wouldn't have minded for myself. But no such luck.

A thought popped into my head as I parked the Prius in Aunt Abby's garage. What was it Wendy had said just before she waved good-bye? Something about not needing any luck now that a new judge had been found. Did she mean now that Polly was out of the judging? That was an odd thing to say, especially since she'd claimed she didn't know Polly.

Too tired to think, I dragged myself out of the car, while Dillon helped his mom out of the backseat.

"Mom," Dillon said, "how about making some hot chocolate?"

Aunt Abby and I looked at him in horror.

"Seriously?" I said.

Aunt Abby shook her head, then gave me a hug and sent me on my way to the RV.

I was totally chocolated out. I had one philosophy about food and that was "you can never have too much chocolate." But tonight I'd reached my limit, and even the smell of it coming from the samples in the napkin Dillon had smuggled into the car made me grimace. What was happening to me?

"Get some sleep, sweetie," Aunt Abby called to me. "The festival opens at eleven, and we have lots to do before then."

"G'night," I called back. I walked the few steps to my home-sweet-RV—Aunt Abby's Airstream—which was decorated in contemporary Disney. My aunt was a fan of anything Mickey, Minnie, Donald, Goofy, and the rest of Walt's gang, and had collected a pile of Disneyana—there really is such a thing—from places like vintagedisney.com, nostalgiadisney.com, rememberdisney.com, and of course, eBay. The Cheshire Cat clock that hung over the door of the RV had apparently been a "lucky find." Aunt Abby had discovered it at a local Goodwill store, buried in the kids' toy section. She prided herself on paying "two bucks" for something considered worth a fortune among collectors.

I locked the RV door behind me, glanced up at the

smiling cat, and noted the late hour. Tomorrow I'd need a good dose of the Coffee Witch's Voodoo Vente— a latte with a double shot of espresso and a melted Mars bar—to function in the morning, after all that wine at the party.

I changed into the Tinker Bell nightshirt Aunt Abby had given me, climbed into my cozy bed, and was half-asleep when something at the back of my mind nudged me awake.

Two chocolate contest judges were now dead.

A coincidence?

What were the odds?

I got out my laptop to do a search for Delbert Morris, the judge Reina had mentioned as the replacement for Polly Montgomery. I'd asked Aunt Abby on the ride back if she'd heard of him. She hadn't. I typed in the name. Dozens of hits appeared. As odd as it seemed, there were more Delbert Morrises than I'd expected. I tried "Delbert Morris San Francisco," "Delbert Morris chocolatier," "Delbert Morris judge," and a few other combinations, but nothing turned up. The only thing I could find was a website for Toujour Truffles, and all it had was a list of their specialty chocolates, an address, and an e-mail.

Delbert Morris was turning out to be a needle in a haystack—and I couldn't even find the haystack. I made a mental note to ask Reina more about the guy when I saw her tomorrow at the festival. What were his credentials? Where was he from? Had he done any judging before? Not that it mattered, but it would be nice to know who we were dealing with when it came time for the contest.

My mind was still whirling, so I played a couple of games of Spider Solitaire before shutting down the computer. I switched off the lights and pulled up the Disney Princess comforter, snuggling in. While I didn't exactly feel like a princess at the moment, it was kind of nice being surrounded by the Happiest Characters on Earth.

If only Polly had had some pixie dust, maybe she wouldn't have fallen into that vat of chocolate. But not even Walt Disney's Imagineers could help her now.

I thought I was dreaming when I heard the sound of a cell phone. I was trapped on a small boat in a dark tunnel where millions of robotic children were singing "It's a Small World." Talk about a nightmare.

I sat up in the darkness and felt for my cell phone on the small built-in end table next to the bed. Before I could answer, I heard someone pounding on the door of the RV. I grabbed a sweatshirt and pulled it on over my nightshirt, grabbed the first weapon I could find—my hair straightener—and called out, "Who's there?"

"Me!" Aunt Abby called back. "Who else could it be?"

I yanked open the door. Aunt Abby stood there wrapped in a Minnie Mouse–emblazoned red robe, her face makeup-free, her hair in old-fashioned curlers. If I hadn't known it was her, it would have scared the crap out of me.

I frowned. "Are you all right?" I glanced at the Cheshire Cat. Eleven thirty. Really? It felt much later.

"Oh yes, sweetie, I'm fine," Aunt Abby said, climbing the two steps and entering the RV. I could hear excitement in her voice. "Sorry if I woke you. You weren't in bed already, were you?"

Apparently I had hit that pillow hard. "Uh, I was just about to go to bed," I lied, stifling a yawn. "What's up?"

She slid into a booth seat. "Dillon hacked into the SFPD's database."

"What?"

Aunt Abby made a shushing gesture, as if someone might overhear us in the dead of night in the RV. "He read the medical examiner's preliminary report."

Oh my God. That kid of hers was sure to end up in prison one day.

I slid into the booth opposite her. "Obviously he found out something or you wouldn't be here."

She nodded. "According to the report, the ME noted something suspicious on the body."

"He's already done with the autopsy?" I asked, surprised. Like Wendy Spellman, almost all I knew about forensics I'd learned from watching cop shows on TV, and while they tended to speed up the time frames, this seemed too fast for real life.

"No. It's the preliminary exam. And the ME's a she. Guess what she found?" Aunt Abby's eyes twinkled, even without makeup. I had a feeling she was enjoying her new role as Jessica Fletcher.

"What?"

"A contusion."

"A what?" I hated it when my aunt used cop talk.

"A gash. On the top of her head."

I shrugged. "That's probably where the blade hit her and caused her to fall in."

"She noted that the contusion didn't seem to be consistent with the description of the blade. The blade would have hit her along the *side* of the head, but the gash was right on *top* of her head. And it was jagged, not smooth."

I let her words sink in for a moment. "You mean she thinks . . ."

". . . Polly was struck on the top of her head *first.*"

"And then . . . ?"

"And *then* dumped into the vat."

"Which means . . . ?"

"Polly Montgomery was murdered!"

Chapter 8

"Oh my God!" I said. "Are you sure Dillon got the information right?"

Aunt Abby looked as if she'd just solved the case. "That's what he said. It's all in the ME's report."

She rose, retrieved the *Beauty and the Beast* teakettle she'd given me, and filled it with water. Aunt Abby offered full hookups for her RV, including a cord for electricity and a hose for water. Mrs. Potts's smiling face and bright eyes promised a happy cup of tea, and apparently Aunt Abby was going to deliver it. I wasn't about to get back to bed anytime soon.

"So, the ME thinks she was murdered?"

My aunt retrieved two matching Chip teacups from the small overhead cupboard and set them on the microcounter, then rummaged through the pocket of her robe and pulled out two bags of tea. "Peppermint chocolate or chocolate raspberry?" she asked.

Chocolate? I'd had my fill only a short time ago. Funny how that craving reappeared so quickly. I'm not much of a tea lover, but I'll drink anything chocolate. "Where did you get those?"

"Stole 'em from the party tonight."

I pointed to the chocolate raspberry tea bag in her left hand, and she dropped it into one of the cutesy cups, then placed the minty one in the other cup. She sat down to wait for the water to boil.

"Have you talked to Detective Shelton?" I asked. "Does he have any idea who did it?"

Aunt Abby shook her head. One of her curlers came loose, but she didn't seem to notice. "I haven't heard a word from him. He said something about it being a conflict of interest when I spoke with him earlier. But I'm sure he's got a long list of suspects, since it could have been anyone at the party."

Including us, I thought. *Here we go again.*

Aunt Abby sighed. "Polly wasn't very well liked, you know."

"Really?" I said, surprised. "She seemed quite the social butterfly at the party. Why do you say that?"

The teakettle whistled. Steam shot out of Mrs. Potts's trunklike nose. Aunt Abby got up and poured the boiling water into the waiting cups. The scent of peppermint and fruity chocolate filled the small living space.

"I hope that's decaf," I said as I took the cup from Aunt Abby's hands.

"The tea is," she answered as she sat back down with her cup, "but the chocolate isn't." She took a sip and groaned. "Heaven."

I sipped mine and tasted the hint of raspberry mixed with chocolate. I'd had no idea tea could taste this good. Usually tea tastes like ground-up weeds in hot water to me. Not my cuppa.

"So, what makes you think Polly wasn't well liked?" I asked again.

"Well, she was kind of . . . two-faced, I guess is the word," Aunt Abby said, setting down her cup. "I heard she was sweet as sugar to your face, but you couldn't trust her behind your back. God forbid you ever told her something that you wanted to keep secret. She'd blab it faster than a tweet. Someone once told her I thought George Brown was kind of cute, and I found out later she told him! Embarrassed the heck out of me. They say she loved being the center of attention. Maybe she used personal information like that to get it."

Wow, I thought, as Aunt Abby paused to sip her tea. Did everyone think that way about Polly? Or did my aunt have some kind of special vendetta?

"Plus, she was a slut," Aunt Abby added.

I nearly choked on my drink. "Wha . . . at?"

Aunt Abby peered at me over the teacup rim, one eyebrow raised. "I'm just telling it like it is. Er, was."

I shook my head. "How do you know all this?"

"The food-service world is very small in terms of gossip. Word spreads faster than melted butter."

While I didn't think Aunt Abby would deliberately slander Polly or lie about the woman's proclivities, I didn't fully trust her characterization either. Apparently, Polly had crossed Aunt Abby in the past, like she'd crossed me, and when someone messed with Aunt Abby, she wasn't likely to forget. Maybe she was exaggerating about the dead woman. I'd have to ask around to see if I could corroborate any of her claims.

Aunt Abby downed the rest of her tea, then patted

the table. "Well, I'll let you get some sleep. Big day tomorrow. Keep your fingers crossed that our whoopie pies win the competition on Sunday. I'm dying to do that TV show on the Food Network. I have it all planned. Kind of a down-home approach, serving my specialty—America's favorite comfort foods. Enough of those gourmet shows serving rabbit food and calling it art. People are sick of that stuff. They wanna eat!"

She rose, put her teacup in the stainless-steel sink, and started for the door.

"Aunt Abby?" I called to her.

She turned around. "Yes, dear?"

"How, exactly, did Dillon find out all of that information from the ME's office? I'd think the police department computers would be pretty secure."

She smiled and flashed her Kewpie-doll eyes. "Oh, sweetie. Dillon may have his faults—he's a little quirky, and distractible, and preoccupied, and I do wish he'd shower more and clean up his room—but he's a genius, just like Bill Gates and Steve Jobs and Albert Einstein."

Aunt Abby had not only listed several signs of Asperger's syndrome, but she'd also named some of the most famous people suspected of having Asperger's. There was no doubt in my mind that Dillon shared the same traits, but Aunt Abby had refused to have him tested. He "is what he is," she'd said, and she hadn't seen the point in getting any kind of diagnosis.

"You know, Aunt Abby, Detective Shelton may have us on his suspect list."

"That's ridiculous," she said, grinning. "Wes is my

boyfriend, and I'm sure he'll want my help with the case, just like I helped before when there was a murder in the food truck business."

Boyfriend?

"Aunt Abby, he considered you a primary suspect the last time, remember? And, like he said, your involvement may be a conflict of interest for him."

"Oh, I'm sure that was just a little misunderstanding. Wes didn't really suspect me. He was just doing his job. He may look big and scary to most people, but to me he's just a sweet teddy bear."

I held up my hand, not wanting to know anything more about the man who until recently seemed determined to lock up my aunt for murdering a competitor. Maybe Aunt Abby thought she had the detective wrapped around her manicured pinkie, but he was no dummy. I'd have to keep an eye on her so she didn't wind up getting hurt, like she had with the last four "boyfriends." Aunt Abby had a tendency to fall in love quickly, ruled by her heart, not her head. But then, what woman didn't do the same thing? I thought about Jake. I knew better than to get involved with someone so soon after Trevor the Tool, but he was so darn attractive, and sweet, and smart, and . . .

Enough.

If Aunt Abby and Detective Shelton enjoyed each other's company, so be it. They were adults, albeit different as night and day. But then, they say opposites attract. Was that the case with Jake and me?

And would I have a chance to find out?

*   *   *

After a night of restless sleep, I awoke at the crack of dawn and dragged myself into the tiny shower. I dressed in my Big Yellow School Bus T-shirt and black jeans and headed over to the house for coffee and maybe a whoopie pie for breakfast. I was sure Aunt Abby would be running around frantically and could use my last-minute help preparing for the day's festivities. She was a constant whirlwind of energy, and even when she sat down, her legs swung beneath the table and her fingernails tapped on top.

I entered through the sliding-glass back door, but instead of finding her in the middle of a food-prep frenzy, she was sitting stiffly at the kitchen table, her face pale except for the rosy circles of blush she'd added to her cheeks. Her cell phone rested on the table next to her, covered by her hand. Basil was nestled in her lap.

Uh-oh. Not another upsetting phone call.

"Aunt Abby?" I asked tentatively. I sat down kitty-corner to her. "What's wrong?"

Aunt Abby slowly looked up at me and blinked, as if coming out of a trance.

I nodded toward the phone. "Did you get a call?"

She released her white-knuckled grip on the phone and rested her hand on the tabletop, absently petting Basil with the other. "That was Wes. . . ."

Oh God. Not another murder. Who was it this time? Another one of the judges? A contestant in the chocolate competition?

Or had they tracked Dillon's hacking and were coming to get him?

"What happened? What did he say?"

Tears formed in Aunt Abby's eyes. "He . . . he broke up with me," she said.

"What?"

"Wes broke up with me." She shook her head in disbelief. "I called him this morning to see if there were any new developments in the case, you know, but he said he couldn't talk about it."

I placed a hand on her shoulder to comfort her. "It's true, Aunt Abby. He can't discuss an ongoing case with you, but that doesn't mean he's breaking up with you."

Aunt Abby set Basil down, pulled a tissue from her pocket, and blew her nose. "Then he said we can't see each other for a while, not until this situation—that's what he called it, a situation—is resolved."

"Did he say why not?"

She blinked. A tear rolled down her apple cheek. "He said I'm a person of interest!"

I jerked back. "What? That makes no sense at all! You had nothing to do with Polly's death. I'm sure he knows that." I was trying to reassure her, but I wasn't surprised the detective had put her—and the rest of us—on his list.

She got up and grabbed another tissue from a box on the countertop and wiped her eyes, smearing her mascara. "He said he has to investigate all possibilities, which means everyone who was at the party last night is a person of interest—including you, Dillon, Jake, and me."

"Well, I'm sure that's standard procedure. He can't really suspect you. You just happened to be in the wrong place at the wrong time—once again."

"But why did he have to break up with me? We were getting along so well."

"I don't think he actually broke up with you, Aunt Abby. It's probably just temporary."

Aunt Abby dabbed her eyes.

"I didn't realize you cared that much about him."

She raised her head, sniffed, wadded up the tissues and threw them in the trash. "You know what, Darcy? I don't. Not anymore. Detective Wellesley Shelton is dead to me now. I have a competition to win, and I need to focus on my whoopie pies."

In a dizzying about-face, Aunt Abby returned to her trusted domain—the kitchen—washed her hands—symbolically, as well?—and began pulling whoopie-pie components from the refrigerator and freezer. Basil thumped his tail at her feet, no doubt hoping to catch a dropped morsel. I couldn't blame him. Just watching Aunt Abby do her magic made me drool. After pulling out a batch of steaming-hot chocolate cakes from the oven and setting them aside to cool, she filled a large mixing bowl with flour, then added the rest of the ingredients to make more of the little cakes that held the whoopie pies together. Next she whipped up more raspberry filling, using butter, raspberry puree, milk, and powdered sugar. Using a pastry bag, she squirted the filling onto a cooled cake, then topped it with another cake and gently pressed the two cakes together until the raspberry peeked out from the edges. Minutes later she was done with an entire batch and on to the next. It was like watching an engineer, artist, and architect all at once.

When she wasn't looking, I stuck my finger in the

bowl of raspberry filling and scooped up nearly a table-spoonful. The smooth and creamy filling was sweet and tart, and melted in my mouth. Dillon stumbled into the kitchen wearing a threadbare Minecraft T-shirt and *Star Wars* pajama bottoms and helped himself to a box of Lucky Charms, bypassing the standard bowl, milk, and spoon. He spilled a few Charms on the floor that didn't quite make it into his mouth, but they were quickly lapped up by Basil. Finally, he noticed that Aunt Abby and I were staring at him.

"What?" he said, clueless as usual.

"You're not ready!" Aunt Abby said.

"You need a shower," I said, "and a shave and some hair product—"

"And I need help," Aunt Abby said, interrupting.

"Well, I need breakfast, so chill. Can't a guy have some cereal in peace . . . ?" Dillon looked at his mother, then suddenly put down the box of cereal and moved closer to her, frowning. "Mom? Have you been crying?"

Aunt Abby shook her head. "No, no. I just had a little news this morning that temporarily interrupted my food preparations, and now we're running behind. I need you to hurry and get ready so you can help me load up these pies."

"What news?" Dillon asked, missing the point.

"It's nothing," Aunt Abby said, setting out bowls of filling.

Dillon looked at me. His frown deepened. I knew he'd pester us both until we told him.

"Detective Shelton called," I said.

"How come? Did he catch the killer?"

"Not exactly," I said. "It seems everyone who was at the party last night is under investigation for Polly's murder. Not surprisingly, us included."

"That's wack!" Dillon said, his face turning red as he spoke. "Haven't we been through enough already with that detective dude?" He turned to his mom. "I told you not to get involved with him. He's a cop. He can't be trusted."

Oh, like you can, Mr. Computer Hacker? I thought. I bit my tongue. No sense in starting that argument again.

"I don't know who you're talking about," Aunt Abby said lightly as she swiped another creamy spoonful of filling onto a chocolate cakey cookie. "If you mean Detective Wellesley Shelton, that man is dead to me."

"Good!" Dillon said, completely unsympathetic to his mother's feelings—another sign of Asperger's. He resumed his boxed breakfast, pouring another mouthful of Lucky Charms mostly into his mouth. Basil was all over the escapees that landed on the floor. "Let him solve his own damn murder case this time," Dillon continued, speaking around the cereal. "He won't get any help from me. And I know something he probably doesn't know."

Aunt Abby and I stopped and looked at Dillon.

"What?" I asked.

Dillon took the cream-filled spatula his mother had been using and licked it.

Aunt Abby grabbed the spatula from his hand. "Spill it, or you've had your last whoopie pie!"

"Okay. Okay." He licked his fingers where the

creamy mixture had dripped. "I did a little research last night after looking at the ME's report. Guess what I found out."

"For God's sake, Dillon, just tell us," I snapped. If Dillon didn't quit teasing us soon, I was going to spatula him to death. "We don't have all day! We've got a festival to prepare for!"

He took a deep breath, no doubt for dramatic purposes, then said, "Well, it seems Polly Montgomery sent e-mails to the other judges hours before the party."

"How do you know that?" I asked.

He gave me a "duh" look. "I hacked her e-mail, of course."

"You make it sound so easy," I said.

"It is," Dillon replied. "People are lazy, and they want to keep their passwords simple and easy to remember. I could figure out yours if I wanted to."

Aunt Abby's red-rimmed eyes were wide. "We're getting off track. What did you find out?"

"They were kinda weird," Dillon said. "I printed them out. Be right back."

Dillon set down the cereal box and trudged to his room, returning in a few moments with two sheets of paper. He handed one to his mother and one to me. I read mine over:

From: Polly Montgomery
To: Isabel Lau
Subject: A reminder
If you want me to forget what you've done, then don't forget what to do. . . .

I leaned over and read Aunt Abby's paper. The

e-mail was identical, except for the name of the e-mail recipient. It was sent to Simon Van Houten, the other judge. I looked at Dillon.

"This is pretty incriminating stuff!" I said to him, grinning.

"What do you mean?" Aunt Abby said, confusion written on her face.

"Don't you see?" I said. "It looks like Polly had something on the other two judges. Something they probably wanted her to forget. And in exchange, she wanted them to do something for her."

"Like what?" Aunt Abby asked.

I shrugged. "I'm not sure, but I have a feeling it had something to do with the chocolate competition."

"Yeah," Dillon said. "Like sway the vote . . ."

Chapter 9

I pulled out my cell phone and tapped in a saved number.

"Jake?" I said as soon as he answered.

"Hey, Darcy. What's—"

"I need your help," I said, interrupting him. I didn't have time to waste on chitchat; nor was I in the mood.

"Oookay. Good morning to you too," he said. "What's so urgent?"

"Sorry to be so blunt, but it's crazy here, getting ready for the festival, and something's come up. I'm hoping you can help."

"I'll do my best. What is it?"

"Can you talk to one of your cop friends and see if you can find out exactly who's on Shelton's suspect list?"

A moment of silence, then, "Wait a minute. Are you saying you think Polly was murdered?"

He obviously hadn't heard. "Apparently Polly's head wound wasn't consistent with the mixing blades, or something like that. She may have been hit over the head and then pushed into the vat. Detective Shelton is going to call it a homicide."

"How do you know all this?"

"Uh . . . I have connections in the police department?" I offered weakly.

"You mean Internet connections, namely Dillon," he said. "He's going to get himself in big trouble one day."

Too late for that, I thought, remembering that he'd been kicked out of college for hacking.

"So, will you?" I asked.

"Isn't your aunt seeing the detective? Can't she just ask him?"

"No." I stole a glance at Aunt Abby as she listened to my side of the conversation, then whispered, "They . . . broke up."

"Sorry to hear that," Jake offered.

"I have a feeling everyone at the party last night is a suspect, including us and including you."

Another moment of silence. I wondered what Jake was thinking. Finally, he said, "All right. I'll see what I can find out. But Shelton can't be serious about the four of us. He knows us."

"I agree, but he probably has to include everyone anyway. And since Aunt Abby isn't seeing the detective right now, our source has dried up."

"What do you mean, 'our source'?" Jake asked. "You're not getting involved in this, are you?"

"I'm already involved," I argued, "since I'm a suspect in a murder investigation. Until Shelton finds out who killed Polly, that's probably not going to change."

More silence on the other end.

"By the way," I added. "Dillon learned something interesting about Polly that may be related to her death."

"Darcy!" Dillon hissed in the background.

I glanced at Dillon, who was glaring at me. Uh-oh. Had I said too much?

"More hacking, I assume," Jake said.

"No, no. He . . . uh . . . *overheard* something . . . at the party." I wished I were a better liar.

"What?"

I glanced at the e-mail Dillon had printed out. "Uh, something like, 'If you don't want me to forget . . . then don't forget what you need to do. . . .'"

"What's that supposed to mean?" Jake asked. "Makes no sense."

"It does when you hear who she e-mailed—I mean, who she said it to."

"Okay, let's cut the crap, Darcy. Dillon obviously hacked into Polly's e-mail. Who did she send the message to?"

I blushed, caught in my lie. Dillon leaned over as if to grab my cell phone. I stepped beyond his reach. "Isabel Lau and Simon Van Houten—the other two judges."

"Are you sure?"

"Yes. We have proof. But I can't exactly take it to the detective without getting Dillon in trouble."

"So what do you want me to do? I can't just tell him about the e-mails either. He'll want to know how I found out."

"Tell your cop friend you heard that Polly sent some

interesting e-mails and to check her computer," I said. "Maybe that will narrow down the list and we'll be off the hook. If the judges were being blackmailed by Polly for something they didn't want known, then one of them might have killed her. Or maybe they both did it together," I said, thinking of Agatha Christie's *Murder on the Orient Express*, in which Hercule Poirot investigates the death of a disliked victim named Ratchett and learns that nearly everyone in the cast had a motive to kill him, which leads to a clever and twisted ending.

"Okay. I'll pass the word along and try to find out who's on the list, but if Dillon gets in trouble, I can't help him. I'm not an attorney anymore, remember? I'm a cream puff guy. And by the way, there's no legal protection for cream puff guys either. If Shelton gets suspicious about the information, I'm not going to lie."

"I understand," I said.

"Besides, I'm sure he's got his guys on that computer already. If there's something there, they'll find it."

Jake was probably right. Dillon had beaten Shelton to the information, giving us a little head start. He'd eventually find those e-mails she sent to the two judges, and we'd be officially off the hook.

"Thanks, Jake. Call me if you find out anything, okay?"

"Will do," Jake said, then added, "You owe me now, you know. Big-time."

I smiled in spite of my recent irritation over his visits with his ex-fiancée. "I'll give you an extra whoopie pie the next time I see you," I said without thinking.

"Mmm. A whoopie pie," he said, his voice low and sexy.

Leave it to Jake to take it as a euphemism.

I blushed and hung up without saying good-bye.

By ten a.m., Aunt Abby, Dillon, and I had finished preparing for the festival and had loaded everything into Aunt Abby's car. We caravanned over to the Ghirardelli Square area, where the festival would take up a full city block. Aunt Abby was in the lead, with me second in my VW Bug, and Dillon on his dirt bike. I kept checking the clock as if I had OCD, more because I was hoping to hear back from Jake than because I was worried about making it to the event on time. Until I knew what he'd learned from his cop friend, this gnawing anxiety wouldn't go away.

We parked in the lot reserved for staff, and with arms full of whoopie pies, headed for Aunt Abby's school bus, already in its assigned spot. The closed-off street was lined with food trucks, as well as vendor tents filled with chocolate goodies, street foods, crafts, clothing, jewelry, and other merchandise popular at festivals. The rich scent of chocolate made my nose tingle, and I inhaled deeply, wondering if I could get high on just the smell.

The three of us spent the next hour setting up shop in Aunt Abby's school bus, getting ready for the onslaught of chocolate-starved addicts. While my aunt started another batch of pies, Dillon removed the ones we'd already made from their boxes and I arranged them on doilied platters to entice the customers. I caught Dillon sneaking a couple when his mother wasn't looking but couldn't blame him. They were killer.

A few minutes before the event opened at eleven, I stepped outside the bus to see if I could snag a coffee from the Coffee Witch, one of the trucks participating in the festival but not the competition. Maybe I could even get a cream puff from Jake's truck before the feeding frenzy began.

I looked around at the nearby food trucks, each offering some sort of chocolate goody but with its own twist. Wendy Spellman's truck, Chocolate Candyland, was parked next to Aunt Abby's bus, on the right. The colorful truck featured giant pictures of sweets reminiscent of the popular children's game, Candy Land, most dipped in chocolate. The truck itself looked good enough to eat, with all the chocolate-covered candies from my past—lollipops, gumdrops, licorice whips, sour balls, and so on. I couldn't see Wendy through the closed louvered windows and figured she was busy inside, no doubt preparing last-minute delights like everyone else.

Across from her was Chocolate Falls, owned by Harrison Tofflemire. His truck was painted with a giant replica of his chocolate fountain gizmo, whirls of chocolate cascading down to look like a waterfall. His attractive twin daughters were dressed in skimpy brown shorts and low-cut tops, giggling as they set out dipping sticks and imprinted napkins. I caught a glimpse of Harrison leaning out the window, reprimanding the girls, who rolled their eyes as soon as he withdrew his head.

Next to him, directly across from us, was Griffin Makeba's Fill Your Piehole truck. The vehicle was covered with mini pies that appeared to fly around as if caught up in a pie tornado. Griffin stood outside checking out the other trucks, a frown on his face, his arms crossed. Was he worried about the competition? Or was that just his natural facial expression? Some people were like that, always frowning. Others, like Aunt Abby, presented a happy face as their default look. Me? I felt like I showed every emotion, often to my embarrassment.

Frankie Nudo's Choco-Cheese truck was parked next to Griffin's. It was a simple design featuring a giant wedge of cheese, a plus sign, and a chocolate bar, with the words "Choco-Cheese!" scrawled across the top. The thought of combining cheese and chocolate just didn't have any appeal for me, in spite of my love for chocolate and cheese—separately.

Across from him and on our left side was Monet's I Scream Cakes, a reconstructed postal van painted pink with brown polka dots that looked like scoops of ice cream. Monet and Frankie were also out front, and it sounded like they were arguing about something. Whoever put these two in close proximity must not have known their history.

Just beyond her was Jake's Dream Puff truck, and across from him was the Coffee Witch, offering Willow's caffeine-infused magical potions, always my first stop when I arrived at the Fort Mason food trucks.

She'd created a new chocolate coffee drink to sell at the event, hoping to build up clientele. Her latest concoction was a salted caramel and chocolate smoothie she called Devil's Brew. I made a beeline to see if I could snag a cup before the crowds took over.

Suddenly I heard my name being called.

"Darcy!" I looked around and saw Jake's head poking out of the service window of his truck. Hoping he had news, I detoured over.

"What did you find out?" I said to him as he leaned out, his muscular arms propped on the ledge.

"You need to work on your social skills," Jake said. "You might want to start with a cordial opening, like, 'Hello, Jake,' or something along those lines."

"Sorry," I said, looking up at him. "On top of everything—the festival, the competition, the party—this new development about Polly is making me crazy. Not only are we suspects in a murder case, but I'm beginning to wonder if there is a killer on the loose. Two judges are dead, and he may go after others—"

"Two?" Jake interrupted me. He disappeared from the window, and seconds later the door to his truck opened. He bounded down the steps.

"You didn't know?" I said, confused.

"You're not saying you think George Brown was murdered too—do you?"

"Frankly, I don't know. It seems odd that he suddenly gets hit by a car and dies right before the festival. Then, the night before the event begins, another judge is found dead, drowned in a vat of chocolate. Don't you think there might be a connection?"

"George Brown's death was an accident," Jake said.

I shrugged.

"Darcy . . ."

"Never mind that now. The festival is about to begin. What did you find out about Shelton's suspect list? Are we still on it?"

"There is no list," Jake said.

"Yes, there is. Aunt Abby said—"

"Not anymore," Jake broke in.

I frowned, not comprehending the words coming out of his mouth. "Seriously? Why? Did they find out who killed Polly? Was it one of the judges?"

Suddenly, without warning, two SFPD cars pulled up near the back of Aunt Abby's bus, lights flashing.

"Oh my God!" I said. "Aunt Abby!"

I bolted for the school bus, then stopped just as I reached the open accordion doors. Aunt Abby and Dillon came running down the stairs.

"Are you all right?" I said to her. She looked perfectly fine, but something was going on.

"Yes," she said. "Are you?"

I nodded, glanced at Dillon, then saw two uniformed officers appear from behind Aunt Abby's bus, accompanied by Detective Shelton.

Dillon ducked back into the bus.

Uh-oh.

Before I could grab Aunt Abby and wrap her in a protective embrace, the cops made a sudden and unexpected turn to the right. They weren't coming to Aunt Abby's bus to arrest Dillon for hacking.

A small crowd had gathered next door, made up

mostly of other food truckers. I joined them and watched as one of the officers pounded on the door of Wendy's Chocolate Candyland truck, while Detective Shelton stood back with another officer, who had his hand on his holstered gun.

"Police! Open up!" the first cop ordered.

The door to the truck opened and Aunt Abby's friend, Wendy Spellman, peeked out wearing red reading glasses and a candy-decorated apron over her long dress.

She looked absolutely terrified.

Chapter 10

Aunt Abby darted over to Wendy's truck.

"Step back!" the second police officer commanded.

"Wes, what's going on here?" she said to Detective Shelton. When he didn't answer, she turned to Wendy. "Are you all right, honey?" She tried to shoulder her way closer, but the second officer positioned himself in the way, his hand still resting on his gun.

"Stay back, Abby," Detective Shelton told her.

I stepped up by Aunt Abby's side, hoping she didn't do anything to get herself arrested. Dillon, now apparently unconcerned about being arrested himself, joined me, along with Jake.

"Wendy Sue Spellman," the detective began, "you're under arrest for the murder of Polly Montgomery. You have the right to remain . . ."

I didn't hear the rest of the standard reading of her Miranda rights. The words were blocked out by my aunt's shrill voice as she accused the police of everything from harassment to police brutality to incompetence. Dillon held on to her and tried to calm her down.

"Abby?" Wendy pleaded. Her eyes were filled with

fear as she stepped down from her truck. The first officer turned her around and bound her bony wrists with plasticuffs.

"Is that really necessary?" Jake said, his lawyer instincts apparently kicking in. "Look at her. She's hardly dangerous."

"Sorry," Detective Shelton said to Jake. Then he glanced at Aunt Abby. "Just going by the book."

It was hard to imagine this petite older woman harming anyone, let alone bonking them over the head and pushing them into a vat of chocolate. She didn't look like she had the strength, let alone the inclination.

"Can I at least come with her?" Aunt Abby pleaded.

"No, ma'am," the first officer said. "She'll be booked at 850 Bryant. You can see her there after she's been processed."

"But this is ridiculous!" Aunt Abby argued, looking at the detective. "She didn't kill Polly. She had no reason! If anyone is a murderer, you might want to look at the two other judges Polly was blackmailing!"

"Mom!" Dillon tried to hush up his mother. It didn't matter. The cops weren't listening anyway.

"Do you have an attorney?" Jake asked Wendy.

She shook her head, her face a reflection of confusion and terror.

"Don't worry," he said. "I'll find you someone."

She nodded, her eyes glistening. The second cop pulled out police tape and strung it from one end of Wendy's truck to the other, while the first officer began to lead Wendy away. The detective stood a few feet away, overseeing his officers.

Wendy turned to my aunt. "Abby, please help me. . . ."

The officer guided her forward between the two trucks and into the back of one of the waiting patrol cars. The detective climbed into the passenger seat of the car, and moments later, Wendy Spellman was on her way to the San Francisco Police Department.

"This is crazy!" Aunt Abby bellowed, then stood staring after the patrol car, her mouth agape. "Insane! Ludicrous! Absolutely stupid! How could he do this?" she sputtered.

Dillon wrapped his arm around her and led her toward the steps of the bus, then eased her down to a sitting position on the top step. She sat there shaking her head and muttering.

I looked at Jake. "Do you really have a friend who can help Wendy?"

He nodded and pulled out his cell phone, but before he could punch in a number, Reina Patel came storming out of nowhere, her face red, her expression livid.

"What the *hell* is going on here? I saw police cars!"

Frankie and Monet, hovering nearby, pointed to Wendy Spellman's Chocolate Candyland truck. Apparently their argument had been interrupted by the arrival of the police.

Reina turned around and gasped at the sight of the crime-scene tape. "What's going on? Where's Wendy? Why is there police tape on her truck?"

When no one answered, she looked at me. "Tell me! What's happened? Why's everybody standing around?"

I swallowed. "Uh . . . Wendy was just . . ."

"Arrested," Jake said, thankfully finishing my sentence.

Reina frowned. "What for?"

"Murder!" Harrison Tofflemire's voice boomed from a few feet away. He stood among the other food truckers, flanked by his two partially clad assistants. "The cops said she murdered Polly Montgomery!" The girls covered their pouty mouths in some sort of fake sympathy.

Reina shook her head. "No, no, no! This can't be happening. Arrested for murder? Now? It could ruin everything! Oh my God, how am I going to spin this? Think, Reina. Think!" She tapped the side of her head as if to wake up her brain and began pacing back and forth.

Hmm, I thought. Once again, it looked as if Reina was more concerned with the status of the Chocolate Festival than the arrest of an alleged murderer. I was a little put off by her seemingly callous behavior, but then I wasn't responsible for running a festival that would rake in hundreds of thousands of dollars from thousands of people.

Griffin stepped forward, frowning, as usual. "Well, at least they caught the killer, so the rest of us can relax now. I don't see why the show can't go on as planned. I've made a lot of pies for this event, and I'm not about to feed them to the pigeons because of this."

Reina stared at him for a moment, her eyes narrowed. Then she snapped her fingers. "You're right, Griffin. There's no need to panic. We'll open as usual. No one needs to know what happened here."

"What about the cops?" Monet asked. "Surely some of the people waiting in line saw them drive up and then take Wendy away in handcuffs."

Reina spun around. "Yes, Monet, but they don't know *why* Wendy was arrested. And even if they start asking questions, I'll spread the word that she . . . I don't know . . . didn't have a license . . . or . . . tried to bribe a judge—"

Aunt Abby rose from her seat on the bus step. "You'll do no such thing! Wendy Spellman would never do either of those things. I won't allow you to make up some lie about her!"

"Would you prefer they find out the truth—that she was arrested for murdering one of the judges?" Reina said, crossing her arms defiantly.

Aunt Abby looked befuddled.

"Listen, Reina," I said, stepping in for Aunt Abby. "You don't have to say anything. Probably only a handful of people saw what happened, and if anyone asks, we can just claim we don't know anything. Because we don't. Wendy may have been arrested on suspicion of committing a crime, but that doesn't make her guilty."

"Fine," Reina said, dropping her arms to her sides. "Well, it's too late to move her truck, but we have to do something about that hideous police tape. It's disturbing and distracting."

"You can't remove crime-scene tape," Jake offered. "That's illegal."

Reina walked over to Wendy's truck and studied the tape for a moment. Then, with a flick of her finger, she began turning the tape over so the words "Crime

Scene—Do Not Enter" were no longer visible. The now-plain yellow tape was hardly noticeable against the colorful chocolate-dipped candies that decorated the truck. When she was done, she pulled a black marker from a pocket and wrote on the window in giant letters, TEMPORARILY CLOSED DUE TO EMERGENCY.

Reina replaced the cap, then stood back and admired her work. "There. That should do it—at least until the cops come back and search for evidence, or whatever it is they do. Anyway, back in your trucks, people. It's go time!"

We all stood there in a daze for a moment. Then Reina clapped her hands and yelled, "Move it!" The chocolate chefs headed back to their trucks.

"The gall of that woman," Aunt Abby mumbled as she trudged up the bus steps.

I glanced around for Jake, wondering if he'd gotten ahold of an attorney for Wendy yet, but he had disappeared. I figured he was probably back in his truck too, and I hoped he hadn't forgotten to make the call. Reluctantly, I followed Aunt Abby onto the school bus, dreading the start of the festival when I wasn't in much of a festive mood.

"Wendy did not murder that woman!" Aunt Abby huffed as she handed Dillon a napkin. He had helped himself to a whoopie pie and managed to leave telltale evidence on his upper lip and fingertips. I shook my head at him, but he ignored me.

Aunt Abby turned to me, her hand on her hip. "Darcy, I want you to help my friend Wendy."

"Of course, Aunt Abby, although I'm not sure what

I can do. Jake will find a qualified attorney to represent her."

"Yes, I know he will," she said, "but you have a knack for this sort of thing."

"What sort of thing?"

"For solving murders," she said matter-of-factly.

I almost laughed. "You're kidding, right?"

She eyed me, one eyebrow raised to its apex.

"Listen, I only helped out last time because *you* were a suspect. I'm no cop. I'm not even an investigative reporter. I'm a—that is, I used to be—a restaurant critic, and now I'm your assistant in your busterant. I don't know the first thing about finding out who murdered Polly Montgomery. That's Detective Shelton's job, and he's good at what he does."

"I guess you've forgotten. Wes, er, *Detective Shelton*, is dead to me, now more than ever. If it hadn't been for you that last time, I might be serving up beans to dangerous inmates right now."

"But, Aunt Abby—"

"Darcy, I need you." She turned to Dillon. "You too, son. I'm sure you can dig up more on your computer. Let's get through the morning; then, when it dies down, I want the two of you to find out what you can about Polly Montgomery. We already know she's a blackmailer. What other secrets was she hiding? And who wanted her dead?"

I sighed and looked at Dillon. He nodded.

"All right, Aunt Abby. We'll do what we can," I said. "But I think Wendy's best bet is Jake's lawyer friend."

"Do your best. That's all I ask," Aunt Abby said.

"Darcy, you're great at interviewing people for the newspaper. Use that when you talk to people. Dillon, you know what you need to do. Use your computer skills to find out what you can. The real killer has to be someone who was at the party last night, so start there—especially the judges. I still think it's got to be one of them, since Polly was blackmailing them."

A voice came over the loudspeaker, interrupting any more thoughts of murder, motive, and suspects. I recognized Reina's slightly accented voice.

"Welcome, chocolate lovers, to San Francisco's twentieth annual Chocolate Festival!"

Oh boy, I thought. *Let the Chocolate Hunger Games begin. . . .*

If another murder had occurred during the Chocolate Festival rush that morning, I doubt anyone would have noticed. The crowds were overwhelming and kept the three of us hopping in Aunt Abby's bus for four straight hours. Luckily, my aunt had enough whoopie pies to feed the masses—and her twist on the old favorite was a huge hit. Several people used their tickets for seconds and thirds, skipping opportunities to taste other trucks' treats. If the chocolate lovers' reactions to her entry into the contest were any judge, Aunt Abby would win the competition, hands down and thumbs up.

The craving for chocolate started to die down around three o'clock. Either everyone had had their fill, had used up all their tickets, or had crashed from the sugar rush. Fine with me. I craved a break.

"I need caffeine!" I said to Aunt Abby as she dumped

the bucket of collected tickets into a large plastic bag. Attendees had paid twenty dollars for ten tickets, which they used for their chocolate choices. The chocolate vendors would be reimbursed after the festival, based on their total number of tickets. Each vendor received a dollar, while the other dollar went to the event organizers to cover expenses.

"Want anything?" I asked her and Dillon.

"I'll just make some tea here," Aunt Abby said.

"I'll have a double-shot mocha frap with extra caramel," Dillon called out.

I waited a second to see if he'd pull out some dollar bills from his pocket, but of course he didn't. What was I thinking?

"Be back in a few minutes," I said as I disembarked the bus.

I headed straight for Jake's truck to see if he'd heard from his cop friend or his lawyer friend, but the BE BACK IN 5 sign was in the window. I glanced over at the Coffee Witch, thinking he might have stopped there for a coffee, but there was no sign of him. I wondered where he was.

I waited in the short line to order. When I reached the window, Willow gave me a big smile. It hurt to look at the ring piercing her lower lip. I cringed a bit every time I saw it.

"'S'up, Darce?" she asked, leaning her chin on her fist. "Your usual?"

I nodded. "And one of your Alchemy blends—the one with chocolate and caramel—for Dillon. A double, please."

"Gotcha." While she went to work on the coffee drinks, I looked around at the dwindling crowd, then glanced at Jake's truck again to see if he'd returned.

His door stood ajar.

I leaned back to see if I could catch a glimpse of him inside.

Out stepped Lyla, his supposed ex-fiancée.

A surge of heat enveloped me. What was *she* doing in Jake's truck again? What had *they* been doing?

And why had he put the BE BACK IN 5 sign in the window?

"Any dirt on the arrest of the killer?" Willow asked, sliding the two coffee drinks toward me.

"Huh?" I tore my eyes away from Jake's truck.

"You know, Wendy something. The old lady the cops arrested from the candy truck. What's-her-name."

"Wendy. Wendy Spellman. No news that I know of. Have you heard anything?"

Everyone in the food truck business knew that if you wanted information, you bought a coffee from the Coffee Witch and Willow would tell you everything you wanted to know. She usually heard whatever went on around the trucks and was happy to share any news.

"Nada," she said. "I didn't know the murdered lady or that Wendy lady, except for meeting them at the party last night. But the murdered lady was kind of a beeotch. I tried to talk to her and she acted as if I were invisible. The only time she paid any attention to me was when I was talking to the camera guy. He's pretty hot. She came running over and whispered something in his ear and pulled him away like he was her boyfriend or something."

"Really?" Willow had my attention. Did the mature Polly have a thing for the younger J.C.? "Any idea what she said to him or why she did that?"

Willow shook her head. "Nope. I tapped my number into his phone before he left, but then that woman who was in charge—Reena? She pretty much kept him busy the rest of the night."

"Reina," I said, correcting her, pronouncing it *Rayna*. "Did you talk to Wendy last night too?" I asked.

"A little. She was all bubbly and happy. Nice lady. I wonder why she killed that judge. Although, if you gotta die, what a way to go—dipped in chocolate."

Shaking my head, I wrote Willow's insensitive words off to her youth and took the two coffee drinks. I decided to skip Jake's truck—my questions could wait until Drop Dead was gone—but as I turned to head back to the school bus, I nearly bumped into him.

"Whoa!" Jake said, steadying me as I held on to my coffees. "Didn't mean to startle you. You okay?"

I nodded. Luckily, the coffees were lidded and I hadn't spilled a drop. I looked around for his ex. No sign of her.

"I'm fine," I said. "Uh . . . did you get a chance to call a lawyer for Wendy? Or talk to your cop friend about the murder?"

He nodded. "Is there somewhere we can go and talk for a minute?"

Uh-oh.

"Sure. Just let me drop Dillon's coffee off at the school bus. Why don't you find someplace to sit over in the shade and I'll meet you." I gestured toward a lawn area filled with folding chairs for weary chocolate eaters.

I returned to the bus and handed over Dillon's coffee drink through the service window, saying, "I'll be right back."

Jake was sitting in a chair apart from the other people, next to an empty chair. I sat next to him, still holding my coffee.

"So what did you find out?" I asked.

He took a deep breath. "It's not looking good for your aunt's friend Wendy."

"Why? What do the police have on her?"

"They found something at the bottom of the vat of chocolate when they drained it."

"They drained it?" It hadn't occurred to me that the cops would do that, but it made sense. "What did they find?"

"A metal candy mold."

"And . . . ?"

"Shaped like a knife."

Uh-oh. I remembered that Wendy made chocolate novelties using various molds, including ones shaped like silverware. I had snagged a chocolate knife at the party.

"Are the police sure it belongs to Wendy?"

"It looks that way. They tried to get prints from it but couldn't because of the chocolate. Still, if it's hers, if she had her name on it, it places her at the scene *before* everyone entered the room, since no one saw her near the vat afterward."

"But how would one of her molds get inside the vat? Surely she didn't take it with her and drop it in."

Jake shrugged. "It's circumstantial, but Shelton apparently has more evidence."

"Like what?"

"Don't know yet."

"What about the gash on Polly's head? Do they know what caused it?"

"Shelton thinks it's some kind of jagged stick. Could be anything."

"Did they find it?"

Jake shook his head. "They're searching for it."

If they found some kind of heavy stick with Wendy's prints—and it proved to be the murder weapon—that would be the end of it. She'd surely be found guilty. So what *was* the murder weapon—and where was it?

"So Detective Shelton actually thinks little old Wendy hit Polly over the head with some kind of heavy rod or whatever, then pushed her into the vat of chocolate? That makes no sense." I tossed my coffee into a nearby recycle bin, no longer interested in it. "And why the knife-shaped mold?"

"Shelton thinks maybe she meant to stab Polly with it. Apparently, the thing is pretty sharp—like a knife."

"But why would she stab her with something like that when she could use a real knife?" I asked. "Why a candy mold? And why bring along a big stick?"

Jake shrugged. "Maybe it was something nearby, something handy. I don't know."

I thought for a moment. "No. It's all too contrived. I think whoever killed Polly somehow got ahold of the knife mold and dropped it into the chocolate to make it look like Wendy did it, then beaned Polly over the head with something heavy and shoved her in."

"Maybe," Jake said.

"Besides, Wendy doesn't have a motive. I mean, why would she want to kill Polly?"

Jake looked away.

"Jake? What aren't you telling me?"

He shrugged. "Apparently, Shelton's tech team found something on Wendy's computer."

My breath caught. I immediately thought of the blackmail messages to the other two judges. "What was it?"

"An e-mail Polly sent to Wendy."

Uh-oh. My heart raced. "What did it say?"

"Something like, '*If you want me to forget what you've done, then don't forget what to do. . . .*'"

I gasped. "So Polly wasn't only blackmailing the judges—she was blackmailing Wendy too?"

"Sure looks that way," Jake said.

I wondered what Wendy had done that was so awful that she'd become a victim of Polly's blackmail scheme.

Chapter 11

"What are you talking about?" said a voice behind me. Startled, I spun around in my chair.

"Aunt Abby! What are you doing here?"

"Checking on you," she said, hands on her hips. "What's this about Wendy?"

I glanced at Jake. He stood. "Detective Shelton found an e-mail on Polly's computer, sent to Wendy."

"You mean like the others?" Aunt Abby asked.

Jake cleared his throat before answering. "I'm afraid so. It sounds like Polly was blackmailing her too."

"That's ridiculous!" Aunt Abby said. "I've known Wendy for years. True, we lost touch for a while, but I told you we reconnected, and she's the same old Wendy I knew from high school. She has nothing to hide. Wes is dead wrong about her."

Jake stole a glance at me. Aunt Abby caught him. "I mean it. She's innocent."

He shifted his weight.

"Is there something else?" she asked Jake.

"The cops found one of her candy molds at the bottom of the vat of chocolate," he told her.

Aunt Abby frowned. "Well . . . that's easy to explain."

Oh really? I thought.

"Someone dropped it in there to frame her," Aunt Abby said. "I saw something like that on *Castle*. Murderers are always trying to frame innocent people, and the cops always fall for it."

Jake pressed his lips together, as if to keep from arguing with her.

Aunt Abby turned to me. "Darcy? You don't believe all this bull-snot, do you? You met Wendy last night and you've heard me talk about her. Surely you could tell she wouldn't do anything like that, right?"

I opened my mouth to speak but didn't know what to say. I had met the woman only briefly. I certainly couldn't have passed judgment on her.

"Listen, Darcy," Aunt Abby said. "You've got to get to the bottom of this."

"And how do you suggest I do that?" I asked.

"Start sniffing around, like the good reporter you are. Find out who *else* had a reason to kill Polly. And get some evidence—right, Counselor?" she said to Jake.

Jake nodded.

"All right, now go! The crowds are down and the event will be closing for the day soon. I really don't need you back at the bus until tomorrow morning. Dillon and I can handle it until then. And if there's anything Wendy's hiding, I'm sure Dillon will find out. Which she isn't."

"You'll need help to make more whoopie pies tonight," I argued. "And you'll need help getting ready for the competition tomorrow night."

"Tomorrow morning will be fine. Helping Wendy is more important than winning a contest."

She was right. But although I'd been a reporter, I was no detective. And while Jake had been an attorney, he was no cop. We'd been lucky once, solving a murder when the police were stumped. Would we be able to do it again?

And what if Aunt Abby was wrong about her friend Wendy?

What if Wendy Spellman had a dark side that included an incident she'd kept secret—and a penchant for murder? I tried to recall what she'd said just before we drove away last night, after dropping her off. . . .

"We'll do what we can," Jake said, glancing at me.

I forced a reassuring smile.

"Good," Aunt Abby said. "I'll tell Dillon to find out what he can. Text me when you learn something, and I'll keep you posted on what Dillon discovers." With that she headed back to the school bus.

"She's something else," Jake said, grinning.

"Tell me about it," I said. "Now what?"

"I suppose we ask around, see if we can find out more about Polly, see what she might have had on those judges. And who else she might have been blackmailing."

"Any idea where to look?"

Jake nodded. "I have an idea."

He took my hand and started to lead me off. I stopped abruptly and let go of his hand.

"What's the matter?" he asked.

"What about your ex?"

Jake frowned, puzzled. "What about her?"

"I saw her coming out of your truck when I went to get a coffee. Doesn't she need you?"

Jake smiled. "Darcy, are you still worried about her?"

"Of course not! I'm just asking because I know she wants your help, and if you need to go—"

He held a finger up to my lips to shut me up.

Half of me wanted to bite it, and the other half wanted to kiss it. God, he was aggravating.

"Lyla's fine. I'm taking care of things. Now, come on. Let's go do what we can to help your aunt's friend."

"What about your truck?"

"The festival is closing in an hour. I've already put a sign in the window."

I nodded.

He smiled again, and I melted like a cream puff under a hot sun.

Jake led me through the food trucks to the back entrance of the festival, behind the fence, to a trailer parked not far from the staff parking lot. A large plastic sign was draped along one side of the trailer, with giant brown letters that read SAN FRANCISCO CHOCOLATE FESTIVAL. On the door of the trailer was a smaller magnetic sign that read OFFICE.

"I didn't know this was here," I said.

"It's Reina's office trailer. I brought my registration here." He stepped up the stairs and knocked on the metal door.

I heard indistinct murmurs inside.

Jake pushed on the door handle and opened it.

"Hello?" he called, leaning in. He turned and pulled me up by the hand, and we entered.

Reina Patel sat behind a large metal desk covered with stacks of papers. Her desk was surrounded by boxes filled with more papers—flyers for the festival, entry forms, tickets, et cetera. The walls were bare—the place was obviously temporary—but the floor was crowded with signage, rolled-up posters, and other festival paraphernalia. Along one shelf were trophies for the contest—a big one for the winner, the other two smaller for second and third places.

J.C. sat across from her, slouched in a folding chair, his legs stretched out in front of him, his camera in his lap.

Reina was talking on a tricked-out cell phone covered in rhinestones. As soon as she saw us, she abruptly set down the phone. J.C. sat up in his chair.

"Can I help you?" Reina asked, tilting her head.

Jake stepped forward and reached out a hand, accidentally knocking some papers off one of the stacks and onto the floor. "Sorry," he said, kneeling down and retrieving the papers. He set the mess on the desk and tried to restack them.

"Just leave them!" Reina snapped. "What do you want?"

"I'm Jake Miller, from the Dream Puff truck." He stuck out his hand again, this time avoiding another avalanche of papers.

She reluctantly took it.

Jake turned to me. "This is Darcy Burnett, from the Big Yellow School Bus. We have trucks at the Chocolate Festival. And we're contestants in the competition."

Reina frowned and steepled her hands. "I remember you. From the party. What can I do for you, Mr. Miller? I'm extremely busy trying to run this festival and dealing with all these unexpected glitches. . . ."

Glitches? A woman found dead and another arrested for murder were glitches?

"I'm sure you are," Jake said, "and I won't take up much of your time, but I understand Wendy Spellman from the Chocolate Candyland truck was arrested this morning. I wondered—"

She cut him off. "Very unfortunate, but at least we can put that behind us and move on with the festival. The police certainly did their job well this time. And quickly too."

"Yeah, about that," Jake said. "I think Wendy may have been arrested by mistake."

Reina frowned; then the frown dissolved and she offered a condescending smile. "Well, I'm sorry you feel that way, Mr. Miller, but I think the police know what they're doing. And we don't need any more unpleasant interruptions that might ruin the rest of the festival. We have a lot invested in this event—and a lot of attendees paying for a good time—so unless you're moonlighting as a police officer and have some knowledge other than your intuition, I'd appreciate it if you wouldn't spread any unfounded rumors. What's done is done. Understand?"

I couldn't hold my tongue any longer. "Listen, Reina. Wendy Spellman is a longtime friend of my aunt Abby, and my aunt says there's no way Wendy would ever hurt anyone. I believe her, and I plan to do what I can to help find out what really happened. We'd like your cooperation, but if you can't—or won't—help us, then we'll do this on our own."

The frown on Reina's face returned. She was staring at me in an odd way.

"You're Abigail Warner's niece?"

I nodded.

In a sudden about-face, Reina sat up, placed her hands on her desk, and with a warm smile said, "Of course I'll help you, if I can. If you think your aunt's friend is innocent, then feel free to investigate. Just please promise me you'll keep your little investigation quiet. Like I said, I don't want anything else to jeopardize this festival. If word gets out a murderer is still lurking about, people will stay away in droves and the festival will lose money that's earmarked for charity. Do you understand?"

I wondered how much she really cared about those charities.

Jake nodded, but I wasn't so ready to be shackled by her demands.

"Did the police question you about Wendy?" I asked, figuring it was time to get this so-called investigation started.

"Yes, but I had nothing to contribute and answered truthfully. I don't know Wendy other than through the festival, and I didn't see what happened to poor Polly that night. . . ." She stopped, seemingly overcome by the memory of the murdered woman.

"You didn't know Wendy before this?" Jake asked.

"No. Only what's on her application. We don't do a

lot of screening of our contestants, other than to make sure they have a licensed truck and a legitimate business."

"And you have no idea why Wendy might want to kill Polly?"

Reina shook her head. She glanced at J.C., who also shook his head.

"Is there anyone else you can think of who might have had a reason to kill Polly?"

"Not really," Reina said. "She seemed to have a lot of friends. She was quite popular. Although . . ."

"Although what?" I asked.

"Well, I'm not one to disparage anyone, especially not someone who's no longer here to defend herself, but I thought I saw her have a little tiff with the other two judges, Simon and Isabel, at the party."

"Any idea what it was about?" Jake asked.

"No. And like I said, I don't listen to gossip. I just don't want all this talk of murder to affect the festival and impact ticket sales. Although I'm sure it's all over the news."

"It won't hurt your festival." J.C. spoke for the first time since we'd barged in. "In fact, it'll be just the opposite. People love to gawk at anything related to a crime. That's why reality TV is so popular. Viewers love it when something bad happens to real people. Remember all the crowds that showed up when that restaurant chef was murdered a while back? The people who bought that place were probably booked up for months afterward. I'm surprised they didn't use crime-scene tape as part of the new decor."

I knew exactly the place she was talking about—the restaurant formerly known as Bones 'n' Brew. The murder he mentioned had occurred right across the street from the Fort Mason food trucks—and my aunt had been on the list of suspects.

Reina shook her head. "What a nightmare this has been. Please," she said to Jake and me, "be discreet, will you? Maybe J.C. is right and this will boost sales, now that the murderer has been caught—"

"Alleged murderer," I said, interrupting her.

"Fine," she said.

I caught J.C. fiddling with his camera.

"You videotaped everything at the party last night, right?" I asked him.

He nodded.

"You made a copy for the police. Any chance you saw something on the tapes that might offer some kind of clue?"

"Nah. I fast-forwarded through the whole thing and didn't see anything other than a bunch of people partying. Nothing like the killer pushing that woman into the chocolate. Sorry."

"Can you make a copy for us?" Jake asked.

"Your brother should have a copy. He downloaded it before I handed it over to the cops."

"He's not my brother," I said, almost laughing at the thought.

"If that's all," Reina spoke up, "I really have to get back to work. I have a lot to do before the competition tomorrow night."

"Speaking of the competition," Jake said, "I'd like to

talk to those other two judges who were at the party last night. Know where we might find them?"

"I'm sorry," Reina said, not sounding the least bit sorry. "I can't give out personal information. Especially not about the judges when you're both contestants. That would be unethical. Besides, they've sequestered themselves until the competition tomorrow. As you can imagine, they're a little shaken up from all that's happened, so they're keeping out of sight until they're needed. You understand."

If she said "you understand" one more time, I was going to smack her.

"Sure," Jake said too quickly. "Well, thanks for your time. You'll let us know if you hear anything?"

"Of course," Reina said. "Just remember, if you do anything to disrupt the festival, I may have to withdraw you from the competition."

Oh no, she didn't just threaten us!

Jake seemed to sense my anger and stepped in front of me to shake Reina's hand again.

"Will do," he said; then he turned and gestured for me to leave. I glared at him but did as he wanted. It wouldn't do any good to call the woman on her threat. After all, she had the power to have Aunt Abby and Jake eliminated from the contest—and my aunt would be devastated if that happened.

We stepped out of the trailer, and Jake closed the door behind us.

"Well, that was a colossal waste of time," I said. "And time is something we don't have. The contest is tomorrow night, and after that everyone will scatter."

Jake gently took my arm with one hand and walked me toward the fence near the back entrance. He kept the other hand down at his side.

"Maybe not," he said when we were out of sight of the office trailer. He stopped, gave his other arm a shake, and turned over his hand. In it he held Reina's rhinestone-covered cell phone.

Chapter 12

"Oh my God! You did not just steal her cell phone!"

"No. I didn't steal it. Although I may have borrowed it," he admitted. "I'll run it back to the trailer in a few minutes, make up some excuse for returning, and sneak it under a pile of those papers. She'll never know."

"You're crazy!"

He shrugged.

"How did you get it?"

"Remember when I knocked those papers off the stack?"

I remembered. "Clever. Now what are you going to do with it?"

"Now we go find Dillon and get him to hack into her phone."

On the way back to the school bus, I wondered if a person could go to jail for "borrowing" someone's cell phone, not to mention hacking into it. This was not good.

We found Dillon sitting outside the bus on the step, holding what looked like a cupcake in a fancy paper wrapper. He took a bite off the top of the chocolaty dessert, then looked at us standing over him.

"What?" he asked in his usual blunt manner. Bits of chocolate dotted his lips.

"What are you eating?" I asked.

"It's an I Scream Cake," Dillon answered, then licked his lips. "It's like half cupcake and half ice cream. It's got chocolate cake at the bottom, then a layer of coffee ice cream, then a layer of grated chocolate and sprinkles on top. Yummy." He took another bite.

I guessed the goody came from Monet's truck. It did look good, in spite of the mess Dillon was making while eating it. "Why aren't you inside helping your mom?"

"It's slow. What's up?"

Jake held the cell phone out toward him. Dillon wiped his hand on his jeans, then took it and looked at Jake.

"Can you get in? I need some information."

Dillon tapped the phone.

The screen lit up. The password prompt appeared.

He tapped in several keystrokes.

Seconds later he handed the phone back to Jake. "You're in."

My mouth dropped open. "How did you do that so fast?" I asked.

"Simple," Dillon said. "I told you people tend to be lazy and predictable. The most common password usually has to do with your partner, your kid, or your pet, followed by a zero, one, or one, two, three."

"Does Reina have a partner, a kid, or a pet?" Jake asked me.

"I have no idea," I said.

"So . . ."

"So the next most common passwords are 'password,' the person's city, or something about their work or hobby. Then they usually add the last four digits of their social security number, their date of birth, or the numbers one, two, three, four. I got it on the fourth try. Hers was 'SF one, two, three, four.'" He took another bite of his treat, then looked up at me. "What's yours, Darcy?"

Talk about predictable. Crap! I'd used the name of my parents' dog—Frosty—plus the numbers one, two, three, four.

While Jake fooled around with Reina's phone, I pulled out my phone, tapped "Settings," and changed my password to the name of Dillon's rat and my aunt's birthday month and date.

Dillon grinned. "Let me see it."

I handed it to him.

He tapped a few keys, then gave it back to me. "You might want to change it again."

I stared at him. "You already figured out my new password!?"

"Ratty," he said smugly. "Five, ten. Piece of cake."

"You're incredible!" I said. "Nothing's safe from you. Now what? Should I just make up a word, add a bunch of numbers, include a few symbols, then try to remember what I've done?"

"You don't have to go that far," Dillon said, standing. "But if you want to keep people out of your personal online stuff—e-mail, texts, banking—you have to be smarter than the hackers. They won't try your bank password. Instead they go to places most people use, like online shopping or e-mail invitations, because those passwords are easy to figure out. Or they might use a system like Brute Force Attack, or an Internet site like insecure.com or passwordcracker.com—places that try thousands of common user names and passwords to find the cookies stored in your web browser."

He was starting to lose me. "So what do I do?"

"Make sure your password is strong by using special characters, like an asterisk or a dollar sign."

"And just hope I don't forget which ones I used."

Dillon stuffed the rest of his I Scream Cake in his mouth and swallowed it. "Okay, first choose something you remember from your childhood, like a favorite toy or game. Then add random caps or change the letter O to the number zero, and include some symbols."

"This is too much!" I said, frustrated. "When did things get so complicated?"

"It's not that hard," Dillon said, taking back my phone. "I use a trick that makes it hard for hackers to break in. It's called a LEET code."

I frowned. Like I had time to learn some fancy code just to protect my password.

"Tell me the name of your favorite toy or game," Dillon said.

I shrugged. "Clue, I guess."

"Now tell me a special date in history that's not personal."

"Uh . . . 1930," I said, remembering the first year that a Nancy Drew mystery was published.

"Now, instead of typing regular keyboard letters, use symbols that *look* like letters." Dillon typed in a few symbols on my cell phone keyboard, then showed me the screen. "What does that look like to you?"

I studied the screen: (|_ (_) 3. "A left parenthesis, a vertical line, a horizontal line, another left parenthesis, another horizontal line, a right parenthesis, and the number three. I'll never remember all of that."

"Now picture them as letters," he said. "What does it *say*?"

I stared at the symbols. "I have no clue."

Dillon grinned. "You're close. Look again."

I shrugged and handed the phone over to Jake to see if he knew.

"Clue!" Jake said after one glance. "The parenthesis looks like a C. The vertical and horizontal lines shape the letter L."

"U and E," I said, finally *seeing* what I couldn't see before. "Clever, Dillon. So this might keep me from being hacked?"

"Bingo!" Dillon said.

I smiled. I had to admit, this was kind of cool.

"I'd better get back," Dillon said. "Let me know what you find out."

"Will do," Jake said. Dillon stepped back into the school bus.

I turned to Jake. "So, now that you're in Reina's phone, what are you looking for?"

He said nothing. Instead he tapped a few keys, then said, "Write this down."

I dug through my purse and pulled out the notepad I always kept for writing down recipes for my food truck cookbook. I found a pen and flipped open the pad.

"Isabel Lau . . ." He reeled off a phone number and address.

"Simon Van Houten." Another number and address.

He shut off the phone. "I've got to run this back. Stay here." He disappeared, headed for Reina's trailer. I wondered how he was going to return the phone without arousing her suspicion.

Meanwhile I pulled out my phone and changed my password again, this time to something no one would ever be able to hack, but would be easy to remember— the name of my favorite reading material as a kid and the year *Murder, She Wrote* debuted—and then encrypted the words in LEET code:

/\/\ 4 |) /\/\ 4 6 4 2 ! /\/ 3–1984

Try to hack that, Dillon.

"Did you return it?" I asked Jake when he came back.

"Yeah. I said I had one more question and slipped the phone under some papers when she wasn't paying attention."

"What are you, some kind of magician? How did you do that thing-up-your-sleeve trick?"

"As a matter of fact, yes. Every boy learns a few magic tricks as a kid. I happened to be pretty good. I called myself Jake the Great."

I laughed out loud. "That's the best you could do?"

"Nothing rhymes with Jake except fake."

I could think of a few—snake, flake, rake. . . .

"Later I'll show you how to make a cream puff disappear," he said.

"I already know that trick." I checked my watch. "So what now?"

"Now we go talk to the two remaining judges."

"But Reina said they were hiding out somewhere," I said. "Even if you have their addresses, they're probably not home."

"She was obviously lying," he said. "She just didn't want us snooping around."

"How do you know she was lying?"

"As attorneys, we're trained to look for tells. She had a tell."

"A tell?"

"You know, like when you play poker. A tell is an unconscious facial tic or expression or gesture that contradicts what a person is saying. You've heard the phrase 'poker face'? That's when you consciously try not to give away what's in your hand by keeping a straight face."

Was there anything this dream puff guy didn't know?

"So you played poker as a kid too?"

He nodded. "With my dad. He had his friends over for regular poker games. He taught me what to watch for when he played with his pals."

"Really? Like what?"

"Well, like, if the person fidgets, or scratches his face, or blinks rapidly, he's hiding a good hand. Or if he just stares straight ahead and doesn't make eye contact. Or if he's overly talkative. All giveaways. Sometimes it's just a change in breathing. So while *you're* trying not to let the other guy know what kind of hand *you* have, sometimes your underlying emotions give you away through physical signals."

"And you looked for these 'tells' in jury selection?"

"Not just in juries. I looked for them in the person who's hiring me to represent them. It's a handy trick in a lot of situations."

I grinned. This was fascinating. "What kind of tell did you get from Reina that told you she was lying about the judges?"

"Remember her hands?" Jake asked.

I thought back. "Not really. She'd had a manicure. Wait! I think they were steepled at some point."

"Good memory. That's when she asked what we wanted. It's a sign of confidence, of being in command. She thought she had the upper hand. Then what did she do when we asked about the judges?"

I thought for a moment, then shook my head.

"She placed her hands flat on her desk, as if to keep them under control. Another dead giveaway for nervousness."

"Wow." I suddenly wondered what kind of tells I'd been giving Jake, but decided not to ask.

"You want to know what your tell is, don't you?" Jake said, reading my mind—or my tells.

My mouth dropped open. I knew that was a huge tell that meant, "How did you know what I was thinking?"

"Don't worry," he said. "Aside from what you just did, you're usually good at keeping your thoughts and feelings to yourself."

I took a deep breath, then wondered what that told him. This was getting to be too much.

"Enough," I said. "Let's go find a judge."

Chapter 13

We hopped in my VW Bug and Jake pulled out his cell phone. He dialed the number I'd written down for Isabel Lau. No answer. He tried Simon Van Houten's number. Again no answer.

"Did you get a number for the new judge—Delbert Morris?" I asked.

"No. She didn't have anything listed."

"What now?"

"I say we head on over to Van Houten's place first and check. Maybe they're just not answering their phones. Then we'll try Lau's place."

He typed Simon's address into his cell phone GPS. A map appeared, leading us from our current location to our final destination—somewhere in The Avenues. The woman's robotic voice began giving us directions: *"Turn left in two hundred feet."*

We were on our way to see Judge Number One—Simon Van Houten.

"Do you know anything about this guy, besides what Dillon's told us?" I asked Jake as I followed the female's instructions to the western side of the city.

"Nope," Jake answered.

I punched in Dillon's cell number using the car's Bluetooth. He answered after four rings.

"Dillon, can you find out anything more about the judges—Simon Van Houten and Isabel Lau?"

"Gimme a couple of minutes." It sounded like his mouth was full. Did the guy ever stop eating?

"Must be nice to have a hacker in the family," Jake said, squirming in the seat as if trying to get comfortable. Being taller than six feet, it was a challenge for him, but I loved my cozy car. There was plenty of room for my five-ten frame.

"I guess he comes in handy now and then."

"Turn right in two miles and keep right," came the GPS voice again. I started to say something, but she interrupted me again. I gave up and just listened for her next command. By the time we took the off-ramp and entered the Sunset/Richmond districts, known familiarly as The Avenues, the fog seemed denser and the air cooler. No wonder, since the area was close to the chilly waters of the Pacific Ocean, and winds gusted regularly off Ocean Beach. The Avenues is mostly residential, but it's close to Golden Gate Park, the San Francisco Zoo, Lake Merced, and the Sutro Baths. It's a different world from downtown San Francisco.

The houses from Second to Forty-eighth are mostly tract and row homes, built after the 1906 earthquake. They're simple in design—three stories with stucco facades—and looked small from the front but ran deep. The neighborhoods were middle-class, originally Irish but now mostly Asian, often handed down through generations, although there's a small population of surfers, who rent, then don their wet suits and head for the waves.

We pulled up to the address I had for Simon Van Houten, a modest narrow three-story home with a one-car garage underneath.

My cell phone rang.

Leaving the ignition on, I answered on the first ring. "Dillon? What did you find out?"

"Not much more than what we already knew," he said. "His father owns a bunch of chocolate companies, all under various corporate names. It won't be easy uncovering every company he owns, since he's got lawyers protecting his business filings. His father is loaded, but most of his money is tied up."

I looked up at the small vertical home we'd parked in front of and frowned. If Simon Van Houten's family was so rich, what was he doing living in a simple home like this? Granted, housing prices were inflated, but this was no Pacific Heights.

"Are you sure he's rich?" I asked.

"On paper, at least. By the way, Simon Van Houten the judge is Simon Van Houten the second."

"Wait a minute," I said. "They have the same name? Have you been checking on the right guy?"

I heard computer clicking noises on the other end of the line, then an airy whistle. "Yep. Simon Number One is the rich dad, and Simon Number Two is the judge who works for his father's company. Everything I can find seems to be under his dad's name."

"Thanks, Dillon."

"Later," he said, and hung up.

"That's odd," I said to Jake, who'd been listening to our call on the car Bluetooth. "Simon's dad is the actual owner of all those secret corporations, but he doesn't seem to be sharing much with his son. If Simon the judge is part of the business, why does he live in such a modest house? And why does he act like he's a big-wig in chocolate?"

"He didn't look too poor at the party last night," Jake said. "He was wearing an expensive suit like the more-affluent attorneys wear."

"Maybe it was for show," I said.

"Or maybe he's got money on paper too, like his father, and can't spend it."

I shrugged. "Well, let's go talk to him and see what he has to say." I opened the door. "I hope he's home."

"He's home," Jake said, getting out of the car.

I closed the driver's side door. "How do you know? You have ESP now too?"

"Nope," he said, waiting for me at the curb. "I saw him peeking out of his window upstairs a minute ago."

I glanced at the window. The curtain fluttered. Hmm, I thought. Nosy? Paranoid? Expecting someone?

"Well, he knows we're here. Let's go," I said, leading the way.

I headed up the front steps and rang the push-button bell. I could hear a muffled ring. After thirty seconds with no answer, I rang it again.

"What do you want?" came a voice from overhead.

I looked up to see Simon leaning out of the second-floor window.

"Simon?" I called up. "It's me, Darcy Burnett, from the chocolate party last night. Remember? And Jake Miller, the Dream Puff guy."

"I know who you are. What do you want?" he repeated. The wind caught the top of his thinning hair and flipped it.

"We wanted to talk to you about something. Can we come in?"

"What about?" he called down.

"I'm not sure you want me to yell it out in front of all your neighbors, but it's important."

He patted his hair down, pulled his head in, and closed the window. I raised an eyebrow at Jake. He shrugged.

Moments later I heard a click at the front door as the door popped open.

I grasped the old-fashioned knob and slowly pushed the door open.

The tiny foyer inside was empty aside from a small table that had collected a stack of rolled-up newspapers. Apparently, reading the *Chronicle* wasn't high on Simon's priority list.

I looked up the stairs. Seeing no one, I called tentatively, "Hello?"

Simon's head appeared again, this time hanging over the short rail at the top of the second floor. "Come up. And lock the door behind you."

We did what he said and climbed the stairs. When I reached the top step, I noticed a lever attached to the wall. It was much like the one my friend had in her Avenue house. Like Simon, she used to look out the second-floor window when anyone knocked on the door in order to make sure her visitor wasn't a serial killer. When she pulled the lever, the door at the bottom of the stairs opened, so she didn't have to run down and open it. It was one of the unique touches of the old Avenue homes that I loved.

"Hi, Simon," I said, entering the main living area. The room was long and skinny, decorated in mismatched Ikea-looking furniture, with bare walls and meager offerings of comfort. This was a single guy's home for sure, and temporary at that, with just the basics.

"How did you find me?" he asked, frowning, hands on his narrow hips. According to Dillon's information, he was about forty, but he looked ten years older, with his thin, drawn face and floppy comb-over that barely covered his bald spot. He was dressed for comfort, in gray sweatpants and a flannel shirt.

"Uh, Reina had your address," Jake said. "She said you were keeping a low profile since the murder, but we need to talk to you."

"What about?" Simon said, not moving.

"You know they have someone in custody, don't you?" Jake asked.

Simon nodded. "Supposedly, although I'm not so sure."

"Any chance you've got a beer?" Jake asked. "Been a long day."

Simon seemed to think about it, then gestured for us to sit in one of his prefab chairs, none of which looked inviting. I had to clear away a couple of jackets from the seat I chose, while Jake moved aside a pizza carton and some used napkins.

Simon returned with three cans of beer, handed one to Jake, then one to me. He sat down on a low-slung futon, popped open his beer, and took a long swig.

"So what do you want?" he asked, wiping the foam from his mouth. "If you came here to try to influence me to vote for you, that's not going to happen. That's why I told Reina not to tell anyone where to find me. It wouldn't look good if I was caught talking to contestants."

"We're not here for that," I said quickly, then changed the subject. "I have to say, you still seem a bit paranoid."

He let out a dry laugh, then drank more beer. "Paranoid? Two judges from the competition are dead, the new guy—Delbert Morris—he just quit, and you wonder why I might be paranoid?"

"He quit?" I asked, surprised.

"Apparently," Simon replied.

"But you know about the arrest," Jake said.

Simon pressed his lips together and shook his head. "Yeah, right. Like that old woman had the strength to push Polly into a vat of chocolate. I'm not going to let my guard down until this festival is over. I wish I'd never signed up for it."

"I heard you didn't like Polly much," I said, remembering the blackmail threat Polly had e-mailed him. It was a safe bet that he wasn't fond of anyone who tried to blackmail him.

"Where'd you get *that* idea?" Simon said. He washed the bitter words down with another gulp of beer. I wondered how many beers he'd had so far. He wasn't slurring his words, but his eyes were glassy and he was pouring down the alcohol as if putting out a fire.

I wondered if I should show my hand and tell him I knew about Polly blackmailing him. He might relax a bit if that was out in the open. Then again, he might get more upset and kick us out. Somehow, I had to get him to say something about his relationship with Polly.

"Were you sleeping with her?" I asked on a hunch. Polly was quite the flirt. Maybe she was fooling around with some of the men at the party.

Jake stiffened and shot me a look. Simon frowned.

"That's none of your business," he said. "The cops questioned me and cleared me, so if you're implying I had anything to do with her death, you're mistaken."

"So you didn't have a relationship with her?"

He took another gulp of beer. "Listen, Polly Montgomery slept with just about every guy she met, and maybe even some gals. That has nothing to do with me."

This was getting nowhere. I had to lay my cards on the table. "Simon, I know you were being blackmailed by Polly."

Simon nearly dropped his beer. "How do you know that?"

"I'm a reporter. I can't name my source. But it's true, isn't it? What did she have on you?"

"Nothing. You've got no proof," he said, scowling.

I raised an eyebrow. "Actually, I do. I have the e-mails Polly sent you."

His face fell. "All right, yes, she sent us judges threatening e-mails telling us how to vote at the competition. But we told her to go to hell. That's when she said she'd tell everyone about . . ." He stopped and downed his beer. "I don't know why I'm telling you all this."

"Simon, I think we can help you. What did she have on you?" I asked.

"None of your business. I think you should leave." He stood.

I remained sitting and tried another tack. "How did she want you to vote?"

He shrugged. "She was going to tell us just before we started the judging."

Why would she wait to tell them?

"And now she's dead," I said.

"Yeah, well, I told you. I didn't kill her. Someone else must have wanted her dead for some reason. She was probably blackmailing them too. With two judges gone, and one dropped out, that leaves the two of us—Isabel and me—and that's why we're playing it safe until the festival is over."

"Do you really think you're safe here?" Jake asked. "Why not ask for police protection if you're that worried?"

He cocked his jaw. "Let's just say I've got my own protection."

I studied his shirt and tried to see if there might be a gun or some other weapon hiding underneath, but I didn't get the impression he was armed. Of course, I could be wrong. Maybe it was time to wrap up this interview. If Simon had a weapon and he thought Jake and I were a threat, he might just use it.

"Well," I said, rising. I set my untouched beer on a nearby table. "Let us know if we can help you somehow. And Isabel. We'd like to talk to her too. Do you happen to know where she is? We tried calling, but there was no answer."

"Simon?" A voice coming from the far end of the long room startled me.

I looked over to see someone standing in the shadows. The dark figure stepped forward into the late-afternoon light of the window—a woman with silver hair that framed her pale face and contrasted with her dark eyes. She was dressed in khaki pants and a Hawaiian shirt and wore flip-flops on her feet.

Isabel Lau.

She had a gun in her hand.

Chapter 14

Jake jumped up, ready for action. I froze and nearly wet my pants.

"Isabel!" Simon cried.

Yep. That was a gun she was holding. And she didn't look happy to see us, if her expression was any kind of a tell.

"Put it down!" Simon ordered.

Isabel stood still, her hand shaking as she pointed the weapon in our direction. I was sure the thing would go off any second—if not on purpose, then by accident.

Simon went over and took the gun from her hand. He lowered it, emptied the bullets, then opened a nearby desk drawer, put the gun inside, and closed the drawer.

"What were you thinking?" Simon asked her.

Isabel's face went white, nearly matching her silver hair. Her lips trembled and her dark eyes watered. Suddenly, all the energy seemed to leave her body and she collapsed in a nearby chair. "I heard voices. . . . I thought . . . ," she muttered.

"I said I'd take care of us, didn't I?" Simon told her.

He rested a hand on her back. "There's no need for violence." He turned to Jake and me. "Sorry about that. I didn't know she had a gun."

Isabel looked up, her eyes red-rimmed. Lack of sleep? "I told you I didn't want any part of this," she said to Simon.

I frowned at the two of them. "Any part of what?" Were they referring to Polly's murder? Had they conspired to kill her because she was blackmailing them? I felt compelled to ask: "Did you kill Polly, Isabel?"

Isabel gasped. "Of course not!"

"No, no!" Simon added. "What Isabel means is, she doesn't want any part of the contest judging, and neither do I. Reina talked her into it, but when George died and then Polly—well, she still thinks someone is killing off the judges, one by one."

"So do you!" Isabel said. "Just because that woman was arrested doesn't mean this is over. George's death may have *looked* like an accident, but Polly's death wasn't a coincidence. I'm sure Simon and I are next!" She looked at Simon for confirmation.

"An accident? A coincidence? Who knows?" Simon said. "But we're not taking any chances anymore, with or without Wendy in jail. The only reason we haven't quit is because Reina promised us substantial bonuses."

"Money's not going to do us any good if someone wants to kill us!" Isabel argued. "That's why Delbert quit. He found out about the murders. Now I want out of this before it's too late."

"It's already too late, Isabel," Simon said. "The competition is tomorrow. If we back out now, we'll lose our reputations as well as the money. Plus, it might look suspicious if we did, since we're the only two surviving judges. And if it gets out that Polly had something on us . . ."

Isabel glared at Simon. "Shut up!"

"Simmer down, Isabel. They already know about the blackmail." Simon glanced at us.

I nodded. "We heard Polly was blackmailing you and Simon so you'd vote her way."

Isabel gasped again. Her cheeks turned pink. A look of terror filled her eyes. "How did you find out?"

I said nothing, not wanting to give up Dillon, and looked at Jake to answer.

Instead, he changed the subject. "Isabel, did Polly tell you who to vote for before she died?"

Isabel shook her head, confirming what Simon had said earlier.

"You don't have any idea who it was supposed to be?" Jake pressed.

"No," Isabel answered. "Polly said she'd tell us right before we were supposed to cast our votes."

"And you would have done what she said?" I asked.

Tears filled Isabel's dark eyes again. "Like Simon told you, she said she'd expose us if we didn't."

"What did she have on you?" Jake asked.

Isabel turned away.

"Maybe we can help," I offered gently.

"How?" Isabel asked, twisting her hands in her lap. "George is dead. Polly's dead. And the police think they have the killer."

"We think Wendy is innocent," Jake said, "and we

mean to prove it. So when we do, the police will come looking for the most likely suspects—the two people Polly was blackmailing."

"Not if you don't tell them!" she said.

I didn't mention the fact that they already had Polly's computer with the incriminating e-mails. "Let us help you," I said.

Simon looked at Isabel, then shrugged. "Maybe they can help us after all." He turned to Jake and me. "Do you mean that? You'll help us if the police think we had something to do with Polly's death?"

"Yes," I said. "If you're innocent, we'll do what we can. Jake's a lawyer." I didn't mention the fact that he was currently disbarred. Jake shot me a look. I ignored it.

"All right . . . ," Simon said.

"Simon!" she admonished him. "No! You promised! You said not to trust anyone."

Simon shook his head. "We have no choice, Isabel. If Wendy really didn't kill Polly, then we might need this guy's help in more ways than one."

Isabel crossed her arms and studied Jake a moment, then me.

"You want to tell them, or should I?" Simon asked.

She looked down at the floor.

"Okay, I will," Simon said. He turned to us. "Somehow Polly found out that Isabel had, well, spent some time in prison."

I blinked with surprise. Isabel being an ex-con wasn't what I'd expected. I was thinking more along the lines of plagiarizing a recipe or maybe falsifying her qualifications to be a judge.

"Why were you in prison?" I asked her.

Isabel shook her head. Simon answered for her. "Homicide."

"What?" I blurted.

"It was manslaughter!" Isabel argued, her face turning a brighter shade of pink. "And he deserved it."

That got my attention. Apparently Isabel Lau was capable of murder.

Simon patted her back. "Isabel's husband was abusive. Used to beat her. When he broke her arm for the second time, she'd had enough. She stopped him the only way she knew how."

Isabel's demeanor abruptly changed. Her eyes narrowed and her nostrils flared. She suddenly looked defiant.

"What did you do?" I asked.

Isabel met my eyes and said, "I stabbed him, right after he passed out from drinking a bottle of whiskey."

I stared at her openmouthed, stunned at this confession. "But why? There are services to help battered women—shelters, counselors, housing. Why kill him? Why not just leave him?"

"Because he threatened to track me down—and he had the resources to do that."

"Why didn't you go to the police?" I asked, puzzled.

"They wouldn't have believed me," Isabel said.

"But you had proof," I said. "Your arm was broken! Twice! Surely the hospital had records of this. The police couldn't ignore that."

Tears filled her eyes. "Tell her, Simon. Tell her why I couldn't go to the police."

Simon cleared his throat before answering. "Her husband was a cop."

Whoa. I glanced over at Jake. He gave a single nod. I gathered he'd heard about situations like this, being in the law profession.

"I'm so sorry," I said, unable to imagine what it must have been like, trapped in a marriage with an abusive man, especially one who was supposed to help and protect people. "That must have been twice as hard for you, not having any support from the police department."

Isabel's hands twisted in her lap. "She ended up serving five years," Simon said.

Wow. Five years of her life for killing a man who'd battered her repeatedly.

"It wasn't so bad," she said. "The prison cook brought me in as her apprentice, so I learned a skill. But when I got out, I couldn't get a job," Isabel added. "No one would hire me. The only thing I could do was cook—it became a passion of mine—but even that didn't get me hired. I began cooking for homeless shelters and women's centers to build my reputation before opening my own catering business. But none of that happened until after I changed my name."

"You changed your name?" I repeated. "How?"

"It's not hard," Jake said. "If you live in California, you have the legal right to change your name simply by using your new name in all areas of your life."

"That's true," Isabel said, "but I wanted to make sure my old name was never discovered, or I'd be ruined in the food business. I went through the official process—getting a court order and filing for a petition to change my name. I had to show cause and fill out a bunch of paperwork. It took a few months, but I wanted to be certain no one would find out."

"Aren't there ways to uncover a person's real name, even after all that?" I asked. "It sounds like Polly must have found out somehow."

Isabel shrugged. "I don't know how she did it. Supposedly, if you're a victim of domestic violence, the court will keep the name change confidential."

"Did you post your intention to change your name in the newspaper?" Jake asked.

"Yes. It was one of the requirements," Isabel said. "But I chose an out-of-area newspaper."

Jake nodded. "Polly probably hired a private investigator to do a background check. PIs have all kinds of ways to access information about anyone—public records, Internet resources, tracing backgrounds, Zabasearch, Pipl. It wouldn't take much, even with information that's supposed to be confidential."

I wondered if Dillon had found out her real name, too, while doing his research, but I doubted it, since he'd never mentioned it.

Apparently, Isabel Lau's new identity wasn't completely safe after all. I thought of Anne Perry, the famous mystery writer once known as Juliet Hulme, who was convicted of killing her friend's mother with a brick when she was a teenager. After she served time in prison, she changed her name, adopted a new religion, and began writing murder mysteries, of all things. Years later her true identity was discovered, not by a private investigator, but by a journalist, just before a movie about the crime was about to be released— *Heavenly Creatures*. And that was back when there were no computer hackers or Zabasearches.

"What about you, Simon?" I asked. "Why was Polly blackmailing you?"

Isabel raised an eyebrow. "Yes, Simon, tell them what you did—and what would happen if your father found out—"

"Shut up, Isabel!" Simon snapped. "At least it wasn't murder!"

Whoa, this was starting to turn ugly. What had Simon done that was so awful it caused such a change in his demeanor?

Isabel's eyes narrowed, but this time there were no tears, only venom, in those brown eyes. "You're a pig, Simon. I can't wait until this is all over and I never have to see you again. I don't know why I agreed to hole up in this crappy little house with you—"

Simon cut her off. "So what are you going to do about it, Isabel? Kill me too?"

"Okay, everyone, calm down," Jake said. "Isabel, chill. Simon, answer the question. Why was Polly blackmailing you?"

Simon sat down, looking as if he'd had the wind knocked out of him. After a few deep breaths, he said, "That witch found out what I did to my dad."

"Tell him," Isabel insisted. "Tell him how you double-crossed your own family and why you're living in a dump like this now."

"Shut up, I said," Simon yelled. "I'm *going* to tell them if you'll let me talk!"

Isabel closed her mouth. We all waited for Simon to begin again. Finally, he said, "Like Frankie Nudo's family, my dad gets his chocolate from the Ivory Coast. But unlike the Nudos, who are getting rich from their business, my father is going broke. He's trying to sell off his chocolate companies as fast as he can, then move to Mexico before his business completely falls apart. And it's all my fault."

"Why?" I asked. "What did you do?"

"He ratted him out," Isabel piped up.

Simon glared at her. "I couldn't live knowing the truth. All those children . . ."

I looked at Jake. He frowned.

"What he means is," Isabel said, "he couldn't live with the fact that his family was using child labor to produce their cocoa on the Ivory Coast. Did you know tens of thousands of kids help supply a third of the world's cocoa? And most of those kids are under fourteen. They don't go to school. They do hazardous work for long hours and little pay. They have health issues. . . ."

I thought of Griffin Makeba, the Pie Guy at the party who'd mentioned child labor, only it sounded like he'd been referring to Frankie Nudo's family.

"Stop, Isabel. I know! That's why I told the International Labour Committee. I couldn't live with it anymore. Child labor has been going on since the early nineteen hundreds and no one's done anything to stop it until recently. Finally people are beginning to boycott these cocoa producers and put an end to child labor. But my father wouldn't listen."

"So you turned him in," Jake said softly.

He rubbed his eyes. "All I did was supply them with some evidence. They promised my name would be kept out of it. I didn't want my father to find out what I'd done."

"What happened?" I asked.

"There was a lot of pressure on him to change the way his chocolate was produced. There were boycotts. Cheap labor disappeared. Costs went up. He stopped making a profit and began losing money. When he tried to sell, no one wanted to buy—not even the Nudos. Now he owes his creditors, his lawyers, his employees. He's lost just about everything, thanks to me." Simon shook his head.

I didn't know what to say. Simon had essentially done the right thing, but he'd destroyed his family in doing so.

"I lost everything too," Simon continued. "No more money coming in from my father. About all I have left is my relationship with my dad," Simon said. "But if he ever finds out what I've done, I won't even have that."

I felt for Simon, and for Isabel. Both had secrets they didn't want exposed, for good reason. But they still had strong motives for killing Polly.

"All right," I said. "If neither of you killed Polly, do you have any clue as to who might have done it?"

"No," Simon said.

Isabel pursed her lips. She looked as if she was about to say something.

"Isabel?" I asked. "Did you think of someone?"

She shrugged. "Maybe. I don't know. Last night, at the party, while Polly made the rounds, chatting up everyone as if they were her best friends, I might have overheard—"

"Isabel!" Simon said, glaring at her.

"You said they might be able to help us," Isabel said to him. "Why not tell them the rest?"

"What did you overhear?" I asked.

"Polly told a bunch of the contestants that she was going to vote for them . . . ," Isabel said.

"Seriously?" I asked.

Isabel nodded. "But only *if* they shared the winnings with her."

Whoa.

"How did you manage to hear all that?" I asked.

Isabel stole a glance at Simon. He nodded his consent.

"I . . . slipped a listening device into her Coach bag—the one she carried all night. Simon bought the device at that Spy Shop on Beach Street. I dropped it in when she wasn't looking; then Simon and I took turns listening to her conversations with an earpiece."

"You're kidding!" I was having a hard time picturing these two as amateur spies.

Simon got up and went to a drawer in the kitchen. He pulled out a tiny earpiece the size of a pea and a small portable microphone. When he returned to the living area, he stuck the earpiece inside his right ear.

"Wow. It's almost invisible," I said, staring at his ear.

He dropped the portable mic in my pocket, then

went down the hall, entered a room, and closed the door.

"Say something," Isabel said.

"Uh, testing, one, two, three . . . ," I said.

Seconds later Simon returned to the living area again. "Testing, one, two, three? That's the best you could come up with?" He pulled a small magnet out of his pocket and held it up to his ear. The tiny pink earpiece popped out and he placed it in his open palm. "It's Bluetooth. State-of-the-art. On sale for two hundred bucks."

Jake picked it up and examined it. "They use these in law enforcement sometimes."

"But why did you listen in on her conversations?" I asked.

"We thought she might say something . . . incriminating. Something we could use to blackmail her back."

"Did she?" Jake asked.

Isabel smiled. "She said a lot. You'd be surprised at how powerful those little mics are."

"What did she say?" I asked.

"Like I said, she told some of the contestants that she would vote for them as long as they split the money with her."

Jake shook his head. "She didn't talk to me."

"I'm pretty sure she didn't talk to Aunt Abby, either." At least, I didn't think so. "Who did she talk to?"

"First it was that pretty gal from I Scream Cakes— Monet," Isabel said. "Then Frankie Nudo. Then . . . let me think . . . Griffin, the Pie Guy. And Harrison."

"And she promised each of them a vote if they'd split the prize money with her?"

"Yes," Isabel said.

"What about Wendy Spellman? Did she try to bribe her too?"

Isabel shook her head. "That's the strange part. Wendy was the only one Polly talked to and told the opposite— that she *wouldn't* be voting for her. I got the feeling something happened between those two in the past and Polly still carried a grudge. Wendy told Polly she didn't need her vote and stormed off."

"Did you tell any of this to the police?" Jake asked.

"Goodness, no!" Isabel said. "That slope is slipperier than a mountain covered in icing. If one thing led to another, that detective would quickly learn too much about us. That's why we kept our mouths shut."

"Then we're back to square one," I said, sighing. "Who killed Polly?"

Simon spoke up. "I still think someone is going around killing the judges. I just can't figure out why. When Wendy got arrested, I briefly wondered if she killed Polly because Polly wasn't going to vote for her. But it's not much of a motive, and I don't really believe it."

"So you two still holed up here," I said.

"Yes," Isabel said. "Better to be safe than sorry. I still think someone is after the last two Chocolate Festival judges. And I don't intend to be next."

Chapter 15

"Do you believe they didn't kill Polly?" I asked Jake when we were back in the car.

"Don't know," he said. "They both have motives, being blackmailed by Polly. Isabel served time for killing her abusive husband, so I suppose she's capable. And Simon doesn't want his father to find out what he did. But is that enough to make him commit murder?"

"They're both pretty angry people. Maybe they did it together."

"It's possible," Jake agreed. "He did get pretty defensive when you asked him if he'd had an affair with Polly."

"Yeah," I said, "what was *that* about? Dillon said Polly was quite the 'party girl,' but would she really have slept with Simon? He's so not attractive."

"Not your type, eh?" Jake said, grinning.

I made a face. "Hey, maybe Simon is sleeping with Isabel and she got jealous."

Jake laughed. "They didn't look like a couple to me. More like frenemies who are only connected by being in the same kind of hot mess."

I started the car, then pulled out my cell phone and punched in Dillon's number using Bluetooth. "Dillon? Can you do some more digging on Simon Van Houten and Isabel Lau?" I filled him in on what we'd learned about Isabel's history and name change and Simon's betrayal of his father.

"Sweet intel!" Dillon said. "How'd you find out all that?"

"If I told you . . . ," I began, mocking his response whenever I asked him where he got his information. "So, let me know if those leads take you anywhere, okay?"

"Later," Dillon said, and hung up.

"If anyone can find out anything more about Simon, it's Dillon," I said. "He's annoying as hell, but he does have his talents."

"So, what's next?" Jake said, giving Simon's house a last glance as I pulled into the street. "By the way, I don't know if you noticed, but they've been watching us from the window."

I couldn't see from my vantage point, but I could picture the two of them peering out from behind the curtains.

I drove down the quiet avenue toward the freeway. "Remember what Isabel said?"

"What?"

"About bugging Polly's conversations?" I asked.

"Yeah, what about it?"

"Isabel said Polly talked to the other contestants in the competition—all but my aunt and you. She told each one she was going to vote for them if they split the prize money with her, remember? Everyone except Wendy."

He nodded. "You think one of the other contestants might have killed Polly?"

"It's possible."

"But why?" Jake asked, frowning. "They had no reason to kill her, especially if she promised to vote for them. Half the prize money is better than no prize money at all."

"True," I agreed. "But maybe one of them *did* have a reason. Maybe the two judges weren't the only ones Polly was blackmailing. Maybe she had something on those contestants too. And maybe she wanted more than just half the winnings."

"Then why would she tell all of them she was going to vote for them and make them winners? They couldn't all win," Jake argued.

"Good question," I said.

I pulled onto the freeway, easing into traffic headed toward Ghirardelli Square and the Chocolate Festival. "I still think we need to talk to the other contestants—Monet, Frankie, Griffin, and Harrison—find out if they had any reason to get rid of Polly. And have Dillon see what he can find out about them."

My cell phone rang. I punched the phone icon on the dashboard and said hello.

"Dude, guess what," Dillon said with no other introduction.

"What? Did you find out something?"

"You might say that," he said. "I hacked into Polly's computer at the *Chron* and checked out the articles she'd been working on. You're going to owe me big-time."

I glanced at Jake. "What did you learn?"

"She was writing an exposé on the Van Houten family chocolate companies. It was all about how they were exploiting child labor at their factories. She had all the deets—names, ages, wages, working conditions. It was going to bring down the house of Van Houten and ruin the company."

"But Simon already turned his father in. What purpose would that serve?" I asked.

"Don't know, but I e-mailed you a copy of the article in case you want to read it. Looks like it was scheduled to run next week, after the Chocolate Festival was over. I wonder if they'll kill it now."

I thanked Dillon, hung up, heard a *ping*, and handed the phone over to Jake so he could open the e-mail.

"Read it to me," I said.

He clicked on the attachment and began reading.

Chocolate Cheaters—A Rich Industry Getting Richer off the Poor

By Polly Montgomery

Readers, you know how much I love chocolate! If I don't have a mocha first thing in the morning, followed by a chocolate croissant from Bean to Bar, I can't function. And while I've heard all the good things chocolate does for a person—especially a woman—I've recently learned some disturbing news about my favorite sin.

*And I heard it from the son of one of the world's most
popular chocolate producers.*

"Whoa!" I said. "She was naming names! Go on."

*Meet Simon Van Houten Sr., who created the Cote
d'Ivoire Chocolate Industries fifty years ago by laying
claim to one of the most productive places for growing
chocolate—the Ivory Coast. That, my friends, is where
one-third of the world's cocoa is harvested. And since
global demand for chocolate far exceeds supply, cocoa
beans are at a premium. Unfortunately, inflation, processing, trade, and exporters have all affected the cost
of the beans and cut into profits.*

*For years, these companies have used child labor to
harvest the cocoa pods, using machetes that can slice
open a hand as quickly as a pod. The work is labor in-
tensive, with long hours, little pay, and many health
issues. In spite of this, child labor continues, due to the
poverty of the laborers and the costs for the manufac-
turers.*

"That's pretty much what Simon told us," I said.
"What else does it say?"
Jake read on.

*Some of the biggest names in chocolate are working
toward ending this blight and funding schools to in-
crease education and living standards. But it's not
happening fast enough.*

The Van Houten family needs to step up, change the

way they do business, and figure out how to provide us chocolate lovers with our fix without taking advantage of these young workers. I want my chocolate, but not at this price.

The irony—most of the workers have never even tasted a chocolate bar.

"Wow," I said when he was finished. "She comes off sounding like the Saint of Chocolate, while slamming Simon's family business. Don't you think it's odd that Simon never told us about Polly's plan to print an article? Was Simon lying to us? Or was it some kind of leverage? Maybe she never really intended to publish that story."

My cell phone rang. Jake answered using the car's Bluetooth.

"Did you read it?" Dillon asked before I could say hello. "Do you think Simon killed Polly to stop the article?"

"It's certainly possible," I said. "We need to tell Detective Shelton about this, if he doesn't already know about Polly's work computer."

"Hold up!" Dillon said. "If Shelton finds out how I got all this dirt, I'm going to jail."

"Oh," I said. "I hadn't thought of that. Well, if he hasn't seen her files yet, I'll figure out a way to get him to look at them."

"Darcy . . . ," Dillon said. I could hear the warning in his voice.

"I'll be careful, Dillon," I promised. Although I had no clue how I was going to tell the detective without putting Dillon in jeopardy. "By the way, see if you can find out more about the other contestants. I have a hunch they may have been under Polly's thumb as well."

"Later," Dillon said, and hung up.

Crap. Another two steps forward and one back. The story of my life.

I pulled into the Chocolate Festival parking area designated for the food truckers and turned off the engine, still puzzled by what I'd learned from Dillon. Simon had told us he'd essentially ruined the family business by alerting authorities his father was using child labor, yet Polly was supposedly writing an exposé on the very same. What was really going on?

Jake and I got out of the car and I turned to him. "So, Simon may have lied to us, Isabel is capable of murder, and they both bugged Polly's purse to see if they could get something to blackmail her with—which they did. They overheard her promise several contestants that she'd vote for them as long as they shared the winnings. My list just grew by two more suspects."

"My money's on Simon," Jake said. "I don't know what else he's hiding, but why would he give up his family fortune so easily? There has to be something else behind it."

"How about we talk to the other contestants Polly tried to coerce and see if we can get them to tell us something. Dillon's doing some digging, but I think a face-to-face works better sometimes. Then we'll talk to Detective Shelton."

Jake checked the time on his cell phone. "It's six. The festival closed down for the day two hours ago, but I'm guessing the chocolatiers are still around, getting ready for day two."

"I say we pay them each a visit," I suggested. I was about to head for one of the trucks when Jake placed a hand on my arm.

"Wait a minute. You're going to need an excuse. You can't just go up to them and start asking pointed questions about Polly's offer to split the money if she agreed to vote for them."

I stopped. "You're right." I thought for a few minutes, then said, "What if we tell them *we* overheard Polly's offer. They won't know we're lying—unless they're good at reading tells. And I've got a good poker face from being a nosy reporter all these years."

"Do you really think whoever is guilty will just fess up?" Jake said, shaking his head. "I doubt they're going to admit they were planning to take the offer and then decided to kill off the offeree."

"Got a better idea?" I asked him.

"It might be smarter to learn what kind of relationship each one had with Polly and see if one of them had another motive to murder her. Offing her because she promised to award them the prize doesn't seem like a very strong motive."

"So what do we say?"

"How about using your cookbook plan? Tell them about the food truck cookbook you're writing and ask them if they want to contribute a recipe. While you're chatting them up, use your journalism skills to bring up Polly and find out what they have to say about her. You're good at that kind of thing."

"Great idea. But aren't you coming with me?"

"Darcy, it's your cookbook. I think it would look odd if I came along."

Disappointed he wasn't going to be my sidekick, I nodded.

"See if you can find out how Wendy is doing," I told Jake. "Aunt Abby will want to know. I'm sure she's crazy with worry."

"Sure."

I was about to head off when Jake took my hand and stopped me again. He pulled me close. The wind brushed my face. The smell of chocolate tickled my nose. My heart raced.

"Be careful," he whispered.

Kiss me, I wanted to whisper back. "I will," I said instead.

"One of those people could be a murderer, you know." He brushed a few hairs away that had blown in my face.

Kiss me, I thought. "I know." I leaned in closer.

"Don't do anything stupid." He looked soulfully into my eyes.

Kiss me, dammit. I barely heard his words. "I won't," I promised breathlessly.

Then he kissed me.

Chapter 16

Jake headed over to the school bus to talk to Dillon, leaving me to check out the food truckers who had been offered bribes by the deceased.

"I'll be right here," he'd said before we'd parted. "Just whistle . . . or scream . . . if you get into trouble, and I'll come running. You do know how to scream, don't you?" He grinned.

"Of course," I said, recognizing his reference to the Bogart/Bacall film. I thought about the time I'd been trapped by a killer, my mouth duct-taped so I couldn't scream. Not gonna let that happen again.

Since the lights were still on inside the four trucks, it was a toss-up, so I eeny-meenied between Frankie, Monet, Harrison, and Griffin. Frankie Nudo won.

I knocked on the door to the Choco-Cheese truck, wincing at the sight of the giant chocolate-dipped cheeses that covered the outside. The window slats were closed, so I couldn't see inside. As soon as Frankie opened the door, the smell of cheese and chocolate hit my nostrils—a very odd combination. One was savory, the other sweet. While that worked in some cases, like chocolate-covered peanuts, I wasn't sure it worked with chocolate-covered cheese.

"Yeah?" Frankie said, looking down at me from the doorway. His black curly hair was disheveled and his five-o'clock shadow looked scruffy, not trendy. He wore khaki shorts and a thin white T-shirt, both covered with an apron that was speckled and smudged in what I guessed—and hoped—was chocolate. On his feet he wore once-white athletic shoes, also decorated in brown splats. He held a pair of chocolate-dipped tongs in one hairy hand.

"We're closed," he said, snapping the tongs.

Apparently he didn't recognize me.

"Hi, Frankie. It's me, Darcy Burnett, from the Big Yellow School Bus." I gestured toward Aunt Abby's bus.

"Oh, yeah, yeah. Sorry. Been a crazy day. You know how it is. What can I do you for?"

"I wondered if you had a minute. I'd like to talk to you about something. May I come in?"

He paused for a second, glancing back into his truck as if to see whether there was room enough for me. Or was he worried about something else?

"Uh, sure. You don't mind if I keep working? Got a lot of balls to dip."

Balls, eh?

"Great, thanks." I stepped up and inside the truck. The place was a chocolate mess. All the counters and the sink were smeared with chocolate, as well as some of the cupboard handles, utensils, and even his cell phone, which lay near the service window. Cheese balls the size of Ping-Pong balls where laid out over giant cookie sheets and shoved into a metal rack that held more than a dozen trays. Another rack behind it was also filled with chocolate-covered cheese balls.

"Looks like you're making progress for day two of the festival," I said, nodding toward the completed racks.

"Yeah, only a few thousand more and I'll be done," he said, grinning. "Are you and your aunt ready for tomorrow?"

"I hope so," I said. Although Aunt Abby had been stockpiling and freezing her whoopie pies for the past two weeks, I had a feeling we'd all be working late into the night finishing up anything more she figured we might need. "Although my aunt is pretty upset about what's happened."

Frankie tried to look sympathetic as he picked up a cheese ball with the tongs and dipped it into a pot of melted chocolate. "I know. I know. It's terrible about Polly. But at least they caught the person who did it. Your aunt should feel a little better about that."

"Do you really think Wendy Spellman could have murdered Polly?" I asked, taking a seat on a nearby stool after wiping it clean of chocolate smears with a paper towel.

He shrugged. "Who knows what someone's capable of, right? Even a woman. Women murder people all the time, just like men."

That was an odd thing to say, I thought. "Did you know Polly very well?"

He dunked another cheese ball into the pan, then set it on the tray next to him to cool and firm up.

"Polly?" he said, not making eye contact. He shifted his weight and wiped a chocolaty hand on his apron. "No, no. I mean, sure, we ran in the same circles. How could we not, in this business? Everybody knows everybody, you know? But I didn't really *know* her."

If Jake was right about people having tells, Frankie was loaded with them. I didn't believe him for a second. No eye contact, rambling, repeating himself.

"What about Wendy? How well do you know her?"

He shook his head. "Again, same circles, but her business is, how should I say, meh. Dipping candy into chocolate? It's amateurish. For kids. My chocolate cheese balls, for example, they're for the mature palate." He turned to me with a freshly dipped ball in his tongs. "Here. Try one."

Before I could refuse, he plopped the ball into a tiny paper baking cup and handed it to me.

"Tell me honestly. What do you think?"

Uh-oh.

I looked at the ball, smiled at Frankie, then steeled myself as if I were about to take poison. I started to nibble off a little of the chocolate when Frankie said, "No, no! Pop it in. Like this." He stuck a chocolate cheese ball in his mouth, closed his eyes as if he were in ecstasy, and moaned. After he swallowed the mass, he said, "You need the flavors to kiss."

Kiss?

I forced another smile—probably my last—and slowly pushed the ball into my mouth. The moment the morsel hit my tongue, it began melting into a cheesy-chocolaty goo that I can describe only as, well, ecstasy. I couldn't help myself. I closed my eyes and savored the delectable blend of tastes.

"Incredible!" I said after I'd swallowed the last bit.

Frankie beamed with pride, displaying a charming gap between his teeth. "I know. I know. Right?"

"Amazing that two such different flavors could go so well together. What kind of cheese do you use?"

"That one was Brie. But I use all different kinds of cheeses."

"Actually, that's why I'm here. I'm writing a cookbook featuring food truck recipes and wondered if you'd like to contribute one of your chocolate cheese ball recipes."

Frankie shrugged. "Sure. Why not?"

"Great!" I dug into my purse and pulled out my reporter's notebook and a pen.

"First you have to find a Brie with some fat, but not too much fat, or the cheese won't hold its shape and will get leaky."

I wrote down "Brie—fat—not too much—leaky."

"Then you gotta freeze the cheese for half an hour or so, so you can cut it; otherwise it's too soft. Meanwhile, you temper the chocolate so when it firms up, you got this shiny coat. Tempering—that's the secret."

I raised my pen. "Sorry, but what's tempering?"

Frankie frowned at me. "You don't know what tempering is? Huh. Tempering makes the chocolate smooth, snappy, and shiny. It's not hard to do, just takes time. You chop up your chocolate block—good-quality chocolate, like Guittard or Scharffen Berger. Don't use chocolate chips—they have additives and don't temper right. Put some of the chopped chocolate in a double boiler— water in the bottom half, of course—heat and stir until it's a hundred and fifteen degrees. Be careful. You can burn it, so keep an eye on the temp. Keep adding chocolate until it's all melted. Then cool it to eighty-eight or -nine degrees. That's it. The chocolate should be shiny and smooth."

I wrote frantically to keep up with his directions. By the time I was done, I'd decided I'd never try to temper chocolate. When I craved chocolate, it was much easier to just buy a Mars bar and eat it.

"Okay, so once the chocolate is tempered," I said, "then what?"

"Roll the cheese into balls or cut them into squares, dip them in the melted chocolate, put them on waxed paper to cool, and voila! You can add sea salt if you like. It's trendy now. Then keep the balls at room temperature or refrigerate them. I prefer my balls at room temp."

"So the secret is tempering the chocolate," I recapped, underlining the word in my notes.

"And using the best chocolate and cheese you can find," he added. "Luckily, San Francisco has lots of choices. You wanna try one of my chocolate goat-cheese balls?"

I patted my stomach. "That last one was so rich, I think I'm good for a couple of hours."

"Yeah, they're rich, all right. So you gonna put that recipe in your book?"

"If you don't mind. You'll get some free publicity and a free copy."

"No money?" Frankie Nudo frowned and grew quiet. He set down the tongs. "You know, I think I changed my mind. If anyone can make my chocolate cheese balls, I could lose business."

"Oh, I don't think that's going to happen. Most people don't even try the recipes."

"Then what's the point?" Frankie said. Something in him had changed. He'd been so animated while talking about his recipe, but once money was mentioned, he'd turned cool to the idea of being included in the book. "Naw, sorry. No recipe. I'm in this business to make money."

I slid off the stool. The party was over. Frankie moved closer to me, no doubt to encourage me to leave, and I began backing toward the door. I really hadn't expected such a negative turnaround, but Frankie was obviously all about the money.

"Frankie," I said as I neared the door. I wasn't done asking him about Polly, and I wasn't going to leave until I did. "One quick question. There's a rumor going around that Polly promised her vote to one of the contestants in exchange for half the winnings. Did you know about this?"

Frankie's frown deepened. His dark eyes narrowed on me, as if he were trying to see through me. "I heard nothing like that. No way. Polly would never do something as stupid as that. Never. I've known her for years and—" He stopped, his eyes wide.

I caught his mistake immediately. "Earlier you said

you didn't know her that well, yet didn't you just say you've known her for years? I'm confused."

"Look, I'm busy here. It's time for you to go," Frankie said, his voice low. "But I will tell you this. I do not associate with people who spread rumors, and if you say that to anyone, you'll regret it. You get me?"

Was he threatening me? I had a feeling if he'd had a rolling pin instead of a pair of tongs in his hand, he just might have used it. Was it time to scream?

I opened the door and flew down the steps, then looked back to see if Frankie was going to follow me. Instead, he stood at the top, glowering down at me. "One more thing I think you should know, lady. I'm gonna win the contest tomorrow, fair and square. I don't need no bribe to win. My cheese balls are the best in the world. And tomorrow you and everybody will see that!"

He slammed the door shut, leaving me with a bitter aftertaste.

I thought about giving up on this whole investigation/ interview thing. I'd gotten nowhere with Frankie, not even a recipe that I could use in my book, and in fact might have made things worse. He probably wouldn't talk to me at all now. If Dillon didn't find out more dirt on him, I just might find myself at a dead end . . . or worse.

I was about to go drown my sorrows in one of Aunt Abby's whoopie pies—and check on Jake and Dillon— when I heard a woman's loud voice coming from the truck next to Frankie's. It was Monet's I Scream Cake truck, painted with inviting ice-cream cones and cupcakes that almost looked good enough to eat. The lights were still on, but the blinds were down, so I couldn't see inside. I wondered who she was screaming at—and why.

I remembered her heated discussion with Frankie earlier and figured she had a bit of a temper. How much of a temper? I wondered. Enough to make her murderous? I recalled hearing that Frankie and Monet were once married but were now divorced. It sounded as if there was still some passion between those two, even if it was on the negative side. Why had they broken up? Too many cooks in the kitchen? Too competitive? Too temperamental?

I'd once done an article on the temperament of chefs, and while the stereotype portrayed the chef as someone who yells at his staff, throws pots and pans, insults customers, and storms out in the middle of a dinner rush, most of the chefs I interviewed weren't like that. If they had been, they'd probably be spending their days in court, not the kitchen, defending their tantrums when being sued. Yes, they're passionate—about food. It's their pride and joy. But when you take into account the fact that they have to deal with long hours, low pay, bloody fingers, and questions from customers like "Does the vegetarian burger have beef in it?" "How is the grilled chicken cooked?" and "Can I have everything on the side?" it's a wonder we don't have more murdering chefs, what with all those sharp knives at hand.

I glanced around to make sure no one would catch me eavesdropping, then stood just below the open louvered window so I could hear better. Maybe Monet was upset about Polly's death and how it might impact her winning the contest. Or had something else made her angry?

After a few seconds of silence, I heard Monet's loud voice again.

"You were sleeping with her!" she yelled.

I wondered who she was talking with.

I couldn't hear the response, only the sound of someone slamming doors and tossing utensils around. Then came, "You sleep with everyone, you pig! You have no standards! You're a man-whore. I knew it the minute I met you!"

Wow. Someone had really pissed off Monet, and it sounded like a lover—or ex-lover. Someone in the food truck business? Specifically, the chocolate-making business? Aunt Abby had said it was a very small world. Lately it had become even smaller.

"I hope you choke on your own food!" Monet cried. "You're a fool! Didn't you know she was practically sleeping with everyone? You probably killed her when you found out you were nothing special to her."

More slamming of drawers, cupboards, and utensils. I wondered what the inside of her truck looked like at that moment.

"No! I don't want to see you. Never again! If you come around, I'll bash your head in with my blender and scramble your brains with my mixer—what's left of them!"

Bash his head in? Wasn't that how Polly was killed?

I listened for a few more minutes, but I heard nothing more. I was dying to know who she'd been talking to, so I took a deep breath, collected my courage, and knocked on the door, ready with my cookbook spiel. I only hoped she wasn't too angry to see me and answer a few questions. Then again, maybe in her state of mind, she'd spill everything, just to vent her anger. A woman scorned often liked to share the details.

The louvered window opened a few inches. "Who is it?" Monet called out, peering through the cracks in the slats.

"It's Darcy Burnett," I said, "from the Big Yellow School Bus across the way. I wondered if I could talk to you for a minute."

Silence. Then the sound of the door opening. Seconds later, there stood Monet, a big smile on her face as if she were thrilled to see me and hadn't been screaming and threatening someone's life only moments before. There wasn't a hair out of place, her makeup was still perfect, and she was wearing bright orange capris and a tank top that showed off her thin but curvy figure.

"Come in, *chéri!*" she said cheerily. "I could use the company while I clean up. The only people I've talked to all day have been customers."

I blinked, surprised she could turn on the sweet charm so quickly. Was that a customer she'd just been yelling at?

I stepped into the truck and glanced around for signs of foul play—a dented blender? A bloody mixer?

The place was immaculate. Not a cupboard door off its hinge or a cooking utensil bent around the faucet. What was up with all that slamming?

Was Monet some kind of Jekyll and Hyde who could easily switch from murderous monster to delightful host at will?

I only hoped I didn't say anything in the next few minutes to make her mad.

Chapter 17

"So, Darcy, will you join me for a drink?" Monet asked, smiling broadly, her perfect white teeth sparkling. "It's my own special concoction. I call it a French Kiss!"

She didn't wait for my response. Instead she pulled down two soda-type glasses from a cupboard and took out a carton of chocolate ice cream from the oversized freezer. She dropped two scoops in the large blender that sat on the counter, poured in a shot of coffee liqueur, a shot of chocolate syrup, a shot of vodka, and a shot of crème de cacao, and whirled all the ingredients until they were smooth and blended. Then she poured the contents equally into the soda glasses, added straws, and handed me a glass. She sucked down half the drink in record time.

"God, I needed that!" she said, taking a breather from all that sucking. "It's been a wild day, hasn't it? First that judge gets killed, and then that old lady gets arrested, and then all those nonstop customers screaming for ice cream cupcakes. I'm exhausted. And we have to do it all over again tomorrow before the contest. I don't know if I'm going to live through all this. How're you holding up in your aunt's school bus?"

I took a sip of the drink and said, "Better now. This is delicious!" I knew I was overdosing on chocolate today, but I couldn't help myself. The drink was dynamite. I just had to be careful I didn't explode.

"So, you sold a lot of your ice cream cupcakes?" I asked, easing into my interrogation. I'd blown it with Frankie and didn't want to find myself at a dead end again.

"Tons!" she said, then paused to down the rest of her chocolate drink. "If the number of tickets I collected are any indication, I just might win this competition tomorrow—" She stopped abruptly and covered her mouth. "I'm sorry. I'm sure your aunt is doing well too. Maybe we'll all win!" Monet busied herself by cleaning her empty soda glass as she backpedaled from her remark about winning.

"The competition is certainly stiff. Everyone seems to be getting big crowds. Jake's Mocha Dream Puffs had long lines. Harrison's Chocolate Falls looks popular. Griffin's Chocolate Pies and Frankie's Choco-Cheeses seem to be a hit. I wonder how Wendy's Candyland Chocolates would have done?" I hoped I'd segued gently into the reason I'd come—to find out what she might know about the murder of Polly Montgomery and Wendy Spellman's guilt or innocence.

"I think you can forget about Frankie's cheesy entries. I don't think he has a prayer of winning. I told him that when he entered this contest, but he wouldn't listen. He never listened to anything I said when I was with him."

"You and Frankie were . . . together?" I asked, trying to sound surprised. Dillon had already discovered that the two had been married, but I wanted to know more. Had he been the one she was screaming at over the phone?

She sighed. "Married, actually. What a mistake that was. Frenchwomen should never marry Italian men. We're much more composed and less temperamental."

She hadn't sounded so composed a few minutes ago.

"So you two are divorced?" I asked the leading question.

Wiping her hands with a dishcloth, she turned around to face me. "Yes, thank goodness. We started our business together, but we disagreed on *everything*. He thought he was a rock star in his chef's whites. Only trouble was, he couldn't keep them on around other women."

I nodded, trying to appear sympathetic. "So his infidelity is really what caused the breakup," I summarized.

"Yes, but let's not talk about that." She waved the damp cloth around airily. "I get angry all over again when I think of it. He actually believed sleeping with one of the judges would help him win the chocolate competition. Now that she's dead, so are his chances. Serves him right, the pig."

Frankie had slept with Polly? Monet had just dropped

a bomb and didn't even seem to know it. I'd heard Polly had gotten around, but apparently so did Frankie. I wondered if Monet could be considered a suspect in Polly's murder, since her ex-husband had been romantically involved with her? Hidden jealousy?

"You don't suppose Frankie might have killed Polly, do you?" I was curious how she'd react to such a pointed question.

"You mean, if Wendy Spellman didn't really do it?" she asked, her pencil-drawn eyebrows raised.

I shrugged.

"You think Wendy's innocent?" It apparently hadn't occurred to her that Wendy might not have killed Polly.

"My aunt thinks so. She knows Wendy well and is sure she didn't do it."

"Is that why you're here?" Monet frowned and crossed her arms in front of her. "You think someone else killed Polly, like Frankie?"

I said nothing.

"You don't mean me?" she said, her voice rising. Where was that composed Frenchwoman I'd been talking to a moment ago?

I shook my head. "No, of course not—"

"How could you think I killed Polly? Because she was sleeping with my ex-husband? You're out of your mind! He's a pig. I loathe him. If anyone had to die, I wish it had been him."   .

"I was just—"

She cut me off. "Why don't you go ask him if *he* killed Polly? He's the one you should be talking to!"

"I did. He said—"

"He said what? That I killed his only chance at winning the contest? That I dumped her in a vat of chocolate because I was jealous? That I'm happy she's dead because . . . because . . ."

The door to Monet's truck burst open. Frankie Nudo bolted inside, his face flushed, his dark eyes wild.

"Go on. Tell her, Monet! We can hear you all over the festival!" Frankie shouted, spittle collecting at the edges of his mouth. "Tell her why you're glad Polly is dead."

Monet grabbed the closest thing at hand—a heavy metal ice cream scoop—and threw it at Frankie. He ducked just in time to avoid being hit in the head.

"Get out of here!" she screamed, searching for another object to throw at her ex-husband.

"Not until you tell her the truth and stop spreading lies!" Frankie yelled back.

Monet pulled out a large knife from a drawer and pointed it at Frankie. I backed up, caught in the middle, and tried to flatten myself against the freezer.

"You can't hurt me!" Frankie hollered. He stepped forward, grabbed Monet's wrist, and twisted her arm, causing her hand to open. The knife went flying and landed an inch away from my foot. I stepped on it to keep the two of them from trying to get it.

Monet tried to slap Frankie, but he held her wrist tight.

"Polly was blackmailing you too—wasn't she, Monet?" Frankie snarled. "Just like she was me. She knew you never attended Le Cordon Bleu, like you've been claiming all these years. You never attended *any* cooking school. And you lied again about your credentials when you signed up for the contest. But she found out, didn't she? Did you kill her because of that, Monet?"

Before Monet could say anything, I felt the truck bounce again. I turned to see Jake enter, followed by a security guard. The tiny truck was getting crowded. We were nearly elbow to elbow.

"What's going on here?" Jake asked. He glanced down at the knife blade under my foot. His eyes widened. "Are you okay, Darcy?"

I nodded and let out a breath.

Frankie released his grip on Monet's wrist and stepped back, his fisted hands at his sides.

"Did he hurt you, ma'am?" the security guard asked. Thin, with glasses, a sparse mustache, and an oversized uniform, he looked dazed, as if domestic violence during a chocolate festival was out of his league. His name tag read CLIFFORD PRICE.

"Of course not," she said. "I can take care of myself." She rubbed her wrist where Frankie had gripped her tightly.

"Hurt her?" Frankie argued. "She threw that metal scoop at me! And she tried to stab me with that knife!"

"Is this true, ma'am?" Clifford the security guard asked while Jake took in the scene.

"Don't be ridiculous," Monet said. "I couldn't possible hurt him with a little ice cream scoop. As for the knife, I simply dropped it."

Clifford combed his thin mustache with his fingertips. "Do you want to press charges?"

"For what?" Frankie asked. "She tried to kill *me*!"

"Assault? Battery? Trespassing?" the security guard offered.

"She invited me in," Frankie said. He glanced at Monet.

She gave a one-shouldered shrug.

"How about disturbing the peace?" Clifford offered weakly.

"No. Just get him out of here," Monet said. She waved him away.

The guard tried to take Frankie's arm, but Frankie jerked away. I felt for Clifford—he was half Frankie's size and carried no visible weapons, unless he planned to hit him with his cell phone.

"Don't worry. I'm leaving," Frankie growled at Monet. He spun around and got in my face. "But watch out for this nosy lady." I knew he was still speaking to Monet, even though he had his finger inches from my nose.

"Why?" Monet asked. "Because she might find out the truth about you? Of course, it's hardly a secret that you've slept your way into the business. Is that what Polly had on you, Frankie? She found out you were cheating on her like you did on me? Did she catch you with one of Harrison's daughters and threaten to tell him?"

Frankie was fooling around with Harrison's daughters? Whoa.

"That's none of your business, Monet. I'm just saying, watch out for this chick. She's desperate to save her aunt's friend. She tried to pin it on me, and I'll bet she'll try to do the same to you and anyone else she feels like." Frankie glared at me. "Isn't that right, Scooby-Doo?"

One more second and I swear I would have scratched his eyes out, but he turned and left before I could get out my claws. Scooby-Doo? Excuse me?

"Come on, Darcy," Jake said, noticing my rising ire. "Let's go see your aunt. I'm sure she's wondering where you've been."

Monet reached a hand forward as if to stop us. "Wait."

I turned back. "Yes?"

"All that stuff Frankie said about me. You don't believe him, do you?"

"It's none of my business whether you went to cooking school or not," I said.

"No, not that. I mean about Polly knowing and trying to blackmail me. . . ." She trailed off.

I said nothing. Monet had a motive to murder Polly—to keep her background safe and protect her reputation while winning a chunk of money and appearing on TV.

But then, Simon, Isabel, and Frankie all had motives too.

Jake and I headed across the way to Aunt Abby's bus, while Clifford the security guard reported in on his walkie-talkie before driving off in his little golf cart. Although there was still a light on inside Aunt Abby's bus, when I tried the door, it was locked. I knocked; no answer.

I looked at my watch. It was past eight. Aside from Monet and Frankie's trucks, most of the lights were out in the other trucks and the festival area looked like a ghost town. "I guess she and Dillon have gone home for the night. They're probably working on more whoopie pies. I should join them. I've had enough 'interviewing' for the night."

"We can do some more tomorrow," Jake said. "You learned a lot already."

"Yeah, that's the problem," I said. "It seems like everyone I talk to had a reason to kill Polly. Apparently she was blackmailing everyone but you, me, and Aunt Abby."

"Don't forget Wendy," Jake said.

I shook my head. "I haven't. She's the reason we're doing all of this."

"Want to come over for a cream puff?" Jake asked.

I was torn. I wanted to spend some alone time with Jake, but I was so tired from the day, all I wanted to do now was go home, see if Aunt Abby needed help, then curl up in bed and start over in the morning.

"I'd love to," I said, "but I should check on Aunt Abby, see how she's doing with those whoopie pies."

"Okay. I'll walk you to your car. It's gotten pretty dark around here."

He was right. It was downright gloomy, even a little creepy, without the customers, vendors, music, and noise. The area was lit by only a few streetlights and the glow from some nearby shops.

Jake took my hand as we headed for my car. It felt both comforting and exciting to walk with him, hand in hand. As we passed between Aunt Abby's bus and Wendy's truck, Jake pulled out his cell phone and clicked the flashlight app to light the way. Walking in the dim light, I didn't notice anything unusual until he shined the flashlight on my VW.

"Oh my God . . . ," I whispered as I stared at it in disbelief.

Someone had poured some kind of dark, slimy ooze on my car. Starting on the ragtop, goo had spilled down over the sides, over the windows, and onto the front and back fenders. It was a thick, drippy mess.

As I got closer, the smell of chocolate filled my nose. I reached out and touched the sticky slime.

Liquefied chocolate.

Something caught my eye. A message, scrawled on the chocolate-covered window:

"I know what you're doing."

Chapter 18

I stood there, speechless and dumbfounded, staring at my chocolate-covered car in the semidarkness.

"Whoa," Jake said. "What the . . . ?"

I felt anger more than anything else. Someone was obviously trying to scare me off, but I was pissed at seeing my cute VW Bug turned into an ugly mess. Tears suddenly sprang to my eyes. "My car . . . It's ruined. . . ."

Jake wrapped an arm around me. "No, it isn't. It'll wash off."

"Chocolate's acidic!" I whined.

"But it's balanced with alkaline. It shouldn't harm the paint job. I'm more worried about the note scrawled on your window. Shelton needs to know about this."

Jake got out his cell phone and took several flash pictures of the car and a number of close-ups of the message written on the front window.

"Do you think they left any fingerprints?" I asked.

Jake peered closely at the window with his flashlight app. "None that I can see left in the chocolate. The techs may find something, but I'm guessing whoever did this probably used gloves."

Jake phoned Detective Shelton and left a message on his cell phone, telling him about my car. Then he e-mailed the photos to him. Jake's phone rang the moment he'd finished sending the last picture.

"It's Shelton," he said to me, checking his cell phone screen. "Detective," he said into the phone.

I scanned the area while Jake explained to the detective what we'd found. I was hoping to catch a glimpse of the—what? Prankster? Stalker? Killer?—but the place was deserted. Only a handful of cars remained in the lot. I spotted a light on at Reina's trailer office a few yards away and figured she was working on tomorrow's festival and contest. I wondered if she might have seen or heard anything.

Jake hung up. "He's coming over with a couple of crime-scene techs. He said there's probably nothing they can do if there are no fingerprints, but he's betting this is related to Polly's murder and doesn't want to take any chances. We'll have to sit tight until he gets here."

I nodded toward Reina's office. "Looks like she's still around. Let's ask her if she noticed anything suspicious."

Jake shrugged. "Worth a try."

We walked the short distance to the trailer and knocked on the door.

I heard noises inside—a drawer slamming shut, footsteps. After a few seconds, a voice called out, "Who is it?"

"Jake Miller and Darcy Burnett," Jake answered.

The door opened a crack, revealing a chain and Reina's

right eye. She closed the door again, unlocked the safety chain, and opened the door.

"It's awfully late," Reina began, skipping a cordial greeting as she looked at her watch. "Past ten. What are you doing here?"

"Sorry to bother you, Reina," Jake said. "Have you been here all evening?"

"Yes. Why?" Her eyes widened, and she suddenly looked alarmed. "Is something wrong?"

"There's been an incident," Jake said carefully. "We wondered if you saw anything suspicious in the parking lot during the last couple of hours."

She shook her head, leaned out, and looked in the direction of the lot. "What happened?"

"Someone vandalized Darcy's car." Jake pointed toward my car. I followed his gaze and realized Reina couldn't have seen my car well from her vantage point, even in broad daylight. It was some distance away and somewhat obscured behind a chain-link fence.

"Vandalized?" Reina rushed down the steps. Jake and I led her to my car. When she got a glimpse of it, she gasped. "Oh my God! What is that stuff?"

"Chocolate," I said.

"You're kidding!" She shook her head. "Who could have done such a thing? Has anything else been vandalized? Any of the food trucks or vendors' tents?" She glanced around.

"I don't think so," Jake said. "We didn't see anything else. So far, just Darcy's car."

Reina frowned and stepped closer to the car window. "Something's written here. . . ." She read the words aloud: "*'I know what you're doing.'*" She looked at me. "What's *that* supposed to mean?"

I shrugged. "I have no idea." Although I had a hunch it had to do with the questions I'd been asking about Polly's murder.

"This is outrageous! Where are the security guards? Where's Clifford? How could he let this happen?" She pulled out her cell phone and punched in a number. Seconds later she snapped, "Clifford! This is Reina! Where the hell are you? You're supposed to be guarding the Chocolate Festival area!"

I couldn't hear his response.

"Well, get over here! Now! A car has been vandalized in the staff parking lot, behind the Big Yellow School Bus!" She hung up. "Did you call the police?" she asked Jake.

"They're on their way," he replied. "So you didn't see anything?"

"No, sorry. But heads are going to roll over this. We simply can't have any more trouble or the festival will be ruined for sure."

It was all about the Chocolate Festival for Reina Patel. Was it the money? The prestige? Either way, I had a feeling Reina couldn't give a rat's ass about my car.

"Do you have any enemies?" she asked. "Someone who thinks you're sticking your nose in the wrong place? I'll bet it has something to do with Polly Montgomery's death. What have you been doing?"

"Just asking a few questions," I replied.

Reina shook her head. "I told you two not to bother people, didn't I? And now look what's happened."

I shot a glance at Jake. He shook his head, as if to say, *"Blow it off."*

Clifford the security guard arrived in his little golf cart, just as headlights appeared from down the street. Moments later an unmarked police car pulled into the lot, followed by a white van that read SFPD CRIME UNIT.

Detective Shelton got out of the car, two techs jumped out of the van, and all three headed over to us.

"Wow," Detective Shelton said. "Somebody likes chocolate."

"Not funny," I said. "The paint on my car's probably ruined."

Jake pointed to the message on one of the windows. "Check this out."

The detective studied the writing, then signaled for his techs to begin work. They took pictures, examined the outside of the car for evidence, looked around for footprints and other signs of the vandal, and did the usual CSI stuff.

Meanwhile, Detective Shelton asked me a bunch of questions like: When did I last see the car before it was vandalized? Who did I think was responsible? Does anyone have a reason to threaten me? Routine. He briefly asked Reina and Clifford if they'd seen anything, but since they said they hadn't, he was done questioning them in a matter of minutes.

Thirty minutes later, the detective said, "The guys have all they need at this point. We'll let you know what we find, but I'm guessing whoever did this covered his tracks well. Meanwhile, Darcy, you need to keep yourself safe and out of any more trouble. Whatever you're doing, you'd better stop."

"I told her the same thing," Reina said.

"I'm just trying to help my aunt Abby's friend Wendy," I argued.

Detective Shelton rubbed his stubbly chin, then asked, "So, how's Abby?"

"Fine," I said lightly. "You know, aside from being worried about Wendy and certain the real killer is running around loose and the police aren't doing anything about it."

He glanced around, avoiding eye contact with me. "Well, tell her hello for me."

"Tell her yourself," I wanted to say, but I just nodded. "Can I get my car washed now, before the paint begins to peel?"

The detective nodded. "We're done here."

Detective Shelton and his techs got into their vehicles and drove off, leaving Jake, Reina, Clifford, and me alone to stare at one another, not sure what to do next.

"I've got to get back to work," Reina said. "Another big day tomorrow. Sorry about your car, Darcy."

Yeah, sure.

"I'll drive you over there, Ms. Patel," Clifford said. He patted the passenger seat of his car. "Make sure you're safe and whatnot."

Reina accepted the short ride to her trailer.

"Get in your car," Jake told me. "I know an all-night car wash. I'll follow you there, then see you home. Unless you'd prefer Clifford . . ."

I laughed. "Thanks, Jake. I'm glad you were here."

"Me too," he said. "But I won't feel good until I know you're safely in your RV."

Three car washes later—that's how many it took to get the chocolate, but not the smell, out of almost every nook and cranny—we arrived at Aunt Abby's house and my cozy Airstream home. I checked to see if the lights were on in her kitchen, figuring my aunt would be up all night finishing whoopie pies, but it was past eleven and dark inside, aside from the back porch light, which she always left on.

"Looks like Aunt Abby's gone to bed," I said to Jake. "No wonder. It's late and she's probably exhausted from the busy day."

Jake nodded and glanced around. I got the feeling he was waiting for an invitation to come inside the RV.

"Uh . . . ," I said, feeling awkward. I'd never invited a guest into my place and wasn't prepared to play hostess. "You want a glass of wine or some coffee or something?"

Jake grinned. "Sure. I've never seen your place inside."

I got out my key and unlocked the door to the RV. "It's not much, believe me. And I have to warn you, my aunt decorated the inside long before I moved in. Be prepared."

I opened the door and stepped in. The blinds were drawn across all the windows and along the front windshield, giving us complete privacy. At over six feet, Jake had to duck to enter the curved Airstream doorway. I watched him as he took in all the memorabilia from Aunt Abby's trips to Disneyland, her garage-sale finds, and her purchases on eBay.

"Wow," was all he said as he glanced around. He smiled at the Cheshire Cat clock, the four hand-painted animation cells from *The Sorcerer's Apprentice*, the *Beauty and the Beast* teakettle, the seven pillows on the couch featuring each of the Seven Dwarfs. "You must feel like you're living in Walt Disney's personal RV."

"It's a bit much," I said, "but Aunt Abby would kill me if I got rid of anything. After all, it's her RV. I'm only living here until I can find a place of my own." I decided not to mention that I also needed enough money for a first and last month's deposit and a regular income to pay the rent.

Jake shoved a few pillows over and plopped down on the fold-out leather couch. "Well, I think it's kind of fun. Reminds me of my childhood. I used to love going to Disneyland. Pirates of the Caribbean was my favorite ride."

I smiled at the memory. "Mine too. And the Haunted Mansion." I opened a tiny cupboard and pulled down a cheap bottle of red wine. "Wine? Or do you want a beer?"

"You sure you don't want to get to bed?" he asked.

I stared at him. Did he mean what I thought he meant?

He shook his head as if he'd read my naughty thoughts. "I meant, aren't you tired? You've had quite a day. We all have."

I exhaled a breath of relief. Although Jake was certainly sexy, I wasn't quite ready to take the next step. "I think I could use a glass of wine. It'll help relax me." It felt as if everything I said was a double entendre. Awkward.

Jake smiled. "Wine would be great."

I poured the merlot into two short water glasses featuring cartoon characters. "You want Goofy or Snow White?"

"Definitely Goofy," he said, reaching out to take the proffered drink. "I'm not really the princess type."

Neither am I, I thought, taking a sip. There was no way I was going to sit around and wait for my prince to come rescue me. I'd learned that the hard way with my ex-boyfriend, Trevor the Tool. If I had to choose a Disney role model at this point, it would be that chick from *Brave.* I admired the fact that Merida was free-spirited and adventurous. Like her, I'd much rather be single than hook up with a boring prince.

"You haven't heard a word I've said, have you?" Jake asked, interrupting my daydream.

I blinked. *Where did that come from? Must have been the wine,* I thought.

"Sorry. I guess I'm more tired than I realized. Maybe this wine is relaxing me a little too much."

Jake downed the last of his and stood up. "I'm going to let you get some sleep."

"You're leaving?" I asked, feeling a tinge of disappointment at his words.

He set his empty glass in the small steel sink. "Let's meet up early and see what we can find out before the festival begins. Once it opens, we'll be swamped until the contest and I doubt we'll get a chance to do much more investigating."

"Early?" I winced as I rose from the comfortable chair. "How early is early?"

"When you hear the knock on your door. That's when I'll be by with cream puffs and coffee."

I smiled.

He smiled.

I took a step closer to him, which wasn't hard to do in the small space.

He put his arms around me and pulled me even closer.

He leaned in. . . .

I closed my eyes. . . .

Then something loud hit the Airstream, startling both of us.

"What was that?" I whispered, frozen to the spot.

"I don't know," Jake said, releasing me. "Stay put." He bounded for the door, opened it, and leaped down the steps. I followed him to the door, remaining safely inside the RV.

"What was it?" I called out.

No answer. Jake had disappeared around the back of the Airstream.

I leaned out. No sign of him. "Jake?" I called.

No answer.

"Where are you?"

No answer.

"Jake!"

Jake suddenly appeared around the front of the RV.

"Did you see anything?"

He stood, frowning, at the front of the Airstream, his cell-phone flashlight shining on the windshield.

"What is it?" I headed down the steps and joined him at the front. "What—" I stopped. "Oh no," I said, my heart sinking. "Not again."

The front windshield was covered with chocolate. Someone had obviously thrown a large bucket of the liquid on the window. The empty plastic bucket lay on the ground nearby. That must have been what hit the Airstream.

I peered in closer. "Is something written there?"

Jake focused the light on the front of the RV. Someone had scrawled something at the top of the window— in chocolate:

"Now I know where you live."

Chapter 19

Jake got out his cell phone.

"Don't," I said, holding up a hand.

He frowned. "We've got to report this, Darcy. It's the second time someone has threatened you."

I sighed and felt my shoulders drop. "I know. But not tonight. Please. Whoever did this is probably long gone and left little evidence of his identity. I'm so tired. Could we call Shelton in the morning?"

"Really?" Jake hesitated for a moment, then tucked his cell phone into the pocket of his black jeans. "Okay, but I'm not leaving you alone tonight."

I nodded. "Thanks."

We headed back inside, and Jake locked the door behind us. He looked at the couch-bed, spotted the lever, and opened up the bed. "Got any extra blankets?"

"Are you sure you want to sleep there?" I said, surprised. "It's not very comfortable." Truth be told, I wouldn't have minded his arms around me while I slept.

"You need sleep, Darcy. And there's no way either of us would get *any* sleep if I come in there with you." He nodded toward the bedroom area.

I smiled. He was right. And as much as I wanted to feel him lying beside me, I was too tired to argue. I yawned, kissed him good night, and went into the bedroom, sliding the door closed behind me.

I changed out of my jeans and Big Yellow School Bus T-shirt and into my long Tinker Bell nightshirt, then fell into the small but cozy bed. I closed my eyes, snuggled down under the covers, and took a deep breath, ready to welcome some much-needed sleep.

Half an hour later I was still staring at the *Peter Pan* wallpaper, my mind wide-awake while my body ached for sleep. Thoughts swirled like churning blades in a vat of chocolate as I wondered who had sent those warnings, why Polly had been killed, and who had drowned her in that chocolate.

I also wondered if Jake was still awake too.

I finally gave up the ghost, got up, and quietly slid open the door to the living area. The soft sounds of Jake's deep sleep were comforting, and I envied him the ability to just check out like that. I'd never been one of those people who falls asleep as soon as my head hits the pillow. Turning off the body was easy. Turning off the mind, not so much.

I got my laptop from the small kitchen table and returned to the bedroom, sliding the door closed behind me. At least I could put my insomnia to good use. While Dillon seemed to be able to find out anything about anybody with his unique but questionable computer skills, my high-tech sleuthing abilities weren't quite as gifted, so I turned to my favorite search engine to see what I could find on my suspects. I'd already talked to Simon and Isabel and knew their secrets—at least, the ones Polly had been blackmailing them for. And Frankie and Monet had let the proverbial cat out of the bag regarding their baggage. But I knew little of Griffin and Harrison, the two other contestants that Simon said were also Polly's victims.

I did a search for Griffin Makeba, the Pie Guy. He had a great rep for his wares, with lots of positive Yelp reviews, but that's all I could find. His Facebook page was strictly self-promoting—that is, pie promoting—with little personal information. I'd have to ask Dillon to dig deeper if I wanted to know what Polly might have had on him. So far, a dead end.

The name Harrison Tofflemire, on the other hand, came up repeatedly on the search engine. I skimmed the usual reviews of his Chocolate Falls business—mostly positive—and read an interview he gave to *Chocolatier* magazine about his success story. It was the usual spiel: Came from nothing. Never went to college. Started his own business. Invented the Chocolate Falls gizmo. Fame and fortune followed. I wondered why he'd bothered to enter the contest. He already seemed to have everything.

An instant message popped up on the side of the screen.

r u there?

Dillon!

Yes, what's up? I answered. As a reporter for the newspaper—former reporter, that was—I had

trouble using text slang in my messages. My old
English teacher, Mr. Tannacito, was always looking
over my shoulder, and I couldn't shake him, even
in a text.

cant sleep, Dillon wrote. been digging into
those contestants u asked abt.

Great! I was just googling Griffin and
Harrison's names but didn't find anything
interesting. You get anything?

I watched the cursor beat for a few seconds, then,
gt the 411. griffin makeba, the dude
protesting the choc from the ivory
coast . . .

What about him???

Guess where he gets his choc . . .

The Ivory Coast!

Bingo, Dillon wrote. he's been buying it from
simon's family for years—at a discount.
apparently he threatened to expose simon
senior's working conditions, so they cut a
deal with griffin 2 shut him up and
decreased the price.

OMG, I typed. I couldn't help myself. Text slang

seemed to be contagious when chatting with
Dillon. So the blackmailee was also a
blackmailer! How did you find out?

2EZ. I knew simon's co has lots of back
doors and fake names. But once u go down
that tunnel, ur bound 2 find gold. Or in
this case, choc. ☺

Great job, Dillon! Thanks! Anything on
Harrison Tofflemire? All I could find was
how smart, savvy, and successful he is—and
most of that came from his own mouth.

HAS. BRB.

Hold a second. Be right back.

I waited, all sleep forgotten at this latest news about
Griffin. I couldn't wait to learn what else Dillon had
found. Seconds later he was back.

looks like HT didn't actually invent Choc.
Falls. got a bunch of lawsuits pending.
Canuck co. claims he stole plans 4 their
Chocolate Cascade. When HT brought his
gizmo out, CC went broke, filed bankruptcy
and lawsuits against HT. He's got high-
powered attys fighting this, all on the
down-low. Sounds like he got rich off
someone else's idea.

You're awesome! I gushed over the keyboard. Both of those guys had secrets they didn't want uncovered, both worthy of blackmail. And according to what Simon overheard at the party, Polly knew all about them. Either one of them could have killed her. Wendy has to be innocent.

Yo, abt tht . . .

Uh-oh. What???

Wendy wrote 4 George Brown's magazine under a fake name.

A pseudonym? What was it? What did she write about?

She called her column Chocolate Crimes, and used the name Candy the Chocolate Critic. Wrote reviews on local choc stuff— companies, restaurants, ppl in the choc bus. None of the articles were very sweet, IYGMD.

I got his drift. Wow. If Wendy criticized everyone in the chocolate business—and word got out who she was—she wouldn't have many friends left. And she might even have a few enemies. Did someone frame her for the murder of Polly Montgomery to get even?

G2G, Dillon messaged. Gaming time w/ the guys. TTYL.

I thanked Dillon again, then switched off the laptop, closed it up, and set it on the small built-in table next to the bed. I wasn't any more relaxed than I had been half an hour ago—in fact, I was more wired than ever—but at least I had information on my last two suspects, Griffin Makeba and Harrison Tofflemire.

I lay down and snuggled into the covers again, hoping exhaustion would take over my brain as well as my body. I must have slept eventually, because the next thing I knew, someone was tapping on my bedroom door. I glanced at the Mickey Mouse night-light/clock. Six a.m.

"You've got to be kidding me!" I called out through the door.

"Breakfast!" came Jake's too-cheery voice. "Time to get up. Detective Shelton is on his way over."

"Seriously?" I grumbled. I threw off the covers and staggered into the tiny shower with the too-sensitive hot/cold nozzle and weak water pressure. Fifteen minutes later, I was awake, clean, dressed in a fresh Big Yellow School Bus T-shirt and jeans, and ready for coffee, if not for the day.

I slid the bedroom door open and shook my head at the sight.

Jake, Detective Shelton, and Aunt Abby were gathered around my small table, drinking coffee and eating a Continental breakfast of cream puffs and whoopie pies. The only one missing was Dillon. Apparently he got to sleep in.

"Good morning, sweetie," Aunt Abby said.

I pulled up the only empty chair left and sat down. "Morning," I mumbled, then sipped the latte that was waiting for me on the table. "Glad you could all stop by."

"Jake told us what happened last night," Aunt Abby said, a worried look on her already made-up face. Over her Big Yellow School Bus T-shirt and khaki slacks, she wore a flowery linen jacket that came from Chico's, her favorite store. The jacket had to be an afterthought for Detective Shelton's sake; otherwise she'd be wearing an apron.

She reached over and patted my hand. "Are you all right, Darcy?"

Detective Shelton also looked spiffy for the early-morning hour, dressed in his usual dark suit, with a red tie and product in his hair. I was beginning to wonder if the detective and my aunt were on some kind of date. As for Jake, he could have worn a torn and mismatched pirate costume instead of the jeans and T-shirt he'd worn yesterday and he still would have looked hot.

"I'm fine, thanks to Jake," I said, then blushed, wondering if she knew he had slept over. Ha. Of course she did. Nothing got past Aunt Abby. But I'd have to set her straight on the sleeping arrangements.

"The crime-tech guys will be here soon," the detective said. "You should have called me last night."

Jake raised a traitorous eyebrow at me.

"Sorry, Detective. I was just too tired," I explained. "I figured it would be much like the vandalism to my car and I could deal with it better in the morning."

"Did you sleep . . . well?" Aunt Abby asked. Her eyebrow was also raised, but for another reason. I knew what she was implying. "You still look a little tired."

"No, I didn't sleep well," I said to her, then blushed again at what she was probably thinking. "I mean, I was on my laptop with Dillon half the night. He found out some dirt on Griffin Makeba and Harrison Tofflemire. So yes, I'm tired." I took another gulp of the latte Jake had made with my one-cup machine and prayed it would help keep my eyes open the rest of the day.

"What did you find out?" the detective asked.

I filled him in about Griffin's connection to Simon's company and Harrison's lawsuit. "Did you find out anything about all this chocolate hurling?" I asked him.

He shook his head. "The techs from last night didn't find any prints on your car. Whoever did it must have worn gloves."

"So there's nothing you can do?" I asked, frustrated.

"We're doing all we can, and we're taking these threats seriously. You should too. I hear you've been asking questions."

"I'm being careful," I said. "So doesn't this mean Wendy Spellman is innocent? She couldn't have left that message on my car and the RV since she was in jail."

"I'm not sure the two incidents are related," the detective said.

"They have to be!"

The detective took a deep breath. "Listen, think of it this way: While we have her in custody, she's safe. But we can't rule out the possibility that she may have an accomplice. Maybe she and someone else committed the murder together, and we haven't caught the other guy yet. For now, that's supposition. I won't know anything for sure until I have all the facts."

More silence and coffee sipping as we pondered the detective's latest theory. An accomplice? Who? Why? The questions popped up faster than chocolate-covered kettle corn.

Finally Detective Shelton pushed back his chair and rose. "Well, thanks for the coffee and pastry. I'll let you know what else the techs learn after I get the next report. Jake. Darcy. Abby." He nodded to each of us, his eyes lingering on Aunt Abby; then he stepped out of the Airstream, leaving a mild earthquake and the scent of a spicy cologne in his wake.

"Well," Aunt Abby said, rising from her seat. "I'd better go finish up my whoopie pies. If today is anything like yesterday, I'll barely have enough. Thanks for the cream puff, Jake. Now I know why Darcy spends so much time at your truck." She shot me a knowing smile.

"I'll come help you in a few minutes," I said. "I have a few things to share with Jake."

Her smile widened. "You two take your time." Somehow that simple sentence sounded terribly suggestive. I felt my cheeks go up in flames. As Aunt Abby headed out of the RV, she left me to face Jake with my bright red tell.

"You were up all night chatting with Dillon?" Jake said, thankfully changing the subject.

"I couldn't sleep," I said.

"It sounds like Polly was blackmailing everyone in

the contest except your aunt and me," Jake said. "Even Wendy had something to hide, which unfortunately still makes her a suspect."

"Maybe they all did it, like those people in *Murder on the Orient Express*," I suggested, although I didn't mean it. While Agatha Christie could get away with something like that, it just didn't happen in real life. Did it?

"What do you want to do now?" Jake asked, finishing his coffee. He cleared his place, rinsed his coffee mug, and tossed the leftover pastry papers into the trash can.

"Go back to bed," I said.

Jake grinned. "Works for me."

I smiled. "Actually, I think I'll talk to Griffin and Harrison. See if I can get them to say something about Polly, why she was blackmailing them, and whether they have a tell that says 'I'm the murderer. Look no further.'"

"That's the spirit, Sherlock. Grill 'em, get a confession, and slap on the cuffs."

"Not funny. What are you doing to help Wendy while I'm putting my life at risk?"

"That's not funny, either," Jake said, turning serious. "This time I'm coming with you. And if anyone tries to throw chocolate on you, I'll kick their ass."

I burst into laughter. Jake pulled me close and kissed me. He tasted like a chocolate cream puff. And I could never have too much of that.

A loud banging on the door startled me. I looked at Jake. He moved me back behind him, then opened the door. Two police techs stood at the bottom of the steps, dressed in white CRIME SCENE uniforms.

"I heard there was another message," the female tech said. I peered around Jake and recognized her from yesterday.

"Yep," I said.

"I'll show you." Jake stepped down from the RV and led the techs to the front of the Airstream. As I walked by, I told Jake I'd be in the house helping Aunt Abby prepare for the day while the techs did their work. We agreed to meet at Aunt Abby's bus an hour before the festival opened and to go together to interview Griffin and Harrison.

When I entered the kitchen, Aunt Abby and Dillon were elbow-deep mixing, stirring, and filling whoopie pies. Basil wagged his tail at Aunt Abby's feet, no doubt hoping for a dropped morsel.

"What can I do?" I asked as I donned an apron.

"Sure you're not too tired from making whoopie?" Dillon said, an evil grin on his face.

I grabbed a sponge from the counter and threw it at him. Hit him right in the butt.

Basil barked.

Food fight!

It was on!

Chapter 20

Aunt Abby nipped the food fight before it got too crazy, but only after Dillon had managed to smear chocolate on my fresh Big Yellow School Bus T-shirt. And *that* was after I got some in his hair.

"You two will be the death of me," she said after we settled down. "Dillon, go wash your hair. And, Darcy, go soak that shirt before the stain sets and get a fresh one."

I hung my head like a disciplined pet and returned to the RV to soak my shirt and get a fresh one, then went back to whipping up whoopie pies. After Aunt Abby prepared the mini cake/cookies and made the mocha buttercream filling, Dillon put the cake/cookies together. My job was to finish them off with chocolate frosting and jimmies. Yep, there's a special name for chocolate sprinkles—jimmies. Who knew?

The work was repetitive, assembly-line style, requiring no mental effort, so I thought about my suspect list, who were all victims of Polly's blackmail scheme.

Simon Van Houten didn't want his father to know he'd ratted out the family company's use of child labor.

Did he kill Polly to keep her quiet—and prevent that article she was saving from being published?

Isabel Lau didn't want anyone to know she'd served time for killing her abusive husband and changed her name to make sure no one would discover her past. Did she kill Polly in order to keep her identity—and past—a secret?

Frankie Nudo was sleeping with Polly, maybe hoping to win her vote. But then, did he kill her when he found out she was sleeping around?

Monet Richards faked her cooking credentials, claiming she'd attended Le Cordon Bleu in Paris, but apparently she'd been lying about this for years. Did she kill Polly to keep her from exposing the truth?

Then there was Griffin Makeba, who had been buying chocolate from Simon's company at a deep discount to keep him from airing the company's dirty laundry. That couldn't have helped the company's profit margin. Did he kill Polly because she found out he was blackmailing the Van Houtens?

And finally, Harrison Tofflemire, who had stolen the plans for his famous Chocolate Falls machine from a Canadian company and was being sued. Did he kill Polly because she found out about the lawsuits and threatened to put a black mark on his reputation?

They all had their reasons. But were those motives strong enough to actually commit murder? Apparently, for one of them, it was.

After finishing up the last batch of whoopie pies, we packed them up and loaded them into Aunt Abby's Prius, filling it to the brim.

"You really need to get an SUV or a van," I said to her when the last of the treats were in place. "This car is too small for your business."

"It gets great mileage," Aunt Abby said. "Those big old SUVs drink gas like it's water. No, thank you. I'll keep my green car."

"You only drive a few miles to the Marina and back! I hardly think you'll go broke with a bigger car."

"If I get a new car, it will be all electric," she said.

I gave up. "All right. I'll see you at the festival. Jake and I are going to talk to Griffin and Harrison before the event begins, so I'll be a little late to work."

"Be careful, Darcy," Aunt Abby said. "I appreciate you trying to help my friend, but those warnings you got on your car and the Airstream make me very nervous. Like they said, they know where you live. I don't want you to get hurt. I couldn't live with myself if you did."

I went over and gave my aunt a hug. "I'll be fine, Aunt Abby. Jake's going to meet me, so I won't be alone. And I'll be careful. I promise."

"You mean the world to me, you know," Aunt Abby said. Were those tears in her eyes? "I love having you here. And not just because you're a big help."

"I love being here too. And I appreciate the job, even though I sometimes don't act like it. Working in your food truck is growing on me."

"I knew it would," Aunt Abby said. "And you're getting better at it every day. You might turn into a good cook after all."

Before I took this job—out of desperation—I barely

knew how to microwave a frozen dinner. But I did have good taste, so to speak, and I read gourmet cookbooks like they were romance novels. Now, thanks to my aunt, I could make a great mac-and-cheese meal—for hundreds of people.

I took off my apron and went into the RV to check on the shirt I'd been soaking. The techs were gone, and so was Jake. However, the stain was still there. I'd have to look into some stain-removal products. I grabbed my purse, stepped out of the RV, and locked it behind me.

I met Dillon and Aunt Abby in the driveway. Dillon pulled on his helmet, hopped on his dirt bike, and sped away. Aunt Abby got in her car and drove off with a cheery wave. I headed for my VW, parked on the street, and noticed the ragtop still had patches of discolor where the chocolate had been. Must really be tough removing chocolate stains if three car washes couldn't do it. I slid into the driver's seat and inhaled the smell of chocolate that lingered inside. It made me hungry for a Snickers bar.

I arrived at the festival gate at ten, drove through after showing the guard my pass, and parked in the staff lot near Aunt Abby's car, where she and Dillon were unloading boxes of whoopie pies. I glanced across the way at Jake's Dream Puff truck, but apparently he hadn't arrived yet, so I grabbed a few boxes and helped carry in Aunt Abby's supplies for the day.

"I'll be back soon," I said to Aunt Abby after we'd hauled in all the boxes. I headed over to Jake's Dream Puff truck to see if he was inside. The sign in the window read CLOSED and the truck showed no signs of life inside. I wondered what had caused him to be late meeting me.

Drop-Dead Gorgeous?

I headed over to the Coffee Witch for one of Willow's magical concoctions, bought two Voodoo Ventes—one for me and one for Jake—then returned to his truck to see if he'd arrived.

Still no sign of him.

I checked my watch. The festival would be opening in forty-five minutes. Time was running out.

I set Jake's coffee on the shelf outside his truck window, wrote MEET ME AT THE PIEHOLE on the outside of the paper cup, then headed over, my own coffee in hand. This time I would step things up in terms of my questioning. The longer Wendy remained in jail and the real killer went free, the worse it would be for her— and maybe the rest of us—in the long run.

I could see through the service window that Griffin was preparing pies for the day's onslaught. Wishing Jake was with me, I knocked on his open door. In spite of the fact that Griffin might be a murderer, I didn't feel that nervous, since there were all kinds of food trucks nearby who would hear me if I screamed.

"Come in!" Griffin called out.

I stepped inside. "Hi, Griffin."

He looked up from the bowl of liquid chocolate, and I immediately thought of the chocolate that had been poured over my car and RV windows. "Oh, hey. You're Darcy, Abby's assistant, right?"

"Yes. I hope I'm not bothering you."

"Not at all. What can I do for you?" he said as he stirred the chocolate.

"Uh . . . I wondered if you might be interested in contributing a recipe to the food truck cookbook I'm writing. I'd love to include one of your chocolate pies. I can't pay anything, but it would be free publicity, and you'd get a copy of the book."

"Sounds cool." He began pointing to the various mini pies he'd lined up along the counter for display. "Which one do you want? I have Death by Chocolate Pie, which is fudgy. Chocolate Addiction, which is chocolate bourbon pecan. My personal favorite—Chocolate Orgasm—that's chocolate banana cream. Or you can have a recipe for Chocolate Crack, aka chocolate peanut butter, or Satan's Chocolate—French Silk, or Chocolate Decadence, which is a chocolate marshmallow mousse pie."

"Wow. That's a lot of chocolate pies. They all sound wonderful. You pick."

"Okay. When do you need it by? I'm kind of busy right now, but I could get it to you next week."

"That would be great," I said. I took a sip of the coffee I was carrying. "That looks yummy," I said, indicating the bowl of chocolate. "Smells good too. What kind of chocolate do you use?"

"Only the best," he said proudly.

"From the Ivory Coast?" I asked, getting to the point.

Griffin stopped stirring and looked up at me. "No!" he said a little too sharply. "Why would you say that?"

"No reason. I thought that particular chocolate was supposed to be the best."

"You've been listening to the wrong people. Did you know that African chocolate is made by children—enslaved children who work themselves to death? I would never be a part of that. My chocolate comes from South America, where it's fair trade. I pay more, but at least I don't feel guilty."

Wow. If what Dillon had learned about Griffin was true, he was a real hypocrite, not to mention a good liar. Not only was he blackmailing the Van Houtens to get his chocolate cheaper, but he couldn't care less about those kids. Despicable.

"Did Polly know where you got your chocolate?" I pushed on, checking to make sure my escape route was clear if I needed to run out quickly.

Griffin frowned. "What do you mean? Why would Polly want to know anything about my chocolate?"

"I heard a rumor that you were getting your chocolate at a discount, while other people had to pay full price. I wondered how you managed that."

Griffin's eyes narrowed. He took a step toward me, a large chocolate-covered metal spoon in his hand.

"I thought you came here to ask me for a recipe. What's with all the questions? It sounds like you're accusing me of something."

Where was Jake when I needed him?

I was ready to flee, but I wasn't leaving until I had some answers. "I just wondered if Polly found out about your special deal and you got angry and . . ."

"You think I *killed* Polly?" He forced a laugh. "That's just stupid! I had no reason to kill her. Where did you come up with such an idiotic idea?" He took another step closer to me. I took a step back.

"I must be wrong, then," I said, trying to defuse the growing anger I saw in his dark eyes. "Sorry. You know rumors. . . ."

"Spreading rumors like that can get you in a lot of trouble, lady," Griffin said. He stared at me as if trying to figure out what I knew—or what he was going to do next. "What happened to Polly could happen to you if you're not careful."

Now, that was a threat.

In the corner of my eye, I saw one of his fists clench.

"You're right, Griffin. I'll have to be more careful. I'd better let you get back—"

He slammed his fist on the counter, scaring the bejesus out of me. I dropped the cup of coffee, spilling liquid all over the floor.

"You're not leaving until you tell me where you heard this ugly rumor," Griffin snarled. He waved the large spoon menacingly in his raised hand.

It was time to go. I spun around and darted for the door.

Griffin grabbed my arm. "I *said*, I want to know who told you I was buying chocolate at a discount!"

I dug in my purse, which was hanging off my shoulder, and pulled out my cell phone. Griffin slapped it out of my hand. The phone went flying down the steps.

He tightened his grip on my arm. "Tell me!"

I shrugged my purse off my shoulder and swung it at him. He ducked and released my arm.

In that split second, I practically leaped from the top of the steps to the ground, barely landing on my feet.

Griffin stood above me, glaring, his brown eyes wild with murderous intent.

Chapter 21

I snatched my cell phone from the ground and backed away, glancing around frantically for help—or at least witnesses—in case he decided to follow through with his threat immediately. I spotted Harrison Tofflemire standing outside his truck, looking in my direction. His two daughters were also outside, but they were too busy flirting with Frankie Nudo to notice me.

I ran to Harrison, hyperventilating from my fight-or-flight reaction to Griffin's anger. "Harr . . . Harrison . . ." I wheezed, and bent over to catch my breath.

"Are you all right?" Harrison said, glancing across at Griffin's truck, then back at me. "What's all the ruckus?"

"Griffin . . ." I puffed. ". . . I . . . he . . ." I looked back. There was no sign of him.

"Here, let me get you some water. I'll be right back."

To be safe, I followed him up the steps of his truck, not wanting to remain outside alone. Not after Griffin's threats and that look in his eye.

Harrison pulled a bottle of water from his refrigerator, opened the cap, and handed it to me. I drank several gulps and felt my heart rate begin to slow down.

"Thank you," I said.

"No problem. What happened? You looked like a frightened rabbit. Something spook you?"

I nodded. "Griffin. I was talking to him in his truck and"—I hesitated, not wanting to tell Harrison the truth—"and he got upset about something, so I left. . . ."

"I heard yelling," Harrison said, "but I didn't know where it was coming from. Chefs around here do a lot of yelling, so I don't pay much mind to it. Did he hurt you?"

"No." I glanced at my wrist where Griffin had grabbed me. It was red, but not bruised—at least not yet. I thought about having him arrested for assault, but what was I thinking? I'd gone in there alone, made some serious accusations, and essentially provoked him. If I called the cops, I'd just make him even angrier, and it would prove nothing.

"He's a hothead," Harrison said. "Always mad about something. He hates Simon Van Houten because he thinks his father's business is involved in child labor. He hates Monet for giving him the cold shoulder. He hates Frankie because Frankie's a player. And he hates me because I'm so successful and my daughters won't have anything to do with him. Just blow him off."

Harrison *was* successful, but according to Dillon, with someone else's invention. This was going to be my opening to question him, but I was still shaking from my encounter with Griffin. Maybe now wasn't a good time. Then again, time was of the essence and this was the perfect opportunity. And Harrison's daughters were around, so he surely wouldn't get violent.

I decided to go for it. Surely I wouldn't be attacked twice in one morning. Would I?

"You've really done well for yourself, haven't you?" I asked him after taking another sip of water.

"I've been lucky," he said modestly. He pulled over a roller cart holding the larger of the two chocolate waterfalls. The stainless-steel appliance, shaped like a pyramid, stood about five feet tall, one of the largest I'd seen. "This baby sold more than a hundred thousand units last year." He patted it as if it were a pet. "I'll be using it for the contest this afternoon. The smaller one is less complicated, so I've been using it for the festival, but I'm bringing out the big guns for the win."

"How did you come up with the chocolate waterfall idea?" I asked, baiting him.

"Simple, really," he said, beaming with pride. "You see, this here's the base, which contains the motor, heater, and the controls." He pointed as he listed the parts. "The motor turns the auger. The auger is like a giant corkscrew that brings the chocolate up from the base to the top. The heater keeps the chocolate melted, and the controls operate it."

Okay, so he knew the basics of a chocolate waterfall. That wasn't what I had asked. I listened patiently as he went on.

"The tiers—these layers here—fill up with molten chocolate. When the chocolate reaches the top tier, it overflows and cascades down, like hot lava, or a waterfall."

He switched on the smaller machine, poured some chocolate chips onto the base, and they instantly began to melt.

"You have to use chocolate that has a lot of cocoa butter, or you have to add oil." He poured in more chocolate chips, and soon the base was full of melted chocolate. "Once it gets going, you can dip just about anything in the chocolate—fruit, cake, marshmallows, your finger." He grinned.

My mouth was starting to water from the smell of the heated chocolate. Harrison switched on the pump and magically, the chocolate began to rise up the central auger—a metal tubelike thingy with small circular blades attached every inch or so—and spill over the top.

"Here. Try some." He opened the refrigerator and pulled out a bowl of strawberries. He handed me a skewer and gestured to the bowl. I stabbed a medium-sized strawberry with the skewer and inserted it slowly into the liquid wall of cascading dark chocolate. When I pulled it back out, the berry was completely coated in chocolate.

"Go on. Eat it," Harrison said, watching me.

I bit into the chocolate-covered strawberry.

Incredible.

I was going to have to get me one of these Chocolate Falls.

"Good?"

"Delicious!" I said after I finished the strawberry. "So, how did you come up with the idea of creating this machine?"

Harrison shrugged. "Just came to me, you know. I

was thinking about how popular chocolate fondue was, but not so easy for a big group of people to enjoy. Then I saw this champagne fountain at a wedding once, and put two and two together. Chocolate Falls! My own invention."

"But there are other chocolate fountains on the market, aren't there?" I persisted.

"Yeah, but mine was the first, and it's the best. I have a secret patent for it that I don't share with anyone."

"Funny," I said. "I thought a Canadian company invented this version in the 1980s. You said you came up with the idea in 2002?"

Harrison switched off the machine. The grin on his face was gone, replaced by a frown. "Where did you hear that?"

"I don't know. I must have picked it up when I was writing food reviews for the newspaper."

"Well, it's not true. It's *my* invention. I created it and I perfected it. Lots of companies have tried to copy me, but none of them know my secret. You'd better check your sources carefully next time."

"I will," I lied. "Oh, I know where I heard it. From Polly Montgomery."

I watched Harrison closely for a reaction. His face twisted in disgust.

"Polly? That drunken old slut? She was nothing but a backstabbing, two-faced gossipmonger who should have been run out of the industry. I don't mean to speak poorly of the dead, but in this case, I'll make an exception. There was no love lost between us."

"Were you and Polly . . . ?" I couldn't bring myself to

say it. I didn't have to. He answered the implied question.

"Yeah, we had a thing, but it was a long time ago," Harrison snapped. "Before I knew what a well-heeled liar she was. I don't know what else she told you, but I wouldn't believe a word of it if I were you."

So Harrison and Polly had also been an item. Was there any man safe from Polly's generous charms?

Before I could ask another question, Harrison said, "Look, I gotta get ready to open. The festival will be starting in a few minutes. Meantime, I'd appreciate it if you wouldn't say anything about me and Polly. My girls don't know, and I don't want them to think casual sex is okay."

"Of course," I lied, figuring his daughters were way ahead of him on that. "I just have one last question."

"What's that?" Harrison said, irritation etched on his face.

"Do you have proof you invented the Chocolate Falls before anyone else?"

"What kind of a question is that?"

I was about to go out on a limb here. "Did Polly have reason to think you might have stolen the idea from that Canadian company?"

"I guess I didn't make myself clear, missy," Harrison said, his eyes narrow and focused on me. "If you say or print anything about me, my relationship with Polly, or even hint that Chocolate Falls wasn't my invention, my lawyer will have you up on slander *and* libel charges faster than you can melt chocolate."

*   *   *

I escaped Harrison's truck without injury, probably because I fled the moment he'd threatened me. As I passed Jake's Dream Puff truck, I saw the CLOSED sign still in his window, along with the coffee I'd left him.

"Aunt Abby?" I said after boarding the school bus. "Have you heard from Jake?"

"No. I haven't seen him, dear," Aunt Abby said. "But I'm glad you're back. Fifteen minutes until showtime and I'm still not ready. Could you unwrap those whoopie pies and put them in the paper cups?"

Nodding, I donned an apron. Dillon opened the boxes of ready-made whoopie pies, while I used tongs to place them in the colorful fluted paper cups, ready for the first wave of festival attendees. "You haven't heard from him at all?"

"Who?" Aunt Abby asked.

"Jake! He's still not in his truck. That's not like him."

"No, dear."

"Dillon?"

"Nope," he replied. "Maybe he had car trouble."

Maybe, I thought. *Maybe not.*

Maybe something was wrong.

It wasn't like him to ditch me when he'd said he'd meet me—at least, not without calling to cancel first. And it wasn't like him to be late opening his food truck, especially today, the second and last day of the festival. If Reina found out he hadn't shown up, she'd have a fit.

My cell phone rang.

"That's probably him now," Aunt Abby said, pulling out more paper cups.

I retrieved my cell phone—which now had a crack

in the glass—and checked the caller ID. Aunt Abby was right.

"Jake! Where are you?" I said a little too frantically. Thinking about the recent threats I'd received, I'd worried he'd gotten some too, since we'd been working on this murder investigation together. "Are you all right?"

"I'm fine, Darcy. Are you?"

"Yes, but you were supposed to meet me this morning."

"I know. I'm sorry. I hope you didn't go ahead without me," he said.

I didn't answer.

"Oh, Darcy, no. Look, this thing is becoming more serious than I realized. I'm at the hospital—"

"The hospital! Why? What happened? Are you all right?"

Aunt Abby and Dillon stopped what they were doing and looked at me, alarmed.

"I'm fine. My cop friend called after you left. There was another hit-and-run accident late last night or early this morning."

"Oh no! What happened? Someone you know?"

"It was J.C. He was run down while walking out of his apartment."

"Oh my God. Is he . . . okay?"

"He's in a medically induced coma. It doesn't look good."

Chapter 22

"What happened?" Aunt Abby said the second I hung up the phone.

"J.C.—Reina's camera guy. He . . . was hit by a car last night sometime. . . . He's at the hospital. . . ." I was having trouble processing the news I'd just heard from Jake. There was no way this was a coincidence. But this time it wasn't a festival judge. If this was deliberate, why had J.C. been targeted?

Had he seen something the night Polly was killed after all? Was it captured on his camera? Had he not noticed it at first?

"The poor thing!" Aunt Abby said. "First George, then Polly, now that young camera boy. Do you think it has anything to do with Polly's death?"

"It has to," I said. "Dillon, you downloaded the party footage from J.C.'s camera, didn't you?"

"Yeah, about that . . ." Dillon said, shaking his head.

"What's wrong?" I asked.

"There was some kind of glitch. It didn't come through."

I sighed, then had a thought. "Could you hack into his computer and download it that way?"

"I could try," he said, "assuming he saved it to his computer. But the festival's about to open. Can it wait?"

"Whenever you can get to it would be great." I looked at my aunt, her eyes as wide as whoopie pies. "Aunt Abby, would it be all right if I went to the hospital to see about J.C.? Do you think you can manage without me for an hour?"

"Of course, dear. Dillon and I will be fine. Things usually start off slowly the first hour. Go see what you can find out. Anything to help Wendy."

"Thanks, Aunt Abby. I'll be as quick as I can."

"Darcy?" my aunt said. "Does this mean the police will let Wendy go? Surely they can't think she killed Polly now that someone else tried to kill that boy."

"Not if the police think it was just an accident and not deliberate. Wendy will still be on the hook."

Aunt Abby sighed and gazed off into the distance. Dillon shot me a worried look. I nodded, letting him know I was concerned about my aunt too.

"I'll be back soon." I gave Aunt Abby a hug and headed out of the bus.

I made my way to the parking lot and found my VW Bug free of chocolate or any other type of vandalism, other than the remaining stain on the canvas top. That was a relief. I only wished Jake had been with me, especially when I questioned Griffin and Harrison, but I'd see him soon enough at SF General.

As I drove up Gough Street on the way to the hospital, I thought about possible reasons why someone would run J.C. down. The obvious motive was that J.C. knew something the killer didn't want him to share. Or was it something on J.C.'s camera that the killer didn't want anyone to see? Something the police might not have seen?

One thought led to another. Had Polly been black-mailing J.C., too, making him another suspect in her murder? Had she been sleeping with him as well? And if J.C. killed Polly, then why would someone try to kill him?

Or was the hit-and-run just an accident? Pedestrians in this city got hit all the time.

I parked in the hospital lot under a sign that read RESERVED FOR ER PHYSICIANS, my thoughts in a jumble, and headed for the emergency-room entrance. Jake had told me to go to the ER waiting room, and he'd meet me there. I found the room quickly and entered, my heart racing again.

"Jake!" I said the moment I spotted him. He was sitting next to an attractive Asian woman in a tailored blue suit, maroon blouse, and sensible black shoes. The rest of the seats were empty.

"Darcy!" He got up and embraced me, then pulled back and turned to the woman next to him. "Darcy, this is Lisa Lee, the cop friend I've mentioned. She was on duty at the time of the accident. Lisa, this is Darcy."

This beautiful young woman with sleek black hair, a perfect complexion, and sparkling brown eyes was his *cop friend*?

Lisa reached out and shook my hand with her strong

grip. "Nice to meet you," she said. "I've heard so much about you."

Really? All I'd heard about her was that she was Jake's "cop friend," who I'd assumed would be a guy. How sexist was I?

"Uh . . . ," I said, trying to gather my wits after meeting this knockout. Jake really seemed to attract them. "How's J.C.? Do you know anything more?"

Before either one could answer, a deep voice came from behind me. "I should have known you'd be here."

Uh-oh.

I turned to see Detective Shelton's large form filling the doorway.

"Hey, Detective," I said. "Any news about J.C.?"

He shook his head and entered the room. "He's still under. We're not going to get anything from him for a while—if at all."

"What do you mean, if at all?" I asked.

The detective shook his head. I caught his drift. "You two might as well go on back to work."

"Detective," I said. "What about Wendy Spellman? Doesn't this attempt on J.C.'s life prove the real killer is still out there? Can't you let her go?"

"Not so fast, Darcy," the detective said. "We don't know anything more than he was hit by a car and the driver took off. Right now it looks like a hit-and-run accident."

"Are you forgetting about George Brown, the judge who was killed right before the Chocolate Festival? That was also a hit-and-run. This has got to be more than a coincidence."

"Brown's death was ruled an accident too, Darcy."

"You're kidding! Don't you see? George and Polly and J.C. are all connected to the Chocolate Festival!"

Jake touched my arm, trying to calm me. I took a deep breath. "Have you at least watched J.C.'s video?"

Detective Shelton nodded. "Several times. Unfortunately, there's no footage of anything that might have to do with the murder. It's just shots of the crowd, Ms. Patel's speeches, and the vat of chocolate *after* Polly Montgomery was dumped in there. If you were hoping for evidence of the killer in action, sorry. That only happens in bad movies."

I shook my head, exasperated.

The detective sighed. "Like I said, there's nothing you can do here."

"Oh my God, I just heard!" came another voice from the doorway. This time is was Reina Patel. In spite of the concerned look on her face, she appeared festive in her silky brown jumpsuit, her signature chocolate-chip-covered scarf tied intricately around her long, slim neck. "What happened to J.C.?"

While the detective filled her in, I watched Reina's expression. Her frown deepened and her mouth tightened. I wondered if she was upset by what happened to J.C. or just irritated she'd lost future footage of the Chocolate Festival. It was tough to tell.

"What about his camera?" Reina said, confirming my worst suspicions. "Did they find it?"

The detective looked over at Lisa Lee.

"We found it a few feet from the body. It was in pieces," she said.

Reina shook her head. "How sad. He never went anywhere without his camera." She checked her watch. "Well, if there's nothing I can do, I need to get back to the festival. And so do the two of you." She pointed back and forth between Jake and me. "We opened half an hour ago, and you need to be there. I don't want a bunch of disappointed customers complaining on Yelp."

I rolled my eyes at Jake.

Reina started to leave, then turned back. "Officer, are we in any danger? I thought you had the killer in custody."

"It's Detective Shelton," he replied, setting her straight. "We'll have extra police presence at the festival, but I don't think you're at risk. It was probably an accident, but we're not ruling anything out. Stay alert; be smart."

Reina nodded. She pulled out her cell, tapped in a number, and said as she walked out the door, "Yes, I'm calling to see if you have someone who can record an event today. . . ."

Wow. She was already calling for J.C.'s replacement so she could continue her one-woman show. Nothing got in the way of Reina's obsession with making a behind-the-scenes documentary out of this situation. And she'd probably have no trouble selling her story to the Food Network. Like J.C. had said, viewers love real-life drama, even when it's sprinkled with fiction.

Jake walked me to my car, still parked illegally in a spot reserved for physicians. Luckily I hadn't gotten ticketed or towed, only a raised eyebrow from Jake. As we drove back to the Chocolate Festival in our separate cars, I hoped Aunt Abby wasn't too overwhelmed with customers. I felt guilty leaving her, but she understood that I was trying to help her friend Wendy. Unfortunately, the trip hadn't produced much information as to whether the hit-and-run was an accident or deliberate, but I had learned that J.C.'s camera had been destroyed, and the cops had the flash drive. Hopefully, he had downloaded everything onto his computer. And hopefully, Dillon could retrieve any videos he'd made. Maybe the footage would reveal something that could help find the killer.

We parked in the festival lot and walked together through the back entrance to the food truck area.

"I'd better open up," Jake said, after spotting several people looking at his truck and shaking their heads.

"I'm sure Aunt Abby needs help too," I said, glancing at her line.

"Let's meet up when the crowd dies down," Jake suggested.

I nodded and headed inside Aunt Abby's school bus.

"Thank God you're back," Dillon said, wiping the sweat from his forehead with the back of his arm. "It's worse than yesterday."

Aunt Abby was taking orders, while Dillon filled them as fast as he could. I put on my apron and helped Dillon, who was obviously having trouble keeping up. A nonstop stream of customers kept us busy for the next few hours. Around three o'clock, the crowd finally thinned, and Dillon and I were able to take a short break.

"Bring me a Witch's Brew," Dillon said, getting out his laptop and seating himself on a stool. "I'll see if I can get into J.C.'s computer."

"Great!" I said, then asked Aunt Abby if she wanted anything.

"No, thanks. I'll get an energy drink from the fridge." No wonder my aunt never took a break. She lived on those energy drinks.

I swung by the Dream Puff truck and waved to Jake, who was still dealing with customers, then got in the short line at the Coffee Witch for my afternoon infusion.

"Any news about J.C.?" Willow asked when I reached her service window. "I heard he got in an accident or something."

Apparently word had spread, as it always did in the food truck community. Unfortunately, the news wasn't always accurate.

I shook my head. "Not an accident, exactly. He was involved in a hit-and-run. Did you know him?"

"Yeah," she said, a grin filling her face. "He's hot—don't you think?"

Not at the moment, I thought. "Well, right now he's in a medically induced coma."

Willow's grin vanished. "Holy crap! I hope he'll be all right. We were supposed to hook up again tonight."

That was quick, I thought. "You went out with J.C.?" I was surprised that they knew each other well enough to go out on a date, but I shouldn't have been. In spite of Willow's multiple piercings and tattoos and that wicked short blond/purple hair—or maybe because of that—guys seemed attracted to her. And Willow was quite the flirt herself.

"Yeah, we met at that party, you know, where that judge was killed," Willow said casually. "We went clubbing after the cops were done with us. He's totally hot. I love his tats."

I smiled. If you liked guys wearing baggy jeans and faded T-shirts who have scruffy beards, uncombed hair, arms tattooed with tribal designs, Asian characters, and dragons, and gauged earlobe holes you could fit a finger through, then I guessed he was hot.

"Willow, did J.C. ever say anything about Polly?"

"Nope. Only that he wished he had caught the killer. On his camera, I mean."

"Did you see any of the footage he filmed?"

"Just some of the party stuff. When I was at his place last night, he kept playing one part over and over. I got bored and told him I was leaving. He said he'd come to my apartment later, but he never showed. Guess that's 'cause he got run over."

Run over. I shook my head, but said nothing. It wasn't that Willow was cold; she was just young and a little self-absorbed.

"What part did he keep playing over?" I asked.

She shrugged. "I don't know. I wasn't paying much attention."

She handed me my coffee order—one for Dillon, one for Jake, and one for me—and I paid her, plus tip. I tenuously carried the cups back to the school bus to drop off Dillon's coffee and find out if he'd been able to download J.C.'s party footage. J.C. had been playing a particular part "over and over"—to the point where Willow apparently felt neglected and decided to leave.

What was it that had captured J.C.'s attention?

Something the police hadn't seen? Something that might lead to the killer?

The more I thought about it, the more I became convinced that someone had deliberately tried to kill J.C. because of something on that footage.

Chapter 23

"Dillon, did you get anything?" I asked as I entered the school bus.

"Bam!" Dillon said, pretending to strike his laptop with his fingers as if casting a spell.

"You really are a magician!" I said. "How did you do it?"

"Easy," he said, like he always says when he hacks into another computer. "You just hack into the source computer, find the file, download it, transfer it to the target computer, and that's it."

He really did make it sound easy, but there was no way I could do what he did.

Jake climbed in and joined us.

"Dillon got into J.C.'s computer," I told him. "Willow said J.C. kept watching a certain part over and over. We need to see the footage of the party and try to figure out what he was so interested in."

"It'll take hours to watch the whole thing," Jake said, helping himself to a whoopie pie.

He was right. And with the chocolate contest looming, we didn't have hours. "Can we fast-forward through it?"

Dillon tapped a couple of keys and started the video, then moved it into fast-forward. I caught glimpses of Reina dressed in that gorgeous chocolate-brown ensemble as she welcomed guests to the party. I watched as Polly in her red velvet dress and wobbly heels lay drunk on the table, Reina escorted Polly out, and party guests mingled. Then Reina returned; she gave a speech interrupted by Griffin's outburst and the rebuttal from Simon Van Houten. Unfortunately, I couldn't keep track of who was at the party the whole time and who possibly left for a while.

We fast-forwarded through the first part again, which took place on the veranda at the Maritime Museum. Nothing looked suspicious, other than the argument between Griffin and Simon, captured on the video. I had since learned that Griffin was blackmailing Simon, but I still didn't see what that had to do with Polly. She had her own blackmail schemes going on.

The next bit was taken inside the museum after Reina had gathered the guests to view the giant vat of chocolate. There she was standing next to the vat, her chocolate dress nearly the same color as the molten chocolate. She gave another speech; then J.C. did a panorama of the crowd. Everyone seemed accounted for. Then came Reina's scream. The camera spun away from the crowd and focused on Reina, giving us a close-up of her horrified face, her hand grasping her long, thin neck as if she were choking. Then there was a sudden jerk as the camera moved to the vat of chocolate. J.C. had focused on Polly's chocolate-covered hand, clearly visible through the transparent plastic tub.

If the Food Network got ahold of this footage, it would no doubt eat it up.

Was this footage the reason J.C. was attacked? Did someone want to keep it from going to the TV show? And was the hit-and-run actually meant for the camera and not J.C.?

I asked Dillon to replay the scene where Reina screamed when she discovered the vat of chocolate but saw nothing that indicated a murderer lurking in the area.

I checked my watch. Two hours until the contest.

I handed Jake the coffee I'd bought him. "It's cold," I said, "like this case."

He put the paper cup in the microwave and tapped the coffee icon.

"There's got to be something on that footage," I said. "But if there is, I didn't see it."

Jake shook his head. Dillon shrugged. Aunt Abby frowned.

"I've got to get ready for the contest," Jake said, retrieving his coffee. "Good luck, Abby," he said, and gave her a hug. "I hope you win."

"You too, Jake," Aunt Abby said. "As long as one of us beats those other contestants, I'll be happy."

"See you in a while?" Jake said to me.

I nodded and watched him go.

"Damn!" I said. "I was sure there was something on J.C.'s camera footage."

"Darcy, you've been on this nonstop since it happened, thanks to me," Aunt Abby said. "I'm worried about you. You're not sleeping well. You look exhausted.

Why don't you take a nice break before the contest? We'll be fine here. The crowds are light."

I nodded. "Maybe you're right. Are you sure you don't need me until then?"

"I'm sure. The whoopie pies are ready to go. I'd rather you be rested for the contest."

I gave my aunt a hug, thanked Dillon, and stepped out of the bus, ready to drop. As I walked to my car, planning to go home and take a relaxing shower, I replayed the party scene in my head. But instead of seeing something suspicious, it felt as if something was missing. It was like one of those "Can you spot the differences" pictures, where little changes are made in one of a pair of photos. They were usually things easily overlooked, like a button missing in one picture but not in the other, or a mole on someone's face that's gone in the second picture.

That's the feeling I had about the video.

Something was missing.

Now you see it; now you don't.

On my way to the parking lot, I glanced over at Reina's office and saw a young man leaving the trailer. To my surprise, he slammed the office door behind him and stomped off toward the parking lot. I noticed he had a camera in his hand. Curious, I hurried over to him.

"Are you okay?" I asked, hoping he might tell me what had caused him to be so upset.

"What a diva!" the young guy said. He was heavy, with glasses and curly brown hair and the kind of skin that freckles and doesn't tan.

"Are you the new cameraman?"

"Was," he said, emphasizing the past tense. "She might as well hold the camera herself. All she wants is shots of her. I thought this was supposed to be a gig for the Food Network, but it's all about whatever-her-name-is. I'm an artist. They don't pay me enough to put up with this crap. I'm outta here."

I watched him head for his car. Then I glanced back at the trailer and detoured toward Reina's office.

I knocked. A few moments later the door opened. Reina still looked festive yet professional in her chocolate jumpsuit and designer scarf. "Yes?"

"I just saw the new camera guy leaving the festival. He looked upset. Is anything wrong?"

"He's an idiot," Reina said. "I might as well shoot the event myself. At least J.C. could follow directions. This guy thought he was some kind of Spielberg and—"

"Reina!" I heard a man's voice yell from behind me. I turned to see Harrison Tofflemire walking toward the trailer, his face twisted in rage. "What's the meaning of this?" He held up what looked like a heavy metal rod with spiraling blades. It took me a second to recognize it as part of his Chocolate Falls gizmo that siphoned the chocolate up to the top tier. The auger. What was he doing with it in his hand?

"Calm down, Harrison," she said to him.

"No, I won't calm down. The auger in my deluxe Chocolate Falls machine is missing! The machine I was going to use for tonight's contest."

"Isn't that it in your hand?" she asked, pointing to the metal tube he held.

"No! This is the one from the smaller machine. I need the one for the big machine!" He climbed the steps and pushed his way into the office.

Reina blinked. "Uh . . . Darcy, I'm going to have to deal with this. I'll see you at the competition." With that she closed the door.

Crap. Something was going on and I wasn't invited. What was Harrison all upset about?

The bad thing about trailers and RVs is that they tend to have thin walls. I should know. I can hear Aunt Abby's neighbor blasting his TV every night. The good thing was, I might be able to hear what was going on inside.

I circled around to the back so no one passing by would see me eavesdropping and pressed my ear against the wall.

"What's the problem, Harrison?" I heard Reina say. It sounded as if she were talking into a tin can.

"You know what the problem is!" Harrison bellowed. "I want the part you stole from my big machine!"

Stole from his machine? I'd expected him to demand she find the missing part, not accuse her of stealing it.

Reina laughed. "Why would I want that thing? I have no use for it."

"I don't know how you did it, but somehow you got into my truck and stole it. You knew I was going to use the big machine for the contest, and you sabotaged it because I refused to share the winnings with you. Now, where's my auger?"

Reina? Wasn't Polly the one who was blackmailing the contestants into sharing their winnings?

I was dying to peek through the window overhead and see what was going on, but I didn't want to take a chance of getting caught. Instead, I kept my ear to the wall.

"Look, Harrison, I told you I'd fix it so you'd win the contest—for the right price—but you were too greedy. Now you're on your own. Good luck with that."

I could picture her grinning smugly at him.

"I'm not leaving until I find it!" Harrison shouted.

"Go ahead," Reina said. "Have a look."

I heard rustling around in the trailer, the slamming of drawers, the moving of office furniture. It sounded like he was tearing the place apart.

"It's not here, Harrison," Reina said calmly. "If I had it, and I'm not saying I do, it would be somewhere safe. And since you didn't agree to pay me, if I had it, I'd take it to the police."

"What for?" Harrison said. I could almost see him frowning.

"Because it's the perfect weapon to use as a blunt instrument if you wanted to bash someone over the head. And it's covered with your fingerprints."

Oh my God. Harrison? Had he been the one who hit Polly over the head using a part of his own chocolate machine? That heavy metal tube would make a good weapon, especially with those blades encircling it. But how did Reina know? And why *hadn't* she told the police?

"Where is it?" Harrison demanded. "Tell me, or so help me, I'll bash you over the head with this one."

A chill ran down my spine. If Harrison was the killer, he wouldn't hesitate to kill Reina!

I ran around to the door, leaped up the steps, and burst in. Harrison stood a few feet from Reina, the metal auger at his side, his face red with rage. Reina was leaning against her desk as if she didn't feel the slightest threat.

"Harrison! Stop!" I yelled.

Harrison spun around and raised the auger.

Reina took that second to grab a nearby folding chair. She swung it up and brought it down on Harrison's head.

Harrison Tofflemire crumpled to the floor.

I stared at Reina in shock.

"Darcy! Thank God!" Reina said. "If you hadn't come in just now, he would have killed me with that metal pipe! Just like the one he used to kill Polly."

I frowned, confused at the way she'd seemed so calm just before bashing Harrison over the head.

"It's true!" she sputtered. "He killed Polly. And I have proof!"

Harrison moaned. He lay facedown on the floor, the back of his head bleeding from a large gash.

I knelt down to check on him. "Reina, call nine-one-one!" I ordered.

She paused a moment, then began searching her desk for her phone. When she found it, she lifted it up, paused again, then punched in three numbers.

"Harrison!" I said, bending over him. I patted his

face lightly. "Are you all right?" I looked up at Reina. "I need something to wrap the wound on his head. He's bleeding."

"Like what?" she said, glancing around. The place was full of papers, office furniture, and promotional materials for the festival. I saw nothing that could be used as a bandage.

"Your scarf!" I gestured at my neck. "Give it to me."

She clutched the chocolate-chip-covered silk scarf in her hand as if it were her lifeline. "No! It's hand-painted, one of a kind. Cost me a fortune. I'm sure there's something else you can use."

"There *is* nothing else, Reina, unless you want to take off your clothes! Now give it to me before he bleeds to death."

She slowly pulled off the two-yard-long scarf and threw it down at me. I snatched it and wrapped a good part of it around Harrison's bleeding head as best I could, covering the wound.

He moaned again and mumbled something I couldn't make out.

"Where's that ambulance?" I said frantically. "Reina, do you have a first-aid kit?"

"No, but the security guard probably does."

"Then call him!" I said, puzzled by her lack of interest in Harrison's well-being. Then again, if he'd been about to kill her, I really couldn't blame her.

She punched in some numbers, then told Clifford to bring a first-aid kit to her trailer and hung up.

Harrison began to mumble again. "Liar . . . ," he whispered. "Liar. . . ."

"Yes, you're a liar, Harrison," Reina said, leaning over him. "And everyone is going to know what you did to poor Polly, because I have the proof."

"I didn't . . . kill her. . . ." Harrison continued to mumble and slur his words between moans.

"Shut up, Harrison! You tried to destroy my Chocolate Festival, you killed Polly, and you tried to kill me, but you're not going to get away with it."

Harrison rolled over on his back. "She killed Polly . . . ," he said in a whisper.

I looked at him, then at Reina, who was shaking her head.

"You can't pin this on me, Harrison. I told you. I have proof—that metal pipe from your chocolate machine with your fingerprints all over it. After you bashed Polly over the head with it and stuffed her into the vat of chocolate, you hid it in your big Chocolate Falls machine, thinking no one would find it. But I knew. I saw you in J.C.'s video. That's why you tried to kill him too. So I sneaked in and took it. I was just about to go to the police when you came storming into my trailer. Thank God Darcy was here to keep you from murdering me too."

Harrison groaned. His eyes fluttered. I looked at the scarf. He'd lost a lot of blood.

Where was that ambulance? We needed to get him to a hospital, murderer or not. If he'd killed Polly, I wanted to keep him alive. I still had a lot of questions to ask him.

I thought about the camera footage Reina had mentioned. When I watched it, there had been no sign of Harrison killing Polly or even holding that auger.

Someone was lying. Reina? She said she saw Harrison in the video—doing what? Then she took the murder weapon with his fingerprints all over it and said she was about to call the police. But Harrison claimed Reina tried to rig the contest and get him to share the winnings with her, and when he wouldn't, she framed him with the stolen auger.

Which one was telling the truth?

I checked Harrison's head. The scarf seemed to be helping. Some of the bleeding was abating.

"That blood will never come out," Reina said.

I looked at the scarf, thinking what an odd thing that was to say. I noticed a light brown stain on the end of the scarf that I hadn't used for Harrison's wound. The stain was about the size of a Hershey bar and resembled the stain on my T-shirt, the one left by a smear of melted chocolate during my food fight with Dillon.

Only this one was a little different. I held the stained part of the scarf up to my nose.

It didn't smell like chocolate. . . .

This was a bloodstain.

Reina had been wearing that scarf at the party. In fact, she'd been wearing it every time I'd seen her in her chocolate outfits.

Except once—when she was in the room with the vat of chocolate.

I tried to recall the video and visualized her standing

beside the vat, a look of horror in her eyes, her hand grasping her neck.

Her long, thin, *bare* neck.

What had been different about that picture?

It was the only time she hadn't been wearing that chocolate-chip-decorated scarf.

And now it was stained with blood. Polly's blood?

I looked up at her.

"How did you get this stain?" I asked her, my heart beginning to beat faster.

"What?" Reina said. "I have no idea."

"It's blood, isn't it?"

She shrugged and began stammering. "No. Of course not. Unless it came from Harrison."

I stood up. "This is dried blood, not Harrison's blood. Reina, I saw the video from the party."

She blinked. "You couldn't have. It was destroyed."

I shook my head. "J.C. had downloaded it to his computer before it was smashed by that hit-and-run driver."

"His computer?" she said, her eyes narrowing. "How did you . . . ?"

"Dil—," I started to say, then changed it to "A friend of mine managed to find it. We watched the footage, and there was no sign of Harrison doing what you claimed you saw."

"You must have missed that part," she said, crossing her arms over her chest.

"I don't think so," I said, "because I noticed something else. You were wearing your scarf at the party on the veranda, but when we went into the room with the vat of chocolate, it was gone from your neck."

"So? I took it off. . . ."

"You took it off because you got blood on it when you hit Polly over the head with Harrison's auger and shoved Polly into that vat, didn't you? You only pretended to put Polly in a cab, but you must have put her somewhere else. Where? In your car? Then what? You sneaked out while the crowd was still on the veranda, brought her into the room with the vat of chocolate, hit her over the head with the auger, and pushed her into the vat, getting blood on your scarf. So you took it off and probably stuffed it in your purse to clean later. Then you returned to the party, had everyone come into the room, and pretended to be shocked when you saw Polly's hand pressed against the wall of the vat."

Reina glanced at the ugly-looking auger that Harrison had brought with him. It lay on the floor at her feet. She bent down, grabbed it, and raised it over her head.

Chapter 24

I felt beads of sweat break out on my forehead. My heart was nearly beating out of my chest.

"Reina . . ." I held up my hands as if they'd protect me from the metal pipe. "The police and ambulance will be here any minute. You don't want to make this any worse than it is."

She smiled. "No, they won't."

Uh-oh. She hadn't called them.

She'd only pretended to call 911 and the security guard. I was alone in a trailer with a dying man and a killer who was holding a nasty weapon.

With nothing to defend myself.

Except my big mouth.

"Reina! How are you going to explain two dead people in your trailer? You can't get away with this."

"Easy," she said, lowering the auger a little. "Harrison killed Polly and I have the proof—the other auger with his fingerprints. He came here to kill me and get it back. You got in the way, and he hit you over the head with this one. That gave me the chance to grab a chair and defend myself."

I had to admit, it sounded plausible. Now what?

"At least tell me why you killed Polly." I backed up a step toward the door.

She moved forward a step, holding that menacing auger higher, ready to strike.

"Isn't it obvious? She was blackmailing me, like she was everyone else."

"What for?"

"Why should I tell you?" Reina asked.

"Because in a few minutes I'm not going to be able to tell anyone, so why not?"

"Good point," she said, grinning, no doubt at the thought of killing me too. "Okay, I'll tell you, if you promise not to tell." She laughed at her morbid joke.

I nodded, playing along, buying time.

"She found out I killed George. It was an accident, for real this time. I was over at his place, talking about the festival and whatnot, and she came by. George was quite the ladies' man, you know—or maybe you didn't. Anyway, when she burst in on us, we were sort of in a compromising position. She starting yelling at me and calling George a two-timing jerk. She looked like she might kill someone, so I left before things got ugly. I got in my car, which was parked out front, and apparently he came running out after me. . . . I didn't see him. . . . I backed up and hit him. Unfortunately, Polly saw the whole thing. But instead of telling the police, she wanted money to keep quiet. I didn't feel like paying her, so I thought up a way to get rid of her. Then I framed clueless Wendy. Problem solved."

"You just said it was an *accident*. You should have told the police the truth."

"I know, but believe it or not, it wasn't the first time I'd hit someone with my car. When I was a teenager, I hit a guy on a bicycle. Put him in a wheelchair. It was ruled accidental, but it stayed on my record. Another accident wouldn't have looked good, you know?"

"Why did you try to kill J.C.?"

"You know, I hated to do it because he was a sweet kid, but like you, he noticed the spot on my scarf and mentioned it after he played back the footage and saw I wasn't wearing the scarf during the second half of the party. He was starting to put two and two together, so I told him to bring his camera over and I'd take a look and explain everything. Then I waited outside for him to leave his apartment. And hit the gas. It was almost too easy. I'd planned to break in and get his computer too. But time ran out."

Time was running out for me too. I could feel the sweat dripping down my back. I thought about pleading with her to let me go, but there was no way she would do that. This woman had ice in her veins. It was fight or flight, and neither one looked promising.

I had a sudden thought. "Password!"

"What?" Reina frowned at me.

"One, two, three, four!"

"What are you talking about?"

"Password, one, two, three, four," I repeated. "That's *your* password, isn't it?"

Reina looked stunned. "How did you know that?"

"Jake figured it out. And he knows all about you too," I bluffed.

"No, he doesn't," she said. "You're just trying to scare me."

"How else would I know your password? Remember when we stopped by the office and Jake accidentally knocked some of your papers on the floor? That's when he took your cell phone. He figured out your password and downloaded a whole bunch of your saved messages and contacts and everything. If something happens to me, I'm sure he'll go through all that stuff and put two and two together, just like J.C. And so will the police."

Reina thought for a moment, then said, "Call him."

Uh-oh. Had I just put Jake in jeopardy?

"What for?"

"Get out your cell phone and call him. Tell him to meet you here and that you've learned something. And don't say anything more or I'll kill you on the spot."

I got out my phone and reluctantly punched Jake's autodial number.

"Darcy?"

"Hi, Jake. Uh, can you meet me at Reina's trailer? She has a *tell*. . . ." I glanced at Reina. She waved the auger threateningly. "I mean, she has something to *tell* you about the murder."

Reina nodded and mouthed, "Hang up."

I did as I was told, hoping Jake got my *real* message. I glanced down at Harrison. He'd gone quiet and wasn't moving. If he didn't get help soon, he wasn't going to make it.

"Good girl," Reina said. "Sorry I have to do this, but I don't want you running out the door or screaming when Jake gets here." She raised the auger.

I ducked and ran to the other side of the room behind her desk.

She came at me with a vengeance, growling as she began swinging the metal rod. It came slamming down on her desk, just missing me. She raised it again.

She had backed into a corner.

I looked around for anything, *anything* I could use to protect myself. My purse lay on the floor, next to a bunch of posters. With nowhere else to go, I pressed myself against the back wall.

Where was Jake?

Something bright caught my eye. Lining the shelf next to me were the three trophies Reina would be handing out to the contest winners. I lunged for the big one, three feet high, and grabbed it off the shelf.

Reina's eyes flared. She swung the auger at me, but I blocked it with the heavy trophy. Reina's auger went flying out of her hands.

As she bent down to reach for it, I brought the trophy down on her head.

She collapsed onto the floor, groaning. I sat down on her, hard, knocking the wind out of her. As she gasped for breath, I glanced around for something to tie her up with before she got a second wind.

Nothing.

Then I reached around behind me, slipped my hand up the back of my shirt, and unhooked my bra. With practiced skill, I removed it from under my T-shirt, then used it to tie up Reina's wrists behind her back.

Seconds later there was a knock on the door. I ran over and opened it.

"Darcy?" Jake said from the top step. Behind him stood two police officers

He'd figured out my clue!

"Are you all right?"

"I'm fine. A little shaky, but okay. Reina's the killer. She murdered Polly and tried to kill J.C. Harrison needs an ambulance." I spilled it all out as quickly as I could.

The cops followed Jake inside and took in the scene. One called for an ambulance while the other got out proper cuffs for Reina. I blushed as I untied my Victoria's Secret 34C Dream Angels bra from her wrists.

Jake grinned and checked me out with a raised eyebrow.

"You tied her up with that?" he asked.

"It was all I had," I said, stuffing the bra into my pants pocket.

"Great job," he said. "I got your message. Very clever."

"Thank God!" I said. "And you brought the police."

"Thanks to you," Jake said.

I really should have 911 on my speed dial, I thought.

A few minutes later an ambulance arrived to take Harrison Tofflemire to SF General, while Detective Shelton escorted Reina to the police station. She had a few bruises from where the trophy had hit her, but otherwise she was well enough to go to jail.

I was shaken up, but I wanted to support Abby at the contest after all the work she'd done and headed over after talking to the detective, arriving just in time.

"Aunt Abby!" I called as I entered the bus. "I'm here!"

Aunt Abby looked up from the tray she was arranging and grinned. "Thank goodness. Where have you—" She cut herself off after looking me over. "What happened to you?"

I frowned, wondering what she meant. She pointed to a bruise on my arm and Harrison's blood I had wiped on my shirt. In all the commotion with Reina, I hadn't noticed that I'd somehow hurt my arm and figured I must have bumped it at some point. "I'm not sure about the bruise, but that's not my blood. It's Harrison's."

Aunt Abby's eyebrows shot up. Dillon's mouth fell open.

I realized the shocking statement I'd just made and tried to explain. "Oh, uh, he's alive. They've taken him to the hospital."

"What happened?" my aunt asked, shaking her head. Obviously, the more I said, the more I confused her.

I took a deep breath. "Reina was the one who killed Polly. Then she tried to kill Harrison when he figured out that she'd used part of his Chocolate Falls machine to knock out Polly. She ran down George too, but I don't know if anyone can prove it, and it might have actually been an accident." I was talking fast, worried about making it to the contest tent on time, but I knew Aunt Abby wouldn't go until she'd heard it all. "Then she tried to kill J.C., her videographer, because he *did* have incriminating footage on his camera after all. And then she made me lure Jake over to her trailer, planning to kill both of us, but I beaned her with the trophy you're going to win in a few minutes and sat on her and tied her up with my bra. . . ." I was about out of breath. Reliving the scene brought back the fear I'd felt in the midst of everything, and I suddenly had to sit down.

"Goodness!" Aunt Abby said, wrapping an arm around me. "You poor dear. Dillon, get her a drink of water."

"I just need a second," I said, catching my breath. I downed the bottle of water Dillon handed me and sighed. "Don't we have to get going?"

Aunt Abby looked at the clock. "I suppose, although if Reina's not there . . ."

"I highly doubt she will be, since she's on her way to jail," I said.

There was a knock at the bus door. It was open and Willow suddenly appeared at the top of the steps.

"Hey, guys. There's been a little change in plans," she announced.

"What's up?" Dillon asked. "Is the contest still on?"

"Yeah," Willow said, "but guess who's MC."

No one said anything.

"Me!" Willow announced proudly. "I'm replacing Reina. How cool is that?"

"Cool," Dillon said.

"Don't you want to know why?" Willow asked, excitement evident in her green eyes.

I looked at Aunt Abby and Dillon, then decided to play dumb.

"Sure," I said. "How come?"

"Reina was arrested for murder! Incredible, huh? Apparently, she killed that judge chick and tried to blame it on that old lady, and then she tried to kill J.C.! She was probably jealous that he liked me. Anyway, I gotta tell the other contestants the show is on. See you at the contest tent ASAP. Good luck!"

Willow bounded out of the bus, leaving the three of us a moment to take it all in.

"Well, let's get over there," Aunt Abby said. "We've got a contest to win!"

Aunt Abby, Dillon, and I finished gathering up the whoopie pies and carefully carted them over to the contest tent. As soon as I entered, I spotted Lyla Vassar, dressed in a smart chocolate-brown suit with matching stiletto heels, her hair cascading gently over her shoulders. Once again, she was drop-dead gorgeous—and hard to miss with her cameraman at her side. He was panning the room with his camera. The back of my neck prickled at the sight of her. I forced my gaze away and focused on finding Aunt Abby's table in the crowded room. We located her assigned spot at the far side of the room, sandwiched between two other contestants I didn't recognize.

I tried to ignore Lyla while helping Aunt Abby set up her display, but it wasn't easy and I kept sneaking looks at her. Aunt Abby placed each pie on a petite white doily and arranged them in a circle, with the most perfect one in the middle. I glanced on either side of my aunt's table to check out the competition. A heavyset woman was arranging a platter of classic chocolate chip cookies on the right, and on the left, a man in chef's whites fiddled with raspberries as he placed them on a luscious-looking chocolate cheesecake. My mouth started to water.

As soon as we'd finished showcasing the whoopie pies, I scanned the room for Jake. He was easy to find, since Lyla and her cameraman were now focused on him and his cream puffs. As usual, he looked hot in a fresh Dream Puff shirt stretched across his chest. He smiled as he talked into the microphone Lyla held in front of him. I watched, unable to look away until the interview was over. As soon as the camera turned off, Lyla reached over and touched Jake's arm affectionately. Jake glanced up from rearranging his cream puffs and spotted me watching. I turned away quickly and pretended to busy myself with Aunt Abby's display.

"Where are the judges?" Aunt Abby said, frowning as she searched the tent. "Do you think they might not show up after all?"

I shrugged, wondering the same thing. Neither Isabel Lau nor Simon Van Houten had arrived yet; nor was there any sign of a third judge at the judging table. Would they really be no-shows, in spite of the fact that Reina was in custody? Was all of this for nothing?

While we waited, I checked out the other tables. Among the twelve finalists, only a handful seemed to be real contenders. I discounted the chocolate chip cookie lady, figuring those were a dime a dozen. And while tempting, the chocolate cheesecake didn't seem like anything you couldn't get at the grocery store. I spotted some white chocolate squares that looked about as appealing as ice cubes, some black-bottom cupcakes that had obviously deflated once they left the oven, a batch of ordinary-looking brownies from a guy who was stuck in the sixties (did they contain a little extra ingredient?), and several other offerings that didn't compare to my aunt's pies—or Jake's puffs.

I caught a glimpse of Frankie Nudo and headed over to see how his cheesy-thingies had turned out. Frankie had actually put on a suit for the event, and he looked as out of place in it as he must have felt. His curly dark hair was greased back, and he'd added a couple of gold rings to his pudgy fingers. As I neared the table, Frankie frowned.

"Your cheesy-thingies look . . . good," I said brightly. Truthfully, it was all I could muster.

He grunted something and shrugged his shoulders, as if trying to make the suit jacket fit better. He was clearly uncomfortable, and I wondered if it was more from the suit or the competition. Or was it Monet and her proximity that was causing him discomfort?

"Good luck," I finally said, when he didn't say—or grunt—anything more.

He nodded, not meeting my eyes, then cracked his knuckles. Was this guy tense, or what?

I moved on to Monet's table, next to Frankie's, wondering whose idea it was to put these two so close together.

"*Chéri!*" she said, smiling when she saw me. "I heard about Reina! So glad they found out she was the real killer and took her to jail. I was beginning to think I might be next. Now I can relax, win the contest, and take the next step in my career."

I heard Frankie grunt something but couldn't make it out.

Monet either didn't hear him or ignored him. "Where are those judges? My I Scream Cakes won't last forever, even in this cooler full of dry ice."

Monet's table sported a festive tablecloth and a cupcake tier, ready to take on a dozen of her ice cream cupcakes. Next to it sat the cooler she'd referenced.

"How long will they last in there?" I asked, dying to take a peek inside and see what artistic frosting designs she'd come up with for her contest entries. The ones she'd sold at the festival ranged from patriotic red, white, and blue flag designs to bursting spring flowers to funny animal faces.

"I have no idea!" Monet exclaimed. "This is the first time I've had to use a cooler. I always keep my I Scream Cupcakes in a zero-degree freezer." She looked at her watch. "Those judges had better hurry."

"Can I peek?" I asked. Monet thought about it for a second, then lifted the lid.

"Oh my God!" I gasped as I stared down at the ice cream-cupcake concoctions.

Each cupcake was frosted in chocolate icing and

sprinkled with chocolate jimmies to suggest dirt. Inserted into each one was a gray-frosted Milano cookie, with the letters "RIP" spelled out in black icing across the front.

I looked up at her and tried to shut my open mouth. "Wow," was all I could manage.

"Appropriate, don't you think?" she said, grinning proudly. "I like my cakes to have a theme, and these individual gravestones seemed perfect!"

"Well, good luck." With that I moved on to the next table.

The nameplate read HARRISON TOFFLEMIRE—CHOCOLATE FALLS. But instead of Harrison manning the table, his two daughters were in his place, busily trying to assemble the smaller chocolate fountain. They didn't appear to have a clue how to put it together.

"Angelica, it doesn't go there!" one of them said to the other, who was holding up one of the tiers. I couldn't tell them apart. They looked exactly alike, right down to the moles over their right eyes. And their identical skimpy outfits didn't help either.

"Well, if you're so smart, then where does it go, Anastasia?"

Angelica? Anastasia? Really?

"I'll tell you where it goes . . . ," Anastasia said, giving her an evil look.

"Give it to me, you airhead," Angelica snapped.

"You don't know what you're doing, ditzwad!" Anastasia snapped back.

"Shut up and help me!" Angelica said. Or maybe it

was Anastasia. With all their bickering, I was beginning to lose track.

"I wish Dad was here," one of them whined, trying again to fit in the tier.

"I know. We have to win this for him," said the other.

One of them looked up at me, finally noticing I was there.

"Can we help you?" she asked snottily.

"No. I just came by to wish you good luck," I said.

"Whatever," she said, and returned to making fruitless efforts to fix the machine.

I silently stepped over to Griffin's table. He stood behind his table, looking miffed, as usual, his pies haphazardly set on the table without a thought to presentation. The pies themselves looked a little off too. One was lopsided. Another had spilled over the top. Another had a broken crust rim, as if someone had taken a bite out of it.

"How's it going?" I asked, not knowing what else to say.

"Sucks," he said. "This whole festival has been a nightmare from the start, and none of my pies turned out right. I haven't got a prayer. I don't know why I'm still in this stupid contest."

"I'm sure they'll taste great," I said, trying to give him a ray of hope.

"Yeah, right. Someone stole my good chocolate last night, and I had to use some kind of commercial crap."

"Stole it?" I asked, surprised. Had someone tried to undermine Griffin at the last minute?

"No one stole it, pie pal," Frankie shouted from across the room. "You're too cheap to pay for the good stuff and you blame everyone else, like you always have."

"Mind your own business, cheese ball," Griffin shouted back. "That so-called chocolate you use is nothing but melted down carob chips. It's mockolate."

"Shut your piehole!" Frankie yelled. Before I could blink, Frankie came out from the back of his table and, in three swift steps, picked up one of the chocolate pies and smashed it into Griffin's face.

With these clowns, the event was turning into a real circus.

Chapter 25

It took Clifford the security guard, Jake, and two other guys to escort the two men out of the contest tent. Both were accessorized in chocolate pie filling. And Lyla and her cameraman had captured it all on tape for the late-night news.

A few minutes later, Jake returned. Lyla signaled her cameraman to focus on him. I watched as Jake held up a hand, shook his head, and kept walking toward his table. Lyla grabbed his hand and said something to him I couldn't make out. Jake stopped, turned to her, and frowned, then shook his head again. A look came over Lyla's face that I couldn't quite identify. Incomprehension? Disbelief? Anger?

I stepped up a little closer and heard Jake say, "Look, Lyla, I'm sorry."

Then he turned around, spotted me watching him, and headed directly over.

Uh-oh.

Before I could do anything, he reached me, took my hand, pulled me close, then kissed me right there in front of everyone.

In the background, I thought I heard a burst of applause.

He pulled back and looked at me.

I flushed with embarrassment, and it took me a few seconds to recover from the kiss. Finally, I whispered, "Where did that come from?"

"Come on," he said, taking my hand. He walked me out of the tent and took me aside. Turning to me, he pressed his lips together, looked away, then met my eyes. "Darcy, you were right."

Puzzled, I asked, "I was? About what?"

He rolled his eyes. "Lyla."

My heart skipped several beats. "What was I right about?"

"She was . . . She wanted to get back together, like you said."

I knew it! I said to myself. I felt like jumping up and down. Instead I said calmly, "Oh."

"I was so stupid! How did I not see that? I was sure she really needed my help, and I thought she was just doing the story on my cream puffs to thank me. But I was wrong. Dead wrong."

I smiled gently and pressed his hand.

"How did you know what she was up to?" he asked.

I shrugged. "Who would want to let you go? You're a dream puff."

Jake broke into a big grin, pulled me close again, and gave me a kiss that was as delicious as one of his cream puffs.

*   *   *

"The judges are here!" Willow announced.

The antsy crowd simmered down, and the contestants stood at attention behind their tables—minus a few. Griffin and Frankie had vanished, and the Tofflemire girls had given up on reconstructing the Chocolate Falls machine and had left for the hospital to see their dad. That left Aunt Abby, Jake, Monet, and several others vying for the grand prize. The only real contender I could see who might beat out Aunt Abby was Jake.

One by one the contestants brought samples of their chocolate masterpieces to the judging table. The judges were stone-faced as they tasted each one, making notes on small pads. The suspense was killing me, and by the time they'd tried bites of every entry, my crossed fingers had cramps.

When the judges left the tent to confer in private, I ate three whoopie pies to try to calm my nerves. Instead, I had a stomachache by the time the judges returned. After settling into their seats, their faces as stoic as before, they handed Willow a piece of paper with the name of the first-, second-, and third-place winners.

"This is so exciting!" Willow said, unfolding the paper. She took a dramatic deep breath, leaned in to the microphone, and announced: "First-place winner . . . OMG! Abigail Warner!"

A cheer went up from the audience. I looked at Jake and gave him a sympathetic smile. He nodded and gave me a thumbs-up. I could tell he was genuinely happy for Aunt Abby.

Jake took second—five hundred dollars and a gift

certificate for the local gourmet chocolate store, and Monet won third place—a bottle of chocolate wine and a T-shirt that read: "Chocolate Comes from a Plant, Which Makes It a Salad." Aunt Abby was beyond thrilled, especially about appearing on a future episode of *Chocolate Wars*. I was thrilled for her too, but the extra money she'd planned to share with Dillon and me would certainly come in handy.

I glanced around, suddenly noticing someone was missing. Lyla Vassar, along with her cameraman, were nowhere in sight. Had her supposed feature on Jake and his cream puffs all been a sham to get close to him? It sure looked that way.

The contestants handed out leftovers to the delighted audience, then packed up their displays and headed out. Aunt Abby invited Jake to join us for a celebration at her home, and he agreed to meet us there. But first I wanted to take a shower, put on fresh clothes, and take a Zantac.

When I entered Aunt Abby's kitchen forty-five minutes later, I was surprised to see Detective Shelton and Wendy Spellman at the table, as well as Jake, who had also beaten me there.

I went over and gave Wendy a hug. "You're out!"

She grinned and patted Aunt Abby's hand. "Thanks to my best friend here," she said.

Dillon moved over a chair so I could sit by Jake, and I joined the group at the table. Aunt Abby got up and brought me a cup of coffee to go with the platter of Jake's leftover cream puffs. As soon as the Zantac kicked in, I planned to help myself.

"So what are you going to do with all that prize money?" I asked Aunt Abby, after taking a sip of the warm drink.

Aunt Abby glanced at the detective and smiled. "Well, after you and Dillon get your share, I'm going to upgrade my school-bus kitchen to all stainless steel, put in a popcorn machine, and start serving chocolate-covered kettle corn. Wes loves kettle corn."

Detective Shelton—I would never call him "Wes"—grinned. He smiled so rarely, his face looked odd. Nice, but odd.

"What about you, Jake?" Aunt Abby asked.

Although Jake was runner-up, he was number one in my book. I was just glad we were both still alive to enjoy another round of chocolate.

"Don't know yet," he said. "Pay some bills, probably. Take Darcy out for a nice dinner. Get her some gourmet chocolates." He reached over and took my hand.

I blushed. I'd have to get used to these public displays of affection.

"What about you, Dillon?" Jake asked.

"New laptop, new tablet, new phone, Apple watch, Google glasses," he said, his nose buried in his current cell phone.

"Darcy?" Jake asked.

"I'm saving mine."

"Boring," Dillon said.

Detective Shelton rose from the table. "Well, I'd better be going. Glad you're all safe and we have the killer in custody."

"By the way," I said, "how's J.C.?"

"The doctors are hopeful. He's young and strong, but it'll take a lot of rehab to get him up and around again."

"And Harrison?"

"He's fine. His head injury bled a lot, but it wasn't deep. They'll watch him for another day or so before they release him."

"Before you go, Detective, I want to thank you," Wendy said, "and everyone, especially Abby, for believing in me." She looked tired from her stay in jail, but had stopped by on her way home to see her friend.

"It was mostly them," the detective said, waving a hand at the rest of us. "Abby, Darcy, Dillon, Jake. If they hadn't gotten involved, we might never have discovered that Reina murdered Polly—and tried to kill J.C."

Not to mention George Brown, I thought, although technically that was involuntary manslaughter. Or was it? We might never know.

"Yes, thank you, everyone," Wendy said, "for everything. I'm lucky to have such good friends in Abigail and her family. Bless you all."

In spite of my own close call, it gave me a warm feeling to think we helped in some way.

Detective Shelton looked at Aunt Abby. "See you tomorrow night?"

She gave him her Kewpie-doll smile, dimples and all. "Looking forward to it, Wes."

I'd never get used to her calling him that.

"Well, I'm wiped out," I said to the group, and rose. "I'm going to turn in."

"I'll walk you to your RV," Jake said, and joined me. "I have to make sure it's chocolate-free. At least on the outside."

"Hey, why did Reina pour chocolate on your car and RV?" Dillon asked.

"Just to scare me, I think," I said. "The upside is, my Bug still smells like chocolate. The downside is, every time I get in the car, I want a Mounds bar."

We said good night and headed out the back door.

"Want to come in for a drink?" I asked Jake, not ready to let him go—not after those kisses.

"I'm bushed, but a glass of wine sounds good before bed." We climbed into the rig and I caught him eyeing the couch.

I smiled. "Are you sure you want to sleep on that couch again? It can't be that comfortable."

He pulled me close and tucked my hair behind my ear. "You're right. I guess I should head on home and let you get some sleep."

"I wasn't planning to go to sleep. . . ." I smiled.

He grinned, leaned in, and kissed me.

It was—*mmm*—sweeter than chocolate.

Recipes From the San Francisco Chocolate Festival

Aunt Abby's Chocolate Raspberry Whoopie Pies

If you haven't tried a whoopie pie, you're missing a classic American treat! Traditionally, a whoopie pie is a sandwich of two cakey cookies with a fluffy marshmallow center. But that's just the beginning. Try Aunt Abby's Chocolate Raspberry Whoopie Pies, which took first place at the San Francisco Chocolate Festival competition.

Ingredients for Chocolate Cakey Cookie

¾ cup flour
1 teaspoon baking soda
½ teaspoon salt
½ cup butter, softened
1 cup sugar
1 egg
½ cup unsweetened good-quality cocoa powder

1 teaspoon vanilla
1 cup milk

Directions

1. Preheat oven to 375 degrees.

2. Line baking sheet with parchment paper.

3. Mix flour, baking soda, and salt in a bowl.

4. Combine butter and sugar in a separate bowl.

5. Beat egg into butter-and-sugar mixture.

6. Add cocoa powder and vanilla and mix well.

7. Stir in flour mixture and milk until smooth.

8. Spoon dough into 2 tablespoon-sized balls and place on baking sheet, about 2 inches apart.

9. Bake for 11–13 minutes, until cakes spring back when touched.

10. Cool completely.

11. Spread raspberry filling (below) onto one cakey cookie and top with another cakey cookie.

Ingredients for Raspberry Filling

1 cup softened butter
¼ cup raspberry puree
1 tablespoon milk
1 teaspoon vanilla
3 cups powdered sugar

Directions

1. Beat butter in medium bowl.

2. Add raspberry puree, milk, vanilla, and 2 cups powdered sugar and beat until smooth.

3. Add more powdered sugar as needed to thicken frosting.

4. Spread onto cakey cookie.

MAKES 16 WHOOPIE PIES

Jake Miller's Mocha Mousse Cream Puffs

Cream puffs, like whoopie pies, are so versatile when it comes to mixing and matching the outsides with the fillings. This melt-in-your-mouth puff is perfect with a latte in the morning, a glass of milk in the afternoon, and a bottle of red wine in the evening.

Ingredients for Cream Puff Shell

½ cup water
4 tablespoons butter
Pinch of sugar
½ cup flour
2 beaten eggs

Directions

1. Preheat oven to 350 degrees.

2. Combine water, butter, sugar, and salt in medium pan and bring to boil.

3. Remove from heat and add flour.

4. Place back on medium heat and stir well with wooden spoon for 30 seconds.

5. Remove from heat and pour into bowl; stir 1 minute.

6. Add eggs, half at a time, stirring constantly until batter is smooth.

7. Line baking sheet with parchment paper.

8. Scoop mixture into balls and place on prepared baking sheet. Leave 2 inches between puffs.

9. Bake for 30 minutes, until golden brown, light, and crisp; cool on rack.

Ingredients for Mocha Filling

1⅓ cups heavy whipping cream
6 tablespoons good-quality semisweet chocolate chips
1½ tablespoons sugar
Dash salt
1 teaspoon vanilla
1 teaspoon instant coffee granules
Powdered sugar

Directions

1. Combine 6 tablespoons of cream, chocolate chips, sugar, and salt in a saucepan.

2. Cook over low heat until chips are melted and ingredients are blended.

3. Remove from heat and gradually stir in vanilla, coffee, and remaining cream.

4. Refrigerate for 2 hours.

5. Beat filling until stiff.

6. Spoon mocha filling into puff shells.

7. Dust with powdered sugar, or drizzle raspberry sauce over top.

MAKES 8–10, DEPENDING ON SIZE OF PUFF

Monet Richards's Red, White, and Blue I Scream Cakes

Monet Richards makes these patriotic I Scream Cakes for American celebrations, such as the Fourth of July, and French holidays, such as Bastille Day. Below is the easy version, but you can make everything from scratch if you prefer. *Viva la* Ice Cream Cakes for all occasions!

Ingredients

1 package chocolate cake mix
1¼ cups water
⅓ cup vegetable oil
3 eggs
1 container vanilla ice cream, softened
1 container chocolate fudge frosting

Directions

1. Preheat oven to 350 degrees.

2. Line cupcake tin with 24 cupcake papers.

3. Combine cake mix, water, oil, and eggs in bowl.

4. Beat on medium speed for 2 minutes.

5. Spoon 2 tablespoons of batter into each cupcake paper.

6. Bake 8–10 minutes, until toothpick comes out clean.

7. Cool completely, remove papers, and freeze about 4 hours, until firm.

8. Spoon ½ cup of soft ice cream into each cupcake paper and pack it down.

9. Place in freezer until frozen, about 4 hours.

10. Remove cupcakes from freezer.

11. Remove ice cream patties and place on top of cupcakes.

12. Frost with red, white, and/or blue icing, top with red, white, and blue sprinkles, and serve.

Makes 2 dozen

Hint: There are other ways to combine ice cream and cupcakes. You can bake the cupcake batter in ice-cream cones instead of cupcake papers, frost the cupcakes, then top with a scoop of ice cream and add sprinkles.

For added fun, cut off the top of the cupcake, scoop out a spoonful of cake, then fill with a spoonful of ice cream. Replace top, frost, and decorate. Watch their eyes light up when they realize the cupcake is filled with ice cream!

Frankie Nudo's Choco-Cheesy Brie Bites

Believe it or not, chocolate goes with just about anything, even cheese.

Try Frankie's melt-in-your-mouth Brie bites for a rich, creamy treat. Choose a Brie that's semisoft with a moderate amount of fat.

Ingredients

8 ounces Brie cheese, semisoft
12 ounces favorite gourmet chocolate
Sea salt

Directions

1. Freeze the Brie for 20–30 minutes so it's easier to cut.

2. Melt the chocolate in the microwave oven. (Temper first, if desired.)

3. Cut the Brie into 24 bite-sized pieces.

4. Insert a thin skewer in a cheese piece and dip it into the melted chocolate.

5. Place chocolate-covered cheese on baking sheet covered with waxed paper and sprinkle with a little sea salt.

6. Let set completely at room temperature and serve immediately, or store in the refrigerator in an airtight container, then allow to come to room temperature before serving.

MAKES 24 BITES

Griffin Makeba's Mini Minty Chocolate Pies

Griffin likes to make mini chocolate pies for special occasions and often colors the whipped topping to suit the season—orange for Halloween, red for Christmas, purple for Mardi Gras, and so on. He adds mint to give it an extra zippy and zesty flavor, then serves each one with chocolate curls or sprinkles on top.

Ingredients

1 package refrigerated pie dough
1 package instant chocolate pudding mix
3 tablespoons cocoa powder
1 cup half-and-half
½ cup whole milk
1 teaspoon vanilla
1 cup heavy cream
¼ cup powdered sugar
1–2 teaspoons mint extract
Green food coloring

Directions

1. Preheat oven to 450 degrees.

2. Unroll refrigerator pie crust and cut into 3-inch circles. Repeat until you have a dozen circles.

3. Spray the bottom of a mini muffin tin with vegetable spray.

4. Place the circles on top of the muffin wells and pinch the bottom to form the rim of the crust.

5. Prick each circle with a fork.

6. Bake 4–5 minutes, until lightly browned.

7. Allow to cool. Then gently twist each crust off the tin and turn right-side up.

8. Mix pudding, cocoa powder, half-and-half, milk, and vanilla until blended.

9. Pour into large ziplock plastic bag and refrigerate for 20–30 minutes.

10. Beat heavy cream until stiff peaks form.

11. Add powdered sugar and beat until blended.

12. Stir in vanilla and a few drops of food coloring.

13. Pour into large ziplock plastic bag and refrigerate for 20 minutes.

14. Remove chocolate filling from refrigerator and cut a small hole off one corner of the bag.

15. Pipe filling into pie shells.

16. Pipe mint whipped cream on top.

17. Add chocolate curls, sprinkles, or cut-up bits of thin mints on top.

18. Refrigerate until serving time.

MAKES 1 DOZEN

Harrison Tofflemire's Chocolate Velvet Falls with Fresh Fruit Bouquet

When Harrison presents his Chocolate Falls using a chocolate fountain machine, he does so with flair, so instead of simply cutting up fruit for dipping, create a fresh fruit bouquet to dazzle your guests for dessert.

Ingredients

2 12-ounce bags gourmet chocolate chips
3 gourmet unsweetened chocolate squares, chopped
¾ cup canola oil
¼ cup Kahlua
Styrofoam ball
Lettuce leaves
Fruit, such as strawberries, mandarin orange wedges, pineapple squares, cherries, grapes, apple cubes, banana bites, cantaloupe balls, watermelon balls, and so on
Wooden skewers

Directions

1. Place chocolate chips and squares in a large microwave-safe bowl.

2. Microwave on medium high for 2 minutes, stir, and continue until chocolate is smooth and liquidy.

3. Stir in Kahlua.

4. Pour chocolate into the bowl at the base of the machine.

5. Turn on the fountain so the chocolate begins to circulate. (If it doesn't flow smoothly, add a little more oil.)

6. Slice the bottom off the Styrofoam ball so it will sit flat on the table.

7. Cover the ball with lettuce leaves.

8. Cut the skewers in half.

9. Insert fruit pieces on the skewers. Then insert skewers into ball.

10. Cover ball with skewered fruit.

11. Place next to Chocolate Falls.

SERVES 20

Turn the page for a sneak peek at the next
Food Festival Mystery,

Death of a Bad Apple

Coming from Obsidian in January 2016.

"What smells so good?" I asked as I entered my aunt Abby's home, a San Francisco Victorian, through the back door. The aroma of cinnamon, sugar, and baked apples perfumed the air and made my mouth water. I inhaled deeply, trying to fill my lungs with the intoxicating fragrance.

"Abby's Salted-Caramel Apple Tarts!" she exclaimed proudly as she lifted a tray of steaming-hot pastries out of the oven and onto the stove to cool. "It's my latest creation. I'm using salted caramel in the recipe. I'll let you taste one as soon as they cool down a bit. The flaky crust just melts in your mouth."

"Yum!" I stared at the lightly browned individual tartlets, willing them to cool off faster.

"Sit," Aunt Abby ordered. "You'll get drool all over my tarts."

I obeyed her command and took a stool at the island counter, which occupied much of the kitchen. Basil, my aunt's long-haired Doxie, nuzzled my red Toms.

"What prompted you to whip up something new?"

I asked, petting the dog with one shoe. "Your customers love the comfort foods you already serve. I hope you're not going to replace your caramel-chocolate brownies with these. That could cause a riot."

Shortly after my aunt had retired from serving cafeteria food at the local high school, she'd bought an old school bus, tricked it up, and turned it into a kitchen on wheels. For the past year, she'd been serving "old school" comfort food at Fort Mason, along with a dozen other food trucks. Since I was between jobs, I'd been helping out my aunt by making sandwiches, mixing up mac and cheese, and taking orders from hungry customers. Truth was, I'd recently been let go from my job as restaurant critic at the *San Francisco Chronicle* and hadn't yet finished writing my soon-to-be-bestselling cookbook featuring food truck recipes. Unfortunately, I wasn't much of a cook—I was more of an eater—but I was quickly learning how to make pot pies in bulk.

"No, my *pretty*," my aunt said, assuming the voice of a wicked witch. "These are for something *special*." And then she actually cackled.

I laughed at this somewhat new silly side of my sixtysomething aunt. Yes, she could be eccentric, but there was something mischievous behind those twinkling Betty Boop eyes that even her childlike dimpled cheeks couldn't hide. "What are you up to, Aunt Abby?"

She handed me a newspaper clipping and plopped down on the stool next to me.

I picked up the article and scanned the headline: *"Annual Apple Fest Opening October 1st."*

I frowned at my aunt. "What's this about?"

"Read it!" she demanded, her smile as wide as her eyes were bright.

While I skimmed the article, Aunt Abby hopped off her stool and busied herself making coffee, no doubt to wash down the apple tart I was hoping to taste soon. There was nothing special about the story—just a three-graph piece about a popular attraction in California's gold country.

Nestled in the rolling Sierra foothills of El Dorado County is a wonderland of apple orchards and apple farms and apple wineries and apple breweries just waiting to bring you a variety of sweet, tart, and tempting apple treats. The area, known as Apple Valley, stretches from Placerville to Pollock Pines, providing the perfect place for a fruitful getaway. You'll find apple delights from applesauce to zucchini-apple bread, all prepared from the freshest farm ingredients.

While you're there, be sure to sample homemade specialties such as apple crisps, apple strudels, apple bread, apple donuts, apple butter, apple cider, caramel apples, baked apples, and everyone's favorite—American apple pie.

Take the scenic drive along Highway 50 or ride the shuttle, which begins at Apple Annie's Farm and ends at Adam's Apples, with stops along the way at many apple orchards, food tents and trucks, and the A-MAZE-ing Hay Maze. Come pick your favorite apples and taste the apple treats, all fresh from farm to fork. Remember: An apple a day keeps the doctor away—as long as you buy your apples from an Apple Valley–certified grower!

The piece was included in the "What to Do and Where to Go this Fall" section of the newspaper, and was written by someone calling himself Nathan Chapman, the organizer of the Apple Valley Festival. Although I liked apples as much as the next all-American, I'd never been to the area, about a two-hour drive northeast from San Francisco. I got my apples from the local market—and only the green ones—which I cut and dipped in peanut butter. And sometimes chocolate.

"Is this where you got the idea for your apple tarts?" I asked.

Aunt Abby set a latte down in front of me. I encircled the hot cup with my hands to cut the fall chill and bring on the warmth. Was that cinnamon I smelled wafting from the coffee?

"Not just the idea for tarts, Darcy. I've signed up to serve them during the opening weekend at the Apple Fest in two weeks."

"What do you mean? Are you entering a contest or something?" I asked, puzzled.

"Nope. They're inviting selected food trucks to join in the festivities, and I'm taking the School Bus up for the weekend! Doesn't that sound fun?"

She turned her back before I could make a face. While a weekend in the country sounded nice, I had made reservations at the Butler and the Chef in the South of Market district for Jake's upcoming birthday and had my own festivities planned. I sipped my coffee and watched my aunt drizzle melted caramel on the top of the tarts, then add a dash of salt. When she was finished, she scooped one of the tarts onto a small plate and brought the still-steaming treat to me.

"Seriously?" I said, after inhaling deeply. "You're really doing this?"

"Doing what?" came a sleepy voice from the doorway. Dillon, Aunt Abby's twenty-five-year-old son stood in the entryway looking like a zombie, his dark hair sticking up like a porcupine, two- or three-day stubble on his chin. He was wearing a well-worn *Tom and Jerry* T-shirt and baggy flannel pajama bottoms decorated in Minecraft images. Naturally, he was barefoot, and he really needed to do something about those toenails.

"Dillon!" Aunt Abby said cheerily. "Perfect timing! You'll have to taste my salted-caramel apple tarts."

Dillon had a knack for showing up when his mother was baking. He had some kind of sixth sense when it came to food. He lumbered in and took the stool across from me, then eyed my tart. I pulled it back and wrapped my hands around it like a prisoner hoarding food from other convicts.

"What were you guys talking about? Are we going on a trip?"

Before Dillon had a chance to grab my fork out of my hand, I stabbed the tart, broke off a bite, and ate it. "Mmmmmmm," I murmured, closing my eyes. When I opened them again, Aunt Abby and Dillon were staring at me. "Wow" was all I could add.

Aunt Abby beamed. Dillon turned and looked at her hopefully.

"Here you go, dear," Aunt Abby said, setting a caramel-drizzled tart in front of him. "You want coffee?"

Dillon didn't answer—too busy stuffing his mouth with the warm, fruity pastry. We looked on in awe as he wolfed it down in three large bites. "Good," he said simply. "Can I have another?"

"No," Aunt Abby said. "I'm taking the rest to the busterant this morning to see how the customers like them, before I serve them at the Apple Fest."

I shook my head at Aunt Abby's made-up word, "busterant." Since her food truck was actually a converted school bus and not a truck, she coined the term for her half bus and half restaurant.

"What fest?" Dillon said, getting up and heading for the refrigerator. He opened the door, took out the milk, and drank right from the carton.

I gagged a little.

Aunt Abby explained her plan to Dillon. Opening day of the festival was in two weeks and she'd hoped Dillon and I would join her and help serve her apple tarts. She must have caught my hesitant look.

"Of course, there will be some perks," she added.

"Like what?" Dillon asked.

"I've booked three rooms at the Enchanted Apple Inn, a bed-and-breakfast farm, for the weekend. You'll get to see a real working apple farm."

Dillon and I looked at each other.

"Plus, the fest is offering apple wines and beers, a bunch of craft booths, scooter rides, and a hay maze! Doesn't that sound fun?" Her dimples deepened with her widening grin.

"I don't know, Mom," Dillon said. "I've got a bunch of stuff to do on the computer . . ."

"And I was planning to take Jake out for his birthday that weekend . . ." I said weakly.

"No excuses. Dillon, you can bring your computer with you. I'm sure they have Internet service there. And, Darcy, apparently you haven't talked to Jake this morning?"

"No. Why?"

"He's signed up too."

"Jake's coming?" I asked, surprised. He hadn't mentioned it when I'd talked to him last night.

"So is Wes—if he can get some time off. We'll all be up there together!"

OMG. My nemesis, Detective Wellesley Shelton, had been dating my aunt for several weeks, and I still wasn't used to it. Most of my encounters with the detective had been interrogations about various homicides that had occurred recently. I couldn't imagine sitting around the breakfast table making small talk with the man.

"But—" I started to argue.

She cut me off. "Plus, I'll pay you overtime."

Dillon wiped off the milk mustache. "I'm in."

I sighed. I could truly use the extra money. "I guess we can celebrate Jake's birthday with some apple birthday cake."

"Wonderful!" Aunt Abby said. "Now, let's get to work!"

So much for a romantic birthday weekend alone with Jake.

Also available from

Penny Pike

Death of a Crabby Cook
A Food Festival Mystery

When restaurant reviewer Darcy Burnett gets served a pink slip from the *San Francisco Chronicle*, she needs to come up with an alternative recipe for success quickly. Her feisty aunt Abby owns a tricked-out school bus, which she's converted into a hip and happening food truck, and Darcy comes aboard as a part-timer while she develops a cookbook project based on recipes from food fests in the Bay Area.

But when a local chef turns up dead, Darcy's aunt is framed for the murder. With her aunt's business—and freedom—on the line, it's up to Darcy to steer the murder investigation in the right direction and put the brakes on an out-of-control killer....

"A clever new series that cozy mystery readers will eat up."
—*MyShelf.com*

Available wherever books are sold or at
penguin.com